Legend
of the
Five Rings™

RAB

STAN!

Wizards
OF THE COAST™

CLAN WAR
Fifth Scroll

THE CRAB

©2001 Wizards of the Coast, Inc.

Distributed in the United States by St. Martin's Press. Distributed in Canada by Fenn Ltd.

Distributed to the hobby, toy, and comic trade in the United States and Canada by regional distributors.

Distributed worldwide by Wizards of the Coast, Inc., and regional distributors.

Cover art by r.k. post
First Printing: June 2001
Library of Congress Catalog Card Number: 00-190889

9 8 7 6 5 4 3 2 1

UK ISBN: 0-7869-2620-1
US ISBN: 0-7869-1879-9
620-T21879

U.S., CANADA, ASIA,
PACIFIC, & LATIN AMERICA
Wizards of the Coast, Inc
P.O. Box 707
Renton, WA 98057-0707
+1-800-324-6496

EUROPEAN HEADQUARTERS
Wizards of the Coast, Belgium
P.B. 2031
2600 Berchem
Belgium
+32-70-23-32-77

Visit our web site at **www.wizards.com/fiverings**

For Lisa, who showed me true beauty.
You inspired me with your presence, challenged me
with your absence, and helped me learn again
that a good man working for a good cause
will sometimes do the wrong things.

ACKNOWLEDGMENTS

Special thanks to Paul Adachi, Sara Balcaitis, the Bernard family (Lisa, Jared, Abraham, Joshua, and Jacob), Ed Bolme, Neil & Mary Jo Brown, Jeff & Trish & Sarah Brown, Monte & Sue Cook, Ricko Dakan, Jodi & Jonathan Goldberger, Jeff Grubb, Rob Heinsoo, Steve Horvath, Dave Lemon, Summer Linn, J. Robert King, Mary Kirchoff, Scott Magner, Steve Miller, Erik Mona, Mike Montesa, Kate Novak, Luke Peterschmidt, Jeff Quick, Anaïs Reicher, Thomas M. Reid, Cindi Rice, Mike Selinker, Bill Slavicsek, Sabrina Smith, Ree Soesbee, T'Ed Stark, and Anthony & Mikelann Valterra.

The author owes a debt of gratitude to the artistic visions of Utagawa Hiroshigi, Joe Hisaishi, Katsushika Hokusai, Kazuo Koike, Goseki Kojima, Akira Kurosawa, Toshiro Mifune, Frank Miller, Hayao Miyazaki, Stan Sakai, and William Shakespeare.

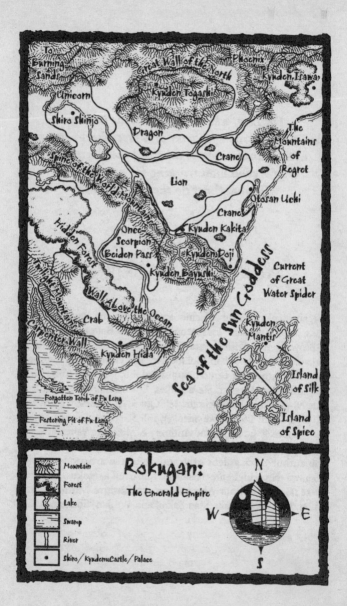

Rokugan:
The Emerald Empire

Mountain
Forest
Lake
Swamp
River
Skiro/Kyudenu Castle/Palace

1 AGAINST THE TIDE

The Wall" was all Hida Amoro ever called it. The three-hundred-year-old, hundred-foot-tall structure ran across the entire southern end of his clan's territory—of the Crab lands. It defined the border the same way it defined the clan itself. The Crab not only stood upon the Wall; they *were* the Wall.

"It is a good day to die," said Amoro as he stood watch. "But it is a better day to crush our enemies!"

"You say that every morning, Amoro-san," Hiruma Waka said with a dark chuckle. He had guarded the Wall longer than any other man in his regiment and was considered a symbolic father by many young samurai. Waka ushered them into the world of the Wall, saw that if they died in those first weeks it was because of the enemy's strength, not their own youthful folly, and eventually set them free to follow their karma. Hiruma Waka was there when Hida Amoro first stepped foot on the Wall, and he watched him grow from an ambitious young samurai to a leather-skinned veteran.

"Have you ever known a morning when I have been wrong?" asked Amoro.

"No," said Waka, "but I have known days when I would rather not think about it. We all know our duty, Amoro-san, but no one relishes it more than you."

"What about my cousin?" Amoro looked Waka in the eye. "What about the Great Bear?"

Waka looked to the west. Fifty yards farther up the Wall was a tower identical to the one on which he and Amoro stood. Identical towers stood every fifty yards for the entire length of the Wall. Each tower stationed two regiments of samurai—one to work the catapults, ballistae, and other siege engines, and the other to take up sword, club, or spear against any creatures determined enough to make it to the top. Most of the infantry samurai stayed within the tower sleeping, drinking, or gambling until the sentries let out the call to arms. Amoro and Waka were on sentry duty at their tower. Hida Kisada, known to all as the Great Bear, stood watch on the tower to the west.

"Your cousin is a great man and an exemplary samurai," said Waka, "but even he does not live for battle."

"What? How can you say such things? He is daimyo of the Crab and yet there he stands on the ramparts, waiting for the enemy. How can you say that he does not live for battle?"

Hiruma Waka put an armored hand on Amoro's shoulder.

"Sometimes it is easier to fight demons than courtiers," he said. "Other daimyo spend half their days in the capital currying favor—the emperor grows old, and they know that his days cannot be many. The Great Bear goes to the Forbidden City only twice a year and spends nearly all that time trying to undo the damage his so-called friends have inflicted on his reputation."

"Bah!" Amoro spit at the mention of the Imperial Court. "The emperor grows senile! Let the courtiers do what they wish—without the Crab they would drown in their own blood."

"I am certain Kisada feels the same as you," Waka agreed. "However as daimyo he *knows* that he must have the cooperation of the other clans. Look out at our enemies, Amoro, look to the Shadowlands!"

Waka pointed to the south. Beyond the Wall, the land itself was tainted. The grass was brittle and gray, the ground soggy and covered with foul-smelling bogs, and every creature the eye could see was heinous and unnatural.

"Once, a very long time ago, that land belonged to my family—to the Hirumas. We Crab stood on a wall at the bottom of Hiruma lands, but our defenses were not strong enough." He looked over the desolate, cursed land before them and tried to imagine what it looked like when his ancestors ruled there. Waka owned several woodblock prints, heirlooms handed down through the generations, that depicted the Hiruma lands as lush rolling hills covered with grass. Peasants tended the fields, birds flew through fantastically blue skies, and the entire countryside rang with song and joy. A chill ran down his spine when he considered that for all he knew they might right now be looking at the exact place that inspired those prints. The Shadowlands taint blighted everything it touched.

"The Crab have but one responsibility—to protect the empire at all costs. To do whatever it takes to keep the Shadowlands out."

"Exactly! So why should we care about honorless dealings among politicians?"

"Because we cannot do this ourselves. We cannot hold the Wall *and* grow our own rice *and* clothe our young. We cannot do it all. We need the help of the Crane, Dragon, Lion, Phoenix, and Unicorn clans. We even need the help of the treacherous Scorpion clan. They are the empire we protect. But they must be reminded from time to time that this protection comes at a price."

"Then let them stand on the Wall, even for a single day, and they will never again forget what it is we do. After they defend the empire from the Shadowlands, perhaps they will stop tearing it apart from within."

"Stop thinking like a politician," Waka chided. "Hold the Wall, let no creature of darkness get beyond us—if there is more than that in your head, you are not doing your job. Life is simple; we always know the best course of action—the *only* course of action.

That is why the Great Bear spends so much time here, I think. When you stand on the Wall, your choices are clear. Live or die. Succeed or fail. As daimyo, your cousin must face problems that have no clear and obvious solution." Waka let out an uncharacteristic sigh.

He feared Amoro was right on several counts. The emperor, the thirty-eighth Hantei to sit on the Emerald Throne, was growing old. Some claimed he was becoming senile, but Waka had his doubts. Such a toothless leader would not be able to command Hida Kisada's respect or obedience, and the Crab daimyo still swore fealty to the emperor. Hantei the 38th had been a strong leader for a long, long time. It was his will alone that kept the petty disputes that constantly flared between the proud clans of Rokugan from erupting into open hostilities. But Hantei the 38th grew old, and his heir was not yet strong enough to ascend. The clans did not dare confront one another openly, but behind the scenes they conducted vicious wars of propaganda and rumor, struggling to gain influence over the young Hantei—the future emperor. Kisada refused to take part in the political nonsense, but it nonetheless left the clan in a precarious position in the walls of the Forbidden City.

After a long silence Waka finally said, "I've read that the problem with being a great leader is that you can no longer simply be a good man."

"Perhaps not," said Amoro, "but you can still be a warrior. Look!"

Waka looked again toward the tower to the west. While he and Amoro talked, Shadowlands creatures had begun to lay siege to Hida Kisada's tower.

A brigade of goblins, with a few skeletons and zombies to fill out the ranks, climbed over one another with amazing speed. They reached the parapet in no time. Sentries banged war gongs in staccato bursts, and the Crab samurai swarmed out from the bowels of the tower.

It was hard to think of the creatures as warriors, or even as individuals. They seemed to come and go in rolling waves. Like the tide, they pounded the Wall night and day, no matter that it had stood for three hundred years or that for every samurai the monsters slew, the Crab killed five of their own.

Amoro watched as Hida Kisada waded to the front of the parapet. He stared in obvious awe at his cousin's ability to lead his troops and to deal death to the enemy. Kisada was a giant of a man who, despite being older than most samurai standing on the Wall, was one of the most lethal warriors in the clan. Every swing of his tetsubo crushed the skull of at least one Shadowlands goblin. The great iron-spiked club was already dripping with the enemy's blood.

As he watched Kisada and his troops battle the ever rising tide of Shadowlands creatures, Amoro panted, as if he desperately wished he were stationed on that tower.

"Oh what a glorious battle!" he said.

"Don't grow too attached to watching," said Waka peering over the side of their own tower. "That wave is about to crash here too!"

Joining his companion, Amoro looked down. A row of zombies leaned flat against the base of the tower as others climbed on top of them. Behind those were one more rank of zombies and then a veritable army of goblins.

Hiruma Waka moved quickly to the brass gong hanging next to the doorway. He banged out a rapid six-beat rhythm three times in succession—the sign to the men below that an attack was imminent.

Samurai flooded out the doorway and took positions around the tower. They were a motley bunch; men and women wearing lacquered armor dyed a cool gray and stained with battle. They all wore a circular insignia depicting a crab with claws raised—the clan *mon*—announcing to the world that they were Crab samurai.

Archers moved to the edge of the parapet and nocked arrows in their dai-kyu. In one fluid motion, they leaned over, fired, and pulled back to reload. Pained groans rose from below, followed immediately by arrows and stones launched at the now-empty air atop the tower. When the air cleared, the Crab archers unleashed another volley of death.

Hida Amoro drew his no-dachi and held the tremendous sword over his head. He focused on the battle ahead. As the goblins grew closer, blood pounded in Amoro's temples. A thin red veil seemed to be drawing slowly across his eyes.

The samurai assumed difficult-to-maintain battle postures. The rhythm of the archers made it easy to lose focus, but battle postures forced the samurai to remain fully alert for the moment when the enemy arrived.

A massive yellow hand reached up and grabbed one of the archers by the head and pulled him savagely over the edge. Where the archer had been, a swarm of pale green goblins scampered up the Wall, waving short swords and spears and shouting obscenities. Before the Crab samurai could move to stem the tide, half the tower was awash in creatures out of nightmare.

The Shadowlands creatures were like a force of nature, or unnature—goblins, zombies, skeletons, ogres, and particularly oni. Oni were tremendous, dwarfing even ogres. Some seemed almost human, others were goblinlike, and still others looked like nothing anyone had ever seen before. Scholars argued whether oni were personifications of human vices or were simply creatures of great power created by the Dark God, Fu Leng. The Crab samurai neither knew nor cared about the answer—all that mattered here on the Wall was how to *kill* them.

Within a matter of moments the tower's stone floor grew slick and tacky with blood. Crab katanas and warhammers and tetsubo beat out a savage and deadly percussion on the Shadowlands forces. But the sheer number of monsters surging over the Wall took its toll on the samurai as well.

No one on either side dispatched foes as efficiently as Hida Amoro. His no-dachi sliced through two and sometimes three goblins at a time. Though, truth be told, he was barely aware of it. The thin red veil across his eyes had become a thick crimson haze. Through it, Amoro could barely tell friend from foe. With each blow, each anguished and brief death rattle, his vision dimmed a little further until he could see no more.

2 THE CLAWS THAT CRUSH

The Great Bear stood amid the chaos of battle and thought, "This is where I belong."

His tetsubo whistled as he swung it in a great arc over his head. It made a delicate sound, like a shakuhachi played under the full moon in a secluded garden. The swing ended by caving in a skull.

Goblins were tenacious, that was certain. Although they had bodies like withered old men, their skulls were unusually thick, and their skin was tough. It took a good blow from a heavy weapon to kill them. Kisada's tetsubo often sent his foes flying so far back that they didn't land until they hit the bottom of the Wall.

As daimyo of the Crab Clan, Hida Kisada spent most of his time traveling up and down the Great Wall of Kaiu, conferring with his generals, speaking to the samurai who swore fealty to him, and observing which stations were in need of repair. He only rarely was allowed the luxury of actually engaging in a battle these days, let alone leading one. He had to look at the war against the Shadowlands from a bigger perspective and could not allow himself to be caught up in the finer details of one skirmish or another. His job was to lead the entire army.

Another goblin came over the rampart and launched itself directly at the Great Bear, striking him in the chest. Kisada wore heavy armor known as haramaki-do. He always wore his armor, whether he was going into battle or not. Haramaki-do, with its wraparound body piece and large shoulder guards, was cumbersome and uncomfortable. It was made of lacquered leather and strips of metal woven together by thick strands of tough silk. Most samurai donned it only before battle, but Kisada wished to inspire his troops. The Crab samurai spent all day every day protecting the empire from the Shadowlands. How could they respect a leader who was not always ready for battle?

Kisada took his tetsubo in both hands and forced it across the slathering mouth of the goblin, which chewed on it ravenously. Some of its sharp teeth bit into the wood of his weapon. Others snapped off against forged iron.

Like most goblins, this one had an almost human countenance. Its bald head, long pointed nose, and tapered chin made it look a little like an old sage, or perhaps a head priest gone mad. But its tall floppy ears and sickly green skin clearly marked it as a creature in the army of Fu Leng.

With a great twist of his mighty arms Hida Kisada turned the tetsubo until the goblin's neck snapped. He stepped forward, swinging the club again, and smashed three goblins that were just cresting the Wall. Their screams echoed as they fell to the ground one hundred feet below.

For a moment there was no one for the Great Bear to fight. He looked around. Although his samurai were not as tall, strong, skilled, or vicious as Kisada, they were more than a match for the goblins. Just by a quick count, Kisada could see nearly two dozen Shadowlands creatures lying dead on the ramparts. No Crab soldiers had fallen to the enemy yet, but one samurai-ko sat slumped against the doorway. The broken shaft of a spear jutted from her thigh, and a diagonal wound crossed her face from the blow that had split her helmet in two. Even in this disadvantageous position the samurai-ko continued to fight. She had abandoned her naginata, a sword-headed polearm, and now fought with her wakizashi short sword.

Three goblins, sensing an opponent they actually had a chance to defeat, moved in on the samurai-ko. Her wakizashi might have been enough to stave off one of them, but never three.

Kisada moved quickly through the chaos of battle, howling like a madman. He swung his tetsubo flat across his body, taking the first goblin's head clean off in a single blow. The second one narrowly dived out of the way of both Kisada's follow-through and his next two strikes. Kisada's third attack caught his opponent across the waist, shattering its hip. The goblin fell to the ground shrieking in pain. One more swing of the tetsubo stopped the shrieking for good.

The Great Bear turned to the injured samurai-ko. A goblin had leaped onto her injured leg and thrust its tanto into her chest. Death must have been nearly instantaneous, but the samurai-ko somehow managed to thrust her wakizashi up into the goblin's throat and through its hideous head.

The two corpses stood locked in a deadly embrace. The young samurai-ko might have given her life, but she did not fail in her duty.

Kisada looked around. The Shadowlands forces were withdrawing just as quickly as they'd come. He spared a moment to look toward the east. The battle on the next tower was already done, but one figure continued to fight on against invisible opponents. He dealt blow after blow to foes whose bodies were already cold. The Great Bear recognized his cousin Amoro.

Amoro was nearly Kisada's equal in a battle—in fact, in any given battle, he might kill twice as many Shadowlands assailants as Kisada. The difference was that when the bloodlust gripped him Amoro also became a danger to his own troops. It was impossible for him to lead others in battle.

Once Amoro struck his first blow, his eyes clouded over, and he was swept up in the fury of killing until there was no one left to kill. If the foes retreated before Amoro's fury was spent, as they had today, his comrades had to withdraw while he sliced his tetsubo again and again into the bodies of the fallen—friend and foe alike. His friends called him a berserker. Others in his regiment called him a lunatic.

Kisada pitied his cousin. It was a shame that one of the most powerful and talented samurai under the Great Bear's banner could not be promoted any higher through the ranks. There was only so much honor a daimyo could heap on an officer who killed half as many of his own men as the enemy.

Of course, he also envied Amoro.

In his youth Kisada had been a wild man. He led assault after assault into the Shadowlands, often against standing orders. His face was a crisscross of scars earned through his various exploits. Many a poem and several Crab drinking songs celebrated the brilliance of the young Kisada's military career. He missed those days of carefree danger and excitement. Amoro certainly was more uncontrollable than Kisada ever was. In fact he might well be insane, but at least he would never have to make that soul-searching choice between the call of battle and the good of the clan.

At fifty, Kisada was ten years past the age when most samurai were urged to leave active service, and ten years short of when they were forced to. As daimyo, of course, he could go on as long as he pleased, but he could never again have the free rein to charge off into battle whenever and wherever he liked. He was the symbol of his clan. Everything the Great Bear did reflected directly on all the samurai under his control.

Hida Kisada was a man of few words, even for a Crab. The other clans said that if you could get a Crab samurai to say three meaningful sentences, you'd hear every word in his vocabulary—well, every word that could be repeated in polite company. The Great Bear was an intelligent, well-spoken man, but he preferred to exercise that skill only when absolutely necessary. "Life is so much simpler," he would say, "when all anyone expects you to do is grunt and nod your head. You would be amazed at how many people act as though you cannot hear simply because you do not speak."

The Great Bear knelt beside the fallen samurai-ko. "I only hope I die as good a death as yours," he whispered.

Three more goblins landed heavily on his back.

"Curse me for a fool!" Kisada barked.

While he was lost in reverie, the goblins, who had only moments before been running away as quickly as their spindly legs would carry them, were now climbing back over the Wall. They attacked the Crab samurai with a fury born of desperation—or fear. The sniveling creatures kept looking over their shoulders as if fleeing something even more frightening than death by Rokugani steel.

The Wall shook.

At first Kisada thought it was an earthquake. They were fairly common in this part of the empire. But earthquakes rarely came in single sharp jolts.

The Wall shook again. Something was climbing. Something very big.

The next violent shake came when a monstrous hand reached up to grasp the lip of the parapet. It was vaguely human-shaped but was made entirely of fleshy, ropelike tendrils wound tightly over a skeleton. It was the color of mud mixed with blood. As the hand strained to pull the rest of the creature up the Wall the cords pulled taut, making high-pitched stretching and snapping noises.

A second hand grasped the top of the Wall. In a deceptively quick motion, the creature pulled itself up onto the tower. Its body was a fifteen-foot tall crimson, ropy tangle of cords. Its muscles gleamed moistly. It looked as though someone had peeled the creature's natural skin off, leaving only the innards to walk around in a mockery of life. Its eyes were bald yellow patches in its sinewy face, but they focused immediately on the Crab daimyo.

"Hida Kisada," the creature said. Its voice was strained and unnatural, filled with resonant pops and crackles as its sinewy throat mimicked human speech.

The goblins on the Great Bear's back released their grips and fled.

"Oni," Kisada answered, raising himself to his full height. He seemed tiny and insignificant next to the hideous beast.

"I have come for your soul," the oni said.

The Great Bear nodded, almost bowed, to the oni. Then he launched himself through the air, his tetsubo raised overhead. He brought it down with a mighty swing, lodging it in the oni's forehead.

The creature laughed.

Flinging its neck back, the oni snapped the war club out of Kisada's hand. It shook its head wildly, trying to dislodge the weapon, but the tetsubo was too firmly planted in the ropy mass. The oni raised both its hands to its head. The air suddenly fled from its lungs.

Kisada, howling like a wounded bear, had kicked the creature in the gut. It doubled over. He grabbed hold of a tendril in its chest and began climbing toward his tetsubo.

Wheezing in deep, popping breaths, the oni couldn't put up much of a fight, but it did manage to wrap both of its arms around itself, crushing the Great Bear to its chest. It leaned back against the ledge of the tower and squeezed as hard as it could while it gasped.

Kisada could not move and had no weapon.

The oni sputtered, trying to regain its breath while robbing the Crab daimyo of his.

All around the tower, the goblins fled back down the Wall. Many of them merely traded honorable death in combat for an ignominious death on the rocks below. A good half dozen limped back into the gray fog of the Shadowlands.

Freed from assailants, the Crab samurai saw the titanic struggle between Kisada and the oni. What's more, they saw that the Great Bear's eyes were beginning to glass over as he struggled to escape. Without any order, or even a word of discussion, they raised their weapons and charged. They screamed curses that even *they* had not thought of before.

The oni saw the odds arrayed against it. It still couldn't breathe—or even stand—properly. The oni rocked forward, then flung itself back, meaning to launch itself and its captive over the Wall.

The Crab samurai were too fast. They reached the oni and held firmly to the arm pinning Hida Kisada.

The creature had no other choice. It released the Great Bear over the Wall. The samurai let go to catch their leader and pull him to safety. The oni dropped to the ground with a thunderous crash and made off into the mists.

"That was the bravest thing I've ever seen anyone do," one samurai said to Kisada as his eyes began to find their focus again.

"Hai!" they all agreed.

The Great Bear seemed not to hear them at all.

"No!" he screamed and leaped for the Wall as if he meant to spring over it and follow the oni.

"Kisada-sama!" screamed one bushi as he grabbed the obi around his daimyo's waist.

"It's one hundred feet down," another said wrapping his arms around Kisada. "You'll never make it!"

"I don't care!" growled the Great Bear. "Don't you see? That creature—that *thing* has my tetsubo!"

All Crab samurai considered their weapons to be symbols of themselves—of their souls, forged and tempered into living weapons. Parents passed their weapons to their children, who in turn passed them on to the next generation. They became more than instruments of death. They were symbols of a family's history and value.

Hida Kisada stared out into the Shadowlands.

"My tetsubo."

3   DEFENDING THE CODE

Hida Kisada is an uncouth, arrogant bully, and he has no right to embarrass the emperor the way he has!"

Hida Sukune bristled at the accusation being leveled against his father, but more importantly he worried about his elder brother's reaction. Hida Yakamo knelt stock-still next to Sukune, his arms and shoulders twitching slightly. The younger brother was certain that he heard a long, low, animalistic growl escape Yakamo's clenched teeth.

They sat before a council of representatives from the major Rokugani clans—all except the Crab. As was tradition, the council sat on a slightly raised tatami dais, while the Hidas knelt on small mats laid on a hardwood floor. Sukune and Yakamo had come to Otosan Uchi with the belief that they were supposed to fill the Crab seats on this particular council meeting. Upon arriving at the Imperial Palace, they learned that they were actually there to stand in defense of their father and their clan.

"What offense has our daimyo caused, Mirumoto-san?" Sukune asked with as much deference as he could muster. More than any other Crab, Sukune was welcomed in the court of the emperor—indeed, in any court in Rokugan—but there was only so much slander even he would suffer at the hands of these bureaucratic imbeciles. He was smaller, weaker, and more socially adept than most Crab, but he still held the deep-seated belief that samurai from any other clan were merely playacting the roles of bushi—of warriors—and that politicians and courtiers had no right to lay claim to that title at all.

Mirumoto Hitomi, the representative of the Dragon Clan, seemed barely to acknowledge Sukune's presence. She stared unblinkingly at Yakamo as she spoke.

"The same offense *every* Crab daimyo has caused since the beginning of time." Hitomi spoke slowly and purposefully. "The Great Bear follows no one's orders but his own. He fails to spend the required time in the emperor's court. He shows complete and utter disregard for the decisions and jurisdiction of the other clans. He shames us all by using siege engines and other weapons of mass destruction against ordinary troops. He follows none of the rules of etiquette or manners prescribed in the code of bushido. All in all, I ask you what he does that is *not* offensive in some way or another?"

The other members of the panel looked at one another with slightly dismayed expressions. Clearly Kisada's arrogance was the subject about which they wished to speak, but the young Dragon was pressing the point too hard. While they all wished the Great Bear would at least make a show of being more mindful of tradition and etiquette, none of the others would question his dedication to bushido, the way of the warrior. What's more, Hitomi seemed to take particular glee in provoking Yakamo.

"One inoffensive action? Is that all you want?" Sukune asked. His temper too was rising, but his tactical mind told him clearly this was not the time or place to give in to the family temper. "Perhaps orchestrating our entire defense against the Shadowlands gives *you* offense, Mirumoto-san, but I doubt you speak for everyone on this council. Hida Kisada has personally planned and led every major action against the armies of the Dark One in the past twenty years. It is by his efforts that the empire is not overrun by demons, ghosts, and goblins. This is a task he performs every waking hour of every day. If he has not had time to attend every function the court conducts, it is only for the sake of making sure that uninvited guests from the realm of darkness do not attend either. If you would prefer—"

Without warning, Yakamo rose from his place, spat on the cherry-wood floor of the audience chamber, and began to stalk out of the room.

"You see?" said Hitomi with undisguised revulsion. "You see how his son acts? And this is nothing compared to the father. He comes into this council room wearing full armor, as if to bully us into forgiving all his father's trespasses. He cannot dress for anything but a conflict, and he is so barbaric that he must let his younger brother speak for him in open court. If the Great Bear cannot even train his own cub to act like an honorable, civilized samurai, what does that say for the rest of his clan?"

Yakamo whirled on his heel and snarled at Mirumoto Hitomi. "Civilized? You want us to act civilized when every day we are up to our breastplates in evil so pervasive, so unyielding that its taste fouls our food and its scent clings inside our nostrils?"

With four giant strides he stood immediately before the Dragon councilor. It would be easy to mistake him for a youthful Kisada. Yakamo was not as large as his father, but he still stood head and shoulders taller than most samurai and looked powerful enough to tear a man apart with his bare hands.

"We provide the safety that allows you to *make* these inane rules, defining honor in terms of dress code and public speaking. If it is so important that we follow your rules, then come to the Wall and stand guard while we send our entire army off to learn the art of flower arrangement and extemporaneous poetry. But do not sit here in the shade of our protection and accuse us of disloyalty in the act of providing it! You do not know as much as you think you do, little Dragon."

Like his father, Yakamo generally preferred to speak as little as possible. However, as the members of the council now knew, this did not mean he was tongue-tied. Yakamo could be quite eloquent, and he was maturing into a skillful leader. When the Great Bear finally decided to leave his seat of power, his first son appeared to be more than ready to fill the void.

Hitomi and Yakamo stared furiously at one another for a long few moments. At first it seemed, with the Crab towering over the kneeling Dragon, that he was in the dominant position. But it soon became clear that Hitomi's calm, centered focus and knowledge of exactly what she was doing at least evened the score.

Yakamo turned so quickly and with such force that some of the other council members thought he had struck Hitomi.

"Come, Brother," Yakamo growled as he passed Sukune, still kneeling in a supplicating position. "We are done here."

Sukune did not follow immediately, however. He sat in his place until after Yakamo stormed out of the room. Only then did he bow and say, "I hope that the members of this council will forgive my brother for his outburst." His voice dripped sarcastic sincerity. "Perhaps the strain of defending the empire has become too much for him. Perhaps you would be wise to have both him and my father removed from the Wall. But I ask you, where else would you put such men? Their spirits are unbreakable. Where would you prefer they be, on the border defending all our lives or here in your midst trying to find some outlet for their warriors' spirits?"

With that, Sukune bowed even more deeply, rose, and followed Yakamo out of the castle.

4 THE CRAB AND THE DRAGON

When Rokugani spoke of the Crab Lands, they almost always meant the Great Wall of Kaiu, which many simply called the Carpenter's Wall. The truth was that the clan controlled a great swath of the empire's southern region. Most of this territory was rocky and uninhabitable, but that was to the Crab's liking. Their land was as tough and unyielding as their warriors.

Between the Twilight Mountains and the Hidden Forest was a long, thin strip of rich soil. Crossing that plain was like riding past one tremendous rice paddy. So great was the Crab army's demand for rice that every available inch of usable land was devoted to the task. It was still nowhere near enough, but the farmers knew their efforts were just as important as those of the samurai on the Wall. Without their rice, the samurai would have no strength to lift their weapons, and without the Crab samurai the tide of the Shadowlands would roll across all of Rokugan. The defense of the empire was *their* responsibility. Without Crab farmers, the Emerald Empire would fall. At least that was how the commoners saw it.

Samurai from other clans who visited the Crab Lands saw it differently. They said, "Even the peasants are arrogant, rude, and far too proud."

Crab samurai were proud of their common folk, who worked twice as hard as those in any other territory. They told stories of farmers who, in years of hardship and drought, offered to commit seppuku to atone for the shame of having a poor crop. No clan was as dedicated to a single purpose as the Crab, and no clan was as tightly knit top to bottom.

A pair of Crab samurai rode along a plain of rice. The farmers who worked the paddy did not kneel as in other regions of the empire. Rather, they stood tall and waved. One shouted, "Ho, Brother! How goes the war?" and another, "A bowl of my rice will strengthen your sword arm!" Such familiarity got commoners slain in lands belonging to other clans. These two samurai simply waved back and continued their journey.

Neither Yakamo nor Sukune had spoken a word after the first day of their journey back from the capital. Seven days of silence— it seemed to Sukune a test of wills. Clearly there was more between Yakamo and Mirumoto Hitomi than met the eye, but his brother did not want to talk about it. Sukune, on the other hand, did not want to talk about anything else.

On the first day of their journey he'd raised the subject every way he could think. Each time Yakamo responded with an angry grunt and urged his steed from a trot to a gallop. From then on, they rode and camped in silence, neither one willing to back down from his own personal wall.

When they were young, Yakamo could always beat Sukune at any physical test. The younger brother had been frail and sickly since birth. He never attained the size or strength of his brother or even his sister—though Hida O-Ushi was never a dainty chrysanthemum. Sukune did, however, show a great aptitude in the tactical arts. While Yakamo would chase dogs, cats, and other children around with a stick, pretending it to be a tetsubo, Sukune would spend hours reading about military strategy. He used pebbles and twigs to re-enact famous battles of ancient generals, and more than a few of his father's own campaigns. He could usually see ways to improve on the historical results.

As they grew, Sukune learned the martial arts required of every Crab samurai, though he did not excel at any of them. He was not afraid of combat and proved himself quite able to defeat even much more skilled opponents if he had time to discover their weaknesses. Yakamo, on the other hand, was always at the top of his class in military training. He was bigger, faster, and stronger than anyone else.

It surprised no one that Kisada favored his elder son. Yakamo turned into the spitting image of his father. No one ever expected Kisada to find the same connection with his younger son, not even Sukune himself. But the daimyo still found it difficult not to look at his second son without lingering disappointment. Sukune found glory on the battlefield, garnered fame with his writings about Crab army tactics, and was an immeasurable help in planning strategy against the Shadowlands. It was not enough. He was a tactical genius, but he did not have the physical presence of a Crab, let alone that of a son of the Great Bear.

Sukune's only other advantage over his brother was his unending patience. He drew on this gift during the ride back from Otosan Uchi. He would not utter another word until his brother told him the provocation behind the confrontation in that council chamber, even if it meant not speaking to Yakamo for weeks after they returned to the Wall.

As it turned out, he needed to wait no longer than that very evening.

While Sukune silently fanned the flames under a small castiron pot filled with rice and wild vegetables, Yakamo grabbed his tetsubo and stood. For a minute he didn't move at all, at least not voluntarily. Sukune could see that the muscles of his arms and neck were twitching. For a minute he thought that something in his elder brother's mind had snapped—that instead of giving in, Yakamo would fly into a murderous rage.

Though he seemed about to win their personal competition, Sukune decided it was better to lose. He could allow his brother to save face but still encourage Yakamo to tell his tale.

"The dinner is almost cooked, Brother," said Sukune hunkering closer to the fire. The night air gave him chills. Even all these years later, his early birth and weak constitution still plagued him. Sukune fought a chronic cough and was susceptible to disease.

Yakamo turned to his younger brother, the spasms in his neck subsiding, and a smile crawling across his face.

"Couldn't take the silence, eh?" It was not in Yakamo's nature to win gracefully. He had to gloat at least a little. "I don't blame you, it was starting to drive me crazy as well."

"Then why don't you tell a story?" Sukune suggested. "Perhaps why Mirumoto Hitomi hates you enough to antagonize you in open court."

Yakamo looked at Sukune, shocked.

"Is that why you've been giving me the silent shoulder?" Yakamo laughed. "I thought you were displeased with how I handled myself back there!"

Sukune shook his head. "I have no idea why a Dragon samurai-ko would bear you such ill will. What did you do to her?"

"Oh, not to her," Yakamo whispered conspiratorially. "To her brother."

▲▲▲▲▲▲▲▲

It was not easy being the son of a great man. Hida Yakamo never really understood the truth of that statement until the final year of his training. By that time he was beginning to really look like his father. Even his friends began to tease him about being the "Young Bear." This was all good-natured, but it still bothered Yakamo. He wanted a chance to be himself—to prove his value as a samurai based on his own skills and merits, not his relation to the Crab daimyo.

During most Crab samurai's training they remained sequestered from interactions with members of the other clans. Unless all of a student's energy was focused on his lessons, he would not be prepared for the overwhelming, never-ending responsibility that was every Crab's birthright. Too much contact with the less-disciplined clans could lead a young Crab to place undue importance on etiquette or decorum. The Crab mission was to hold the Great Wall of Kaiu by any means, and adherence to the foppish niceties could be deadly.

By the time Crab reached their final year of training, though, the relative value of gentility had been burned into their brains. It then was time to take them out into the world and allow them to test themselves against their counterparts in the other clans. In the spring of the year, tournaments were arranged with the training schools of the Crane, Lion, and Unicorn (with visits to other clan training facilities if they were possible). This afforded the students opportunities to observe and compete against different fighting techniques. It also allowed them to learn something about their own weaknesses—a vital element of every samurai's training.

When it came time to make the pilgrimage, Hida Yakamo was more excited than anyone in his class. He had been waiting all his life for a chance to prove himself against real opponents.

The experience did not live up to young Yakamo's expectations.

At each school a different set of rules applied. Often particular rituals of attack and defense were prescribed—the students *had* to fight a certain way. Most schools banned the use of the larger heavier weapons, Yakamo's specialty. "We are here to test the keenness of your mind and the sharpness of your skills," a Crane sensei told him, "not the depth of your brawn."

As a result, Yakamo found himself losing duel after duel. He had practiced with the katana and mastered the basic stances of competitive fighting, but then his training had taken a more practical approach. Emphasis had been placed on learning to read what your opponent expected you to do next and constantly surprising him. He was no good at this formalized, artistic form of fighting. His size and bulk, which served him so well in duels with other Crab, seemed to work against him at inter-clan tournaments. More often than not, Yakamo was knocked out of competition in the very first round.

He could hear the students, sensei, and onlookers whispering.

"Is that the son of the Great Bear? How can he be such a failure?"

"Can Kisada's son really be useless with a sword? Look how much he seems like his father? Where did all the skill go?"

"Perhaps this means that the Crab are not as mighty as they claim. If this is the son of their greatest warrior, perhaps they are all bumbling idiots dancing around on that wall like drunken monkeys."

This last comment hurt the most. The one thing that Yakamo feared above anything else was being unworthy of his legacy.

Yakamo began to feel haunted. Soon, whatever castle or dojo they visited, everyone already knew about his problems. They talked behind his back before he even arrived. Nowhere did he feel this more keenly than at Kyuden Bayushi—the castle of the Scorpion daimyo.

As a symbol to their clan's dedication to secrecy and subterfuge, Scorpion samurai all wore masks of one description or another. Some were beautiful, others grotesque. They all obscured the faces of their owners, leaving only their emotionless eyes for the world to see. Those eyes—as near as young Yakamo could tell—were all trained on him.

That night, he visited his sensei. "In our dojo I was the strongest of our class, but here I cannot even win a single match. Why have my skills deserted me?"

Yakamo's sensei looked him dead in the eye and said, "They have not, Young Bear." This sensei was the only one who could call him by that name and not risk his anger. "You are learning exactly the lesson this trip is intended to teach. It is *most* important that you learn it better than any of your fellows. As the future ruler of the clan, you will be called upon to use this lesson every day of your life."

"But what is the lesson, Sensei?" Yakamo was desperate. So far the only lesson he'd learned was that he was a failure.

"If you play the game by your opponent's rules, he has already won half the battle," said the sensei. "In the dojo, you can win a fight but lose the match. But when you fight for real, whether it is on the Wall or anywhere else, remember that the *only* thing that matters is who walks away from the contest and who is dead. Do not let your opponent goad you into limiting yourself. You have the skills to beat these opponents, but they will not let you use your skills."

Yakamo considered these words long into the night. The next day he would duel for the entertainment of Bayushi Shoju, the Scorpion daimyo himself. Yakamo planned to put this lesson to the test.

When he arrived at court, Yakamo discovered that Bayushi had arranged a special match, not against a student from another clan's school, but rather with Mirumoto Satsu, heir of the Dragon Clan daimyo. Mirumoto was roughly ten years older than Yakamo and had spent those years building up a reputation as one of the most deadly swordsmen in the empire. The Young Bear did not find that hard to believe. Just watching him warm up, he could see Satsu's incredible balance and skill.

The court was host to visitors from all the major clans and several of the minor ones. Everyone whispered about the equity of pairing a student against a seasoned warrior. Still, they all agreed there was a certain excitement about seeing two future daimyo facing one another on the field of battle. Through it all, Bayushi Shoju remained silent and unreadable behind his mask.

The duel, like most on Yakamo's journey, was to be fought with bokken—wooden practice swords. The purpose was to test one's skills, not deprive the empire of the services of its brightest students. A sensei from the Crane clan was chosen as a referee, and he reviewed the very strict list of maneuvers that would be considered legal.

Crab and Dragon bowed to each other, then to the Crane sensei, and finally—and most deeply—to their host. The Scorpion daimyo nodded curtly, and the match began.

Satsu took a classic ready stance holding his bokken directly between him and Yakamo, the blade nearly perpendicular to the ground. Yakamo abandoned the standard dueling pose and held his bokken loosely in one hand flipping it to and fro in a relaxed manner. The onlookers might have thought he was delaying the start of the match except for the fact that the Crab held the Dragon fast in his steely gaze.

Tense moment's passed as Satsu waited for Yakamo to adopt some accepted fighting posture. Finally the Mirumoto could wait no longer. With a thunderous "Kiii-aiiii!" he charged his opponent.

Yakamo reacted by swinging his weapon not like a sword but like a club—as though the bokken were a greatly shortened tetsubo. He deflected Satsu's blow but left his rear unguarded as the Dragon moved past on his follow-through.

Satsu's eyes widened. The entire gallery gasped. Yakamo would never be able to recover from that swing quickly enough to block a reverse slash from the Dragon samurai.

The young Crab had no intention of defending against the blow. As his opponent moved by, Yakamo did not even attempt to recover his fighting position. Instead he pivoted on his front heel and slammed his foot into the small of Satsu's back, sending the Dragon flying face first to the ground.

"Foul!" cried the Crane sensei.

Yakamo was not listening. He followed his kick by bringing his club—that was what he now considered the bokken—down hard across Satsu's shoulder blades.

"Forfeit!" yelled the Crane sensei. He threw his body over Mirumoto in a protective and quite embarrassing manner. "Hida Yakamo used a banned technique and struck with a weapon other than the bokken. He is disqualified. Mirumoto Satsu is the winner."

A restrained cheer went up from the crowd while a wild roar came from the Crab contingent.

Yakamo stood there grinning a foolish grin. He had lost the match but won the fight.

Seating himself beside his sensei, he said, "I now understand your lesson."

"No, Young Bear, you do not," his sensei replied. "But very soon you will."

Yakamo pondered the matter as he sat through the rest of the matches. His reverie was interrupted occasionally as friends congratulated him and detractors berated him. All eyes were on him again, but this time the young Hida didn't mind at all.

When the day's matches were through, Yakamo's fellow students convinced him to go drinking with them. Though he ate twice what his teachers usually allowed on a training regimen, and though his sake cup never seemed to be less than half-full, Yakamo still felt empty inside. Nothing about the evening seemed real to him. He drank and caroused till late in the night and knew he would remember none of it.

The next morning Yakamo awoke earlier than anyone else in his group. The sensei's words still rang in his ears. He wandered off to the castle's garden and tried to clear his mind—they still had one more day of duels in the Bayushi court before they left for home. Despite his victory the day before, Yakamo wanted to leave this place as soon as possible. No peace of mind was to be found in the garden, so he made his way slowly to the main court.

The day's matches were already underway. Two students, one Crane and the other Lion, battled.

Yakamo entered eating an apple he'd plucked from the garden. He swaggered toward his friends, his tetsubo slung casually across his shoulder. Since he was not scheduled to fight today, he was free to carry his real weapon instead of his training bokken.

The crowd recognized the young Hida. Hushed conversations sprang up across the court. Soon even the duel stopped. Everyone turned to look at Yakamo.

"There! That is the man!" said a maiden from the Dragon Clan as she stood and pointed squarely at Yakamo.

He laughed.

"Surely, I am a man," he joked, but no one laughed.

Mirumoto Satsu stood, fire in his eyes.

"I should have known," Satsu growled. "It's true, isn't it?"

Yakamo disliked the tone in the Dragon's voice.

"What?" was all he said.

"My bride-to-be tells me that last night you—" Satsu looked around the court, and his cheeks flushed. "Drunk on sake and some misplaced sense of victory after our duel yesterday, you impugned her honor . . . hers and that of her handmaidens."

Yakamo laughed.

"Dragon women are too delicate for a Crab samurai," he finally said. "And why would I risk your anger, Mirumoto-san, when you so roundly 'beat' me yesterday?"

"You mock the seriousness of these accusations?" Satsu said incredulously.

"No," Yakamo answered. "I dismiss the accusations—I mock you."

"I challenge you!" the Dragon screamed. "Hida Yakamo I challenge you to a duel of honor, if you have any. I will leave you with a scar more permanent than the bruise you placed on my back—and *my* honor."

"Very well," said Yakamo. He might have been in a contemplative mood before, but this Mirumoto was now quite annoying. "I will be glad to put an end to your dishonor."

Only then did Satsu noticed he had no swords tucked into the obi of his kimono. The only weapon he carried was the tremendous tetsubo slung over his shoulder.

"Someone fetch the Bear Cub's swords," laughed Satsu. "I want everyone to know I beat you in a fair duel, not because you used a weapon too big for you to swing!"

"This is the only weapon I will wield," Yakamo said calmly. "If you will not face me using this, then we have nothing more to discuss."

Satsu laughed even louder. "I fear I won't be able to stop myself from killing you if you cannot parry my blows."

"Then kill me, little Dragon," Yakamo said dismissively. "Kill me or go home. Or is your honor only worth defending when *you* set the rules?"

"Very well," Satsu snarled. "I just wanted to give you the chance to save your life—if not your honor."

Yakamo tossed his half-eaten apple to another Crab student. "I'll want that back when we're done."

The Dragon and the Crab faced one another. Satsu adopted the same pose he had in their practice duel. Yakamo held the tetsubo with one hand, arm extended straight out to his right side. Satsu shifted his stance so that both hands held his katana parallel to the ground at about chest height. Yakamo did not move.

Long moments passed.

Finally, just as he had the day before, Satsu gave a mighty "Kiiii-aiii!" and charged his opponent. This time, instead of trying to strike on a passing run, the Dragon stopped short of Yakamo and swung directly at the tetsubo. Obviously he planned to take advantage of the Crab's one-handed form to knock the weapon free.

Yakamo stepped into the wind behind Satsu's swing closing the distance between them. He did nothing to block the Dragon's mighty blow. The tetsubo twisted in his hand and appeared as if it were going to fall. At the last instant, Yakamo reversed his grip and pivoted his entire body. He was now standing next to a startled Satsu, who had nothing—not a weapon or even a semblance of armor—between him and the blurred wood-and-iron club. It streaked toward his chest.

Yakamo's blow hit with the sound of overripe oranges thrown against a stone wall. Satsu flew through the air and landed in a bloody heap fifteen feet from where he'd started. He did not move. No one there had any illusion that he ever would again.

The students of both clans let out a shocked gasp. The woman who earlier had stood and pointed at Yakamo fainted dead away.

Yakamo went to his compatriot and retrieved his half-eaten apple.

"You cheated!" came a cry from the Dragon ranks.

Yakamo turned to see a girl charge toward him, brandishing a wakizashi.

"Satsu was my brother, and you cheated!" the girl screamed as she struck at her enemy. "You don't fight duels with tetsubo. Everybody knows that! Now my brother is dead, and it's all your fault."

Her blow cut Yakamo's kimono but did not bite skin. He wasn't about to let the tiny Dragon have another shot.

With a flick of his arm, he struck her blade aside with his tetsubo. Her wrist twisted painfully, and the short sword flew.

"I will not kill you now, little one, but you will remember that I could have." Yakamo said with no compassion in his voice.

"I will!" Tears had begun to form in the girl's eyes, but she bravely held them back. "I will remember everything about today.

My name is Mirumoto Hitomi, and by all the honor of my clan, I swear to avenge my brother's death. I will find you one day, Hida Yakamo. I will find you, and I will kill you!"

She fell to her knees and wept bitterly.

"I'll be where all good Crab can be found—on the Great Wall defending the empire!" Yakamo turned and walked back toward the Crab camp. "Seek me there, if you dare."

"Now you understand my lesson, Young Bear," said Yakamo's sensei placing a hand on his student's massive shoulder.

"Yes, Sensei," Yakamo said proudly. "Yes, I believe I do."

▲▲▲▲▲▲▲▲

"How long ago was that?" asked Sukune.

"Nearly ten years ago," answered Yakamo. "She has not forgotten her brother's death. Mirumoto Hitomi has grown into a fine warrior!"

"Yes," agreed Sukune, "but she still wants your head!"

"She knows where to find me." Yakamo yawned. "I suppose it doesn't matter whether I die at the hands of a goblin or a Dragon— as long as I die on the Wall."

5   FORM AND FUNCTION

Pitch the daimyo's tent there!" It was an order that Kuni Yori needn't give. These servants followed Hida Kisada as he traveled up and down the length of the Carpenter's Wall. Everywhere he stopped, they turned a local grotto into the Crab Clan strategic headquarters. "Make sure the daimyo has access to both the courtyard *and* the command tent!" Kuni Yori was well aware the servants knew where everything went, but giving orders, particularly pointless ones, reinforced the distance between Kisada and his servants.

Workers pounded tall stakes into the hard earth. On them they hung a long single bolt of silk, emblazoned with the Crab Clan *mon*. An impromptu courtyard and reflecting garden took shape for the daimyo's use.

Hida Yakamo strode up to where Yori stood. "You waste your time and everyone else's with this cheap theater dress courtyard!" As always, he made no effort to hide his disdain for Yori's sense of decorum.

Kuni Yori was the Great Bear's closest adviser, but no man in the Crab army was more dissimilar to Hida Kisada. Yori was a slight man with a pallid complexion, which he accentuated by painting it spectral white. He was a shugenja, and certain eccentricities were to be expected of magic users, but Yori made himself a mask more complex than many Scorpions wore. He claimed it was a mystic symbol that gave him power over creatures of the Shadowlands. The unnerving symbol, along with Yori's naturally domineering personality, gave him power over nearly everyone.

"Yori, you are a skilled shugenja and a gifted tactician," said Yakamo. "You could talk a hawk out of the sky, but you are far too taken with polite culture. Why does my father need a courtyard when he spends most of his days actually on the Wall? The power of his office lies in his strong right arm, not in the bowing and scraping of supplicants. Does he look like that weakling who sits on the Emerald Throne?"

"The daimyo needs a courtyard because of what it represents to the soldiers and commoners around him," said Yori. "The courtyard is a place where life and death decisions are made, Yakamo-san. It is a place of mystery that most of them will never see, but if they do, it will change their lives completely. To generals it is a place where they can show deference in the way befitting their commander. To the other clans it is a place where the daimyo rules absolutely—even the emperor would not dare enter this courtyard and order your father about. It creates the image of a great man and a great leader."

"Bah!" spat a gruff voice from within the makeshift courtyard. "I do not want to 'create the image of a great man'—I *am* a great warrior. Let the world think what it will!" The Great Bear pushed his way through the silk barrier—he was still covered in blood and ichor from today's battle. Something about his posture didn't look right.

"Kisada-sama," Kuni Yori began, bowing deeply, "of what use is might or skill if no one respects them? Yes, the other clans are peacocks strutting gaudy feathers of 'culture,' but we can use their fawning traditions against them."

Kisada's confidence in his own abilities allowed him to keep an advisor who saw things completely differently. Today, as always,

Kuni Yori showed Kisada opinions he would *never* come to on his own. But the Great Bear was barely listening.

"When did you arrive?" he asked his son.

"Just past midday," Yakamo replied.

"And Sukune?"

"My brother is in his tent recovering from his hard ride," Yakamo sneered.

Kisada sighed, his shoulders drooping slightly—a posture he often adopted when talking about his youngest son.

"Wake him," the Great Bear ordered. He shouldered his way into his command tent.

▲▲▲▲▲▲▲▲

"We need to reinforce the position," Sukune's sharp voice rang clearly, though he had not yet reached the command tent. "Transfer a second regiment to that tower, perhaps more. The enemy has sensed a weakness and will continue to strike there until we show them it is useless."

"As usual you miss the point," barked Yakamo. He burst through the tent flap, not bothering to hold it open for his brother. "A single regiment of Crab warriors can defeat anything the Shadowlands throws at us. If we move forces to bolster certain areas, the enemy will attack places where our troops are thinnest."

"But we will suffer needless losses with your plan," Sukune muscled into the tent, though with considerably less ease and bluster than Yakamo. "Good soldiers will die because you wanted to prove a point."

Behind them both came the even smaller form of Kuni Yori. The hood of his shugenja robes was pulled tight around his head. He said nothing. It was quite possible neither Hida brother realized he was there.

"Every man or woman on the Wall is prepared to die for the sake of that point!" said the larger samurai. "If we stand firm and defeat them with an ordinary unit, they will fear every regiment! Every samurai who dies will do so that all other Crab strike fear into the heart of the Shadowlands. That is a death replete with honor."

Kisada glowered from a corner of the tent. He stood with his hands clasped behind his armored back and considered them ruefully. His attendants had cleaned the gore from his armor and skin. There was still something odd about his appearance. "Is this the same argument you were having when you rode out of camp nearly a month ago?"

"It is the same argument we've been having since the day Sukune joined our forces," said Yakamo.

"And it's the same one we'll have for as long as I serve here," replied Sukune.

Kisada laughed, though his heart did not seem in it. "Just the way I want it!" He laughed louder but no more convincingly. "So tell me, what news have you brought from Otosan Uchi?"

"The other clans continue to whine like spoiled children," said Yakamo. "They say you are too bold. That your efforts to defend the empire are not enough; you must also pay personal respect to the emperor every two months. They expect the Great Bear to act like a whipped cur!"

"Is that all?" asked Kisada. "With the urgency they attached to that summons I'd have thought they'd come up with some *new* complaints! I've been brushing those same ones off for over two decades! I daresay you, my son, will have to do the same when you lead the clan."

"We could make it easier on both ourselves and the other clans," Sukune pointed out. As usual his father and brother were in complete harmony, and his was the dissenting voice.

"How?" demanded Kisada. "By following their pointless dictates? You're beginning to sound just like Kuni Yori!"

Sukune took a sharp breath. He distrusted Yori and his hidden games. The shugenja's advice always felt tainted with some spiritual poison that someday would lay low the Great Bear, and perhaps the entire Crab Clan. Sukune was about to protest his father's insult but stopped, cocked his head, and examined the Great Bear from head to toe.

"Where is your tetsubo?" Sukune asked.

Kisada set his jaw and narrowed his eyes, but he did not answer.

"Your tetsubo!" gasped Yakamo.

"Of course!" muttered Yori.

That was what had been so different about the Great Bear's bearing—he hadn't been carrying the tremendous spiked club when he returned from the Wall.

"It was," Kisada paused, uncertain how to explain his loss, "taken from me in battle."

A slew of questions burst from their lips. How did it happen? What did it mean? Was this a harbinger of the fall of the Crab Clan?

Kisada silenced them with one steely gaze. "Tomorrow we will get it back!"

▲▲▲▲▲▲▲▲

"Nothing ever changes in the land of Fu Leng!" Hida Kisada reached down from the saddle, grabbed the goblin that was chewing on his leg, and lifted it clear over his head. The creature wailed pitifully and squirmed in his hand, but the Crab daimyo held on with a death grip. "Kill one beast and another rises. Shatter one fortress and a new one takes form. Death and taint—nothing can change that."

It had been years since Kisada led troops into the Shadowlands, but it might as well have been yesterday. The very land itself was blighted with the taint of evil. No tree or blade of grass grew straight or had the proper color. Everything was crooked and gray. A bone-chilling mist clung to the ground even as the midday sun beat down on the Crab daimyo and the hundred samurai he'd brought into the heart of enemy territory. From cracks in the ground, things scuttled forth to assail them—things like this piteous goblin.

The Great Bear tightened his fingers around the goblin's throat, and he could feel the warmth of the creature's blood trickling across his fist. He growled savagely as he crushed the life from the little monster.

With Yakamo at his side, Kisada had ridden across the desolate plain, following the instructions Kuni Yori provided. In the light of the rising sun, the shugenja had cast a spell that led them toward the missing tetsubo. The magic would bring them within a mile or so of the weapon but could not pinpoint its precise location. Kisada was not worried. The oni was sure to have the tetsubo—either in its possession or still impaled in its forehead. Finding a creature as horrendous as that would be easy, even in the midst of a Shadowlands army. Defeating it was another story, but Yori assured Kisada that he had "something special" prepared for the occasion.

They topped a plateau and found it full of Shadowlands troops. The samurai dismounted. Crab samurai always preferred to fight on foot. From every direction monsters converged on the tight-packed Crab force.

Skeletons clawed at the Great Bear's torso, their bony hands chipping and bending the layers of his heavy armor. A zombie that might once have been a Crab samurai latched onto Kisada's right wrist. Its weight forced the daimyo to release his hold on the no-dachi he carried—secretly, he was glad. The tremendous blade was a fine weapon, but Kisada found it a barely acceptable replacement for his lost tetsubo. Kisada shifted his stance and began crushing skulls with his fist.

Yakamo fought nearby, using his tetsubo to shatter the skulls of three skeletons at a time. His form and savage fury gave Kisada a rush of pride. He was a fine warrior and would make a good daimyo after the Great Bear fought his final battle.

Kisada had left Sukune behind, entrusting him with the management of the forces on the Wall. It was not that Kisada did not trust Sukune in battle—he had proven himself time and again to be brave and resourceful—but the young man's frailty would be too great a hindrance. In the heart of the Shadowlands, the forces of darkness could *see* a warrior's weakness. If Sukune's fragile constitution finally snapped here, it would cost more lives than just his own.

The Great Bear shattered the last of the skeletons clinging to his lower half. That left only the zombie that had his right arm pinned to his side.

The undead thing didn't notice its comrades had been dispatched. Zombies were near brainless monsters. They could follow simple orders given by their masters, but they could not adjust their strategy when the tide of battle shifted. Rather than trying to bring Kisada down, the creature just clung to the Great Bear's arm like a geisha pleading with her lover.

Kisada laid the flat of his palm across the top of the zombie's head. It looked up. The Crab daimyo twisted his wrist violently and pulled the zombie's head and neck clean away from its shoulders. The body fell, and he threw the head the opposite way.

Kisada looked out at his contingent. His samurai were hip-deep in fallen enemies. Shattered skeletons, gutted goblins, and dismembered zombies littered the field as far as the eye could see. Nowhere did Kisada find even a hint of the red, ropy horror that had stolen his tetsubo—that had taken his soul.

"Just like old times, eh, my old friend?"

Kisada turned, shaken from his reverie. On the slope of the hill stood Hiruma Waka, one of the few samurai on the Wall who had more experience than the Great Bear himself. Waka swung a no-dachi nearly identical to the one Kisada had dropped earlier. He showed just how effective the blade could be. Each of his swings cut clean through an opponent *and* wounded the next one in line.

"No, Waka," answered Kisada. "Until I get my tetsubo back, *nothing* will be the same."

As if in response to Kisada's comment, a great commotion arose across the plateau. Goblins ran screaming away, and even skeletons and zombies shambled off faster than usual. The reason soon became clear.

A tremendous, crimson-sinewed creature rose out of the mist and stepped onto the plateau. It lumbered forward, swinging its ropy arms back and forth with each step. Wading into Kisada's troops, it flung samurai through the air like leaves on an autumn breeze. Each of the oni's movements came with a series of pops and crackles. A deep, grating sound, disturbingly like human laughter, escaped its clenched teeth.

"My tetsubo," Kisada hissed.

The oni's forehead bore an ugly, weeping gash where the Great Bear had struck it, but the tetsubo was no longer lodged in the wound. The beast held the weapon in its right fist. It was too small for the creature to use it effectively in battle—more a distraction than an aid—but the sight of their daimyo's tetsubo in the hands of the enemy stunned the troops into momentary inaction.

Except for Kisada. The Great Bear charged, howling like a wild dog under the full moon. He launched himself into the air and landed on the oni's chest, knocking the fifteen-foot-tall monstrosity off its feet.

Kisada grabbed the creature's arm and bit into it as hard as he could. Steaming hot blood as black as pitch gushed from wound and flowed across the Great Bear's face.

The oni yelped, more in surprise than pain, and released its grip on the tetsubo. The Great Bear scooped up his beloved weapon and leaped free. He held the tetsubo aloft the way a father would hold his newborn son to the kami for inspection. Then he locked eyes with the oni.

It was as if all the other combatants, all the samurai and every last monstrous Shadowlands warrior, disappeared completely. There was only Hida Kisada and the foul creature. The Crab daimyo did not see his closest adviser moving around the oni and pouring a coarse white powder in a circle. He did not hear his eldest son, his heir and the future daimyo clan calling his name and urging him to get back. The only thing in his eyes, the only thing in the world was his enemy.

The oni returned his glare with equal ferocity.

Snarling, the two leaped at one another, the Great Bear with his tetsubo poised to strike, and the oni with its massive hands ready to crush him.

Kisada swung.

The oni grasped.

Lighting shot from the sky, dancing in circles around the oni. White energy traced the exact path the shugenja had walked mere minutes earlier. It exploded so brightly that the assembled onlookers could see *through* the combatants. They became shadows of themselves, frozen scant inches away from one another.

Momentarily blinded, Hida Kisada bounced off the oni and landed unceremoniously on his rump. For the second time in as many days he lost his grip on the tetsubo that had belonged to his father, and his father before him. Scrambling, he gathered the weapon up, held it in a defensive posture, and looked for his opponent.

There before him, the oni floated trapped in a sphere of white light.

"Kisada-sama," Kuni Yori said with an exaggerated bow, "the enemy is yours."

6 THE FACE OF EVIL

The plateau, which moments before had been filled with the sound of battle, was now eerily quiet. Not a single goblin, skeleton, zombie, or other creature of darkness remained. Crab samurai milled about uncertain what to do next. The battle was over, but one enemy remained. They knew better than to approach it. The Great Bear had made it clear before the battle began—the oni was *his*.

Hida Kisada looked at the oni trapped in the swirling sphere of energy summoned by Kuni Yori. It sat on its haunches, its massive shoulders brushing the top of its prison. Small bolts of lightning crackled and danced across the sphere.

The oni smiled. It was a horrid sight. The muscles of its face, obviously not used to grinning, groaned and popped as they stretched. The beast seemed unperturbed and comfortable, as if it were in control, as if it wanted to be inside the magical cage, safe from the dangers of the world. All the while it looked Kisada dead in the eye.

The Great Bear and the oni stared at one another, neither willing to break the silence. It was a test of character, one with which Kisada was intimately familiar. It took great concentration and mastery of oneself to lock eyes with a mortal foe and remain as silent as death. Being the first to speak was tantamount to admitting your opponent had greater force of will.

Yakamo likewise remained silent. Kisada had taught this tactic to him at a very young age, always staring the boy down until he confessed some transgression. One of Kisada's proudest moments as a father was the first time Yakamo managed to outstare him. The matter at hand was soon forgotten, but the lesson never would be.

The wind moaned lightly as it stirred the mist. Hidden in that mist were the Shadowlands hordes that recently had been fighting to the death on this plateau. Were they hiding nearby, watching to see the outcome of this titanic test of wills?

"Y-your prison is formed from the elements themselves," said Kuni Yori, unable to wait for this tableau of raw will to play to its conclusion. He looked more physically shaken than either of the combatants. "It will last a thousand years."

As one, Kisada and the oni turned and snarled at the shugenja. The moment had passed. Neither warrior could truly claim victory.

The oni tried to adopt a casual posture within the sphere. In the end it only looked more cramped.

"After five hundred years of senseless battle, I tire of our contest. Perhaps a millennium of rest is just what I need."

"Rest," said Kisada, "is exactly what we intend for you to have—eternal rest!"

"Your life is so short," mused the oni, "and yet you spend it *all* standing upon that fragile structure with no goal other than killing my people. Tell me, Hida Kisada, don't you ever tire of a battle that will never have a final victor?"

"Your 'people'," Kisada said ignoring the question, "are ravenous monsters, and they spend their entire lives trying to climb over our wall and slay every last man, woman, and child in the empire." As he spoke, he drew closer enough to the oni that tiny arcs of lighting leaped to his helmet. The two locked eyes again, but only for the briefest of moments.

"Details," said the oni with a dismissive wave of its disgusting hand. Glistening red sinews popped audibly. "My warriors besiege your wall because I order them to."

The Great Bear grinned triumphantly.

"So without you," he chuckled, "your armies will fall into chaos. *You* are the mind behind their strategy, the force behind their attacks."

"Kill it, Father!" said Yakamo, his eyes gleaming with bloodlust.

The oni yawned.

"Kill me, for all the good it will do you," it said. "These forces may come and go at my command, but after centuries of battle they *want* to kill you as much as you want to kill them. *I* have been the voice of reason, the one telling them *not* to rush your wall with every last goblin and zombie. Surely they could overwhelm you, but in the wake of such an attack, our number would be so reduced that we could not carry the fight to our ultimate goal."

"Otosan Uchi," whispered Kuni Yori.

The creature shrugged.

"I presume so," it said with intense disinterest. "Such things are beyond my knowledge, and concern. My orders were given to me by my master and creator more than five hundred years ago. In the intervening years, Fu Leng has grown bored with my war. He has found other avenues to entertain his thirst for blood. Fu Leng *will* have his vengeance whether one more goblin dies on your wall or not."

The oni leaned closer to Kisada, so close that it singed its face on its new prison. It did not wince and didn't even seem to notice the foul stench of its own smoldering skin.

"Truth be told," it whispered, "Fu Leng could not care less whether *I* die or not. His plans are bigger than my assault on your wall."

"Well then," the Great Bear said, "you are worth *less* than nothing."

"Kill it!" Yakamo urged again. A murmur of agreement! rose among the other samurai as well.

"Yes, by all means, kill me," said the oni. "Of what possible use could I be? I only command the unquestioning loyalty of an army nearly twice the size of your own, Kisada-san. I only have the ability to command my troops to cease their attacks on your positions—and possibly even to fight alongside the Crab forces instead of against them."

Kisada barked a sharp laugh but never took his eyes off the oni.

"What possible use would your goblins be to me?"

"With your wall secured, and your army's number tripled, you could turn your attention to a prize worthy of you—the Emerald Throne itself!"

Another murmur ran through the assembled warriors. Kisada could not tell whether his samurai were outraged at the suggestion or awed by the possibility.

"I have watched you since the day you first climbed onto that wall," the oni said as much to the crowd as to Kisada. "You are different than any other samurai I have ever seen. In five centuries of fighting, you are the only foe I have ever respected. Your skills, your ferocity, and your honor are singular. You do not make alliances and negotiate deals to further your own goals; you fight because it is right. You stand in the face of my numberless horde and never once flinch. *You* are the true embodiment of Rokugan."

The Crab samurai rattled their katana and thumped their polearms on the ground. A chitter of excitement echoed through the mist surrounding the plateau.

The Great Bear chuckled again.

"A very pretty speech," he said. "But why would *I* want the throne? I spend all my time avoiding having to go to Otosan Uchi. If you had been watching me half as closely as you claim, you'd know that such an offer holds no appeal to me."

"What I know is that you are out of favor with the emperor," said the oni. "You have no interest in playing the games of politics and intrigue encouraged in his court. The other clans play them, though, to gain power in the coming days."

Kisada nodded mutely.

"But if you led the empire, you could do away with the posturing and preening in the Imperial Court. You could turn the Forbidden City once again into a true seat of power."

Chants of "Emperor Hida!" began to drift across the plateau and into the misty land beyond.

Though he was as critical of the imperial family as anyone, Kisada did not like the wind of sedition that this creature of darkness was blowing through his troops.

"You would do well," the Great Bear said, "to remember that these 'powerless' Hantei have held the Dark God and all his forces at bay since the dawn of time."

"The reigning Hantei is old, and his heir is weak," the oni grunted, much to the delight of the crowd. "Their hold on power is tenuous. Fu Leng will have his revenge on the hated Hantei, and he is not particular about how he gets it. If someone else sat the throne—someone of true character, whom the Shadowlands knew as a brave and honored opponent—then I could turn his anger. With you on the throne, Hida Kisada, I could promise the continuance of your line, security for your empire, and peace for a thousand years."

▲ ▲ ▲ ▲ ▲ ▲ ▲

"Perhaps it would have been wiser not to laugh quite so uproariously at the oni's proposal," said Kuni Yori as they rode back toward the Crab lands.

"Shut up, magician!" Kisada was not disposed to listen to any further advice Yori had on the matter. "What else would you have me do in the face of so ridiculous a suggestion?"

"If the beast's waggling tongue offended you so, why did you not kill it?" Yori peered at Kisada from within the folds of his shugenja's robe.

The Great Bear said nothing. He could think of several reasons to leave the oni imprisoned in Yori's magical cage rather than killing it outright. None of them had the ring of truth. The truth, as much as he hated to admit it, was that Kisada *was* tempted by the oni's suggestion.

"The oni was right about one thing," Yakamo said hesitantly. "The empire would be better with a warrior like you on the throne."

The Great Bear spun in his saddle and slammed the back of his hand across his son's face. The full battle helmet Yakamo wore softened the blow, but the impact still resonated. Kisada was a demanding leader and a stern father, but he almost never struck his samurai, much less his children.

"The Crab are not politicians, and we are not kingmakers. We do not throw our support behind one emperor and withhold it from the next. Our job is to defend the empire no matter *who* sits on the Emerald Throne." Kisada regretted the act immediately. His son had merely voiced the same thoughts he himself was struggling with. But violent discipline was the only way to deal with such awful temptation. Kisada had to be absolutely resolute in his rejection of this idea. Otherwise it would never go away.

Yakamo said quietly, "If karma ever put one of us on the throne—"

The Great Bear flashed him a cold glare.

Behind them, Kuni Yori smiled with undisguised delight.

"If that ever happens, dark times will have fallen upon the empire, indeed," said Kisada. "The balance between the Hantei and the clans has held for a thousand years. It is the cornerstone of the empire. Anything that undoes that balance can only mean the end of everything that has kept us standing on the Wall for generations."

As if to bolster Kisada's determination, the group crested a small rise, and the Wall came into view. There was a great deal of commotion on the towers, though no battle was underway.

A mile closer, Kisada saw a rider heading toward them from the base of the Wall, pushing his horse as fast as it would go. Soon it became clear the rider was none other than Sukune. He came upon them at a gallop and reined his steed in abruptly.

"What is it, boy?" asked Kisada.

Sukune was nearly as breathless as his mount, but between wracking coughs he said, "A message from the capital. The Scorpion Clan has assassinated the emperor and taken the throne. They hold the Forbidden City and all of Otosan Uchi and demand that all other clans swear allegiance to Bayushi Shoju as the new emperor of Rokugan! The Hantei have been overthrown! The empire is in chaos!"

7 MARCH OF THE CRAB

The sun will come up in about three hours. That is how long you have to rest!"

Hida Kisada heard his order passed back along the line. It would be several minutes before the last soldier got the news. He watched as four by four, the Crab army dropped their packs. Not bothering to remove their armor, they lay down on the grassy plains to catch what sleep they could. They looked like wheat being blown by a late summer storm. Eventually, the whole force as far as the eye could see were drifting off to sleep. Only sentry pickets remained on their weary feet.

The Great Bear lay down his pack and sat against a thick maple tree. He pulled out a short strip of dried fish and tore off a bit to chew on.

Three days.

It had been three days since he led his troops away from the Wall. For the first time in his memory, the Crab army was going to take arms against other Rokugani soldiers. The question remained—which ones?

As usual, his sons did not agree on the matter. Instead of sleeping, Kisada let his mind drift back three days.

▲▲▲▲▲▲▲▲

"Go up and down the Wall," the Great Bear ordered. "Tell every garrison they are to send two-thirds of their troops to meet us on the road to Otosan Uchi. We will leave in one hour on a forced march. We will not rest until we reach Beiden Pass."

"Hai!" said the runners. Rather than rely on a single messenger to relay important communications, the Crab had a network of runners set up along the Great Wall of Kaiu. Each runner would sprint from one tower to the next, then pass his or her message along to the next runner who would do the same. The effect was that of having a single runner who could sprint at full speed the entire length of the Wall.

"Two-thirds of our troops?" Sukune could not believe what his father had ordered. "You expect us to hold the Wall with two-thirds of our troops off on a fool's errand to the capital?"

Yakamo whirled on his brother, eyes gleaming within the dull gray metal of his helmet.

"Take care with your tone!" Yakamo stood so close to his brother that he looked straight down into Sukune's eyes. "No one questions the daimyo's orders so brazenly, not even his own son!"

"I only meant," Sukune said, standing tall and returning his brother's stare, "that Father says the politics of Otosan Uchi have no bearing on the Crab Clan. It does not matter who sits on the Emerald Throne. Our job is to protect the empire!"

"At any other time that might have been true," Kisada answered, stepping forward to separate his sons. "But the timing of this treachery and the offer I just received from the Shadowlands cannot be coincidence."

"On a forced march it will take you more than a week to get to Otosan Uchi," said Sukune. "By the time you arrive, the Scorpion Coup will either be solidified or eradicated."

"Perhaps," conceded Kisada. "But the chaos created by the loss of the last Hantei will be felt for weeks—perhaps even months. If not settled effectively, this could tear the empire apart more savagely than all the forces of Fu Leng combined."

"We cannot stand idly by while an honorless Scorpion sits the throne!" Yakamo spit the word Scorpion as though it burned his tongue.

"Why not?" asked Sukune. "It makes no difference to the Crab who runs the Imperial Court. We must still guard the borders. If the emperor calls himself Hantei or Bayushi changes *nothing* for our clan!"

"But what if the emperor called himself Hida?" asked Yakamo slyly.

Sukune gasped.

Kisada gave Yakamo a disapproving glance but did not strike him.

"Father!" Sukune exclaimed. "This cannot be your plan!" The young samurai then broke into a fit of coughing.

"Calm yourself, Sukune," said the Great Bear. "I have no desire to sit upon the Emerald Throne. We do not know what is happening in the capital, and that is why I am taking our troops to Otosan Uchi. The other clans can be trusted only so far. It is important that the Crab be there to insure the empire is protected. When all is said and done, we will need a new emperor. If such is my karma, I will humbly accept it."

Kisada paused.

"But I believe it is much more likely that this incident will bring the first Emperor Toturi to power."

▲▲▲▲▲▲▲▲

Kisada left Sukune in charge of the Crab forces that remained on the Wall. His son was among the most gifted tacticians he had ever worked with, and the Great Bear felt certain if anyone could devise a plan to defend the entire length of the Shadowlands border with only one-third the normal troops, it was Sukune.

Now, as he rested in predawn darkness, the Great Bear wished he had brought Sukune along. Of course, Sukune's fragile health could never have sustained the six-day forced march.

The more they marched, the more confounded Kisada became about the dilemma in Otosan Uchi. The Crab daimyo would not know until he actually saw the situation which side his samurai would support.

Kisada had no love for the Hantei. The dead emperor had grown too weak, and his heir was too young. Still, they traced their ancestry back to the original Hantei—son of Lady Sun and Lord Moon. They were born to rule.

If the heir was dead, though, who should assume the throne?

Sukune's point, that it made no difference *who* was emperor, faded as the capital drew closer. This would be Kisada's one chance to have an impact on the day-to-day workings of the empire. With the right person on the throne, he would no longer have to worry about politicians and courtiers undermining his clan's actions. He might even garner greater imperial support for the defense against the Shadowlands.

Bayushi Shoju could be that person. The Scorpion were an underhanded lot, but they were not out to destroy the empire. There was a certain wisdom in placing the most devious person possible on the throne. In the past, one always had to wonder what the Scorpion Clan was up to, but if they were in charge of the empire, then there would be no further need for subterfuge—they would have everything they desired.

On the other hand, how could the clans reward someone for murdering the emperor and stealing his station? The only thing that could come of that was more advancement through assassination. Not that this would affect the Crab. Protecting the empire's border was not a glamorous job, not one that other clans were likely to want. In the end, a political bloodletting might just be what the Forbidden City most needed.

"The sun is about to come up, Father, and you have not slept a wink." It was Yakamo. Kisada could make out his form sitting nearby, but could not see his son's expression—which likely meant the boy could not see his.

"Clearly, then, neither have you," said the Great Bear. Truthfully, Kisada did not feel the need for rest. Even when they stopped, he would rather have pressed on. He knew the wisdom of not pushing his troops to their very limits before a battle—perhaps the most important battle of their lives.

"I have been thinking about the situation in Otosan Uchi," said Yakamo with a faraway sound in his voice. "None of the factions there really deserve to rule Rokugan. They are all there for selfish reasons and would use their usurped power only to further those same selfish ends."

"Which is exactly how the Forbidden City has worked since before I was born." Kisada stretched. The sky was beginning to lighten, and he wanted to be up and ready before the rest of his troops awoke.

"I also keep considering the oni's proposal," Yakamo rose, walked to his father's side, and squatted there. "Clearly, they hope to gain some advantage by having you on the throne."

"Clearly," agreed Kisada.

"Knowing that, you could very easily take their plan and turn it into something wholly to our advantage," Yakamo said slowly, trying to gauge his father's reaction. "Shadowlands oni cannot be trusted, of course, but that does not mean their ideas are entirely without merit."

This thought had occurred to Kisada on several occasions.

"No," he finally said. "I will not seek such a resolution. It would throw the empire into even more confusion. We march to make certain the smoothest, fairest transition of power takes place. If the Scorpion is strong enough to hold the city until we arrive, we will support the sitting emperor. If Bayushi's weak will prevents him from solidifying his hold on power, we will help the other clans dethrone him."

Kisada was making this decision as the words came from his mouth. Seconds earlier, he would not have known where he stood on the matter.

"The most important thing for the Crab Clan is a strong emperor. Exactly who that is matters not at all."

8   STRENGTH

The empire is no more." From the stony hill where Hida Kisada stood, he could see that Otosan Uchi was burning. The capital was still the better part of a day's march away. At least four separate military camps surrounded it. Within its walls, battles raged, but not in the Forbidden City—the walled and magically protected citadel where the emperor and his retinue lived. "The other clans have managed to take back most of the city, but the Scorpion is still secure in his lair. The real battle has not even begun yet."

"How can Bayushi hold out against such overwhelming odds?" asked Yakamo. He had expected to find the city devolved into chaos, with the Scorpion crushed and the other clans fighting among themselves for the Emerald Throne. He never imagined Bayushi's samurai could stand up to a head-to-head confrontation. They were trained for skulking and attacking weaker forces.

Kisada raised his arm and motioned forward. His troops had marched harder than anyone had any right to ask. In only six days, they'd covered the two hundred fifty miles separating the Great Wall of Kaiu and Otosan Uchi. The Great Bear knew that to rest now and watch the turmoil below would only weaken the soldiers' morale. Seeing the capital in flames could push them to even greater physical extremes, but only if Kisada kept them moving.

The Crab army swarmed over the hills, not in a long straight line but in waves that nearly spread from one horizon to the other. Surely Bayushi Shoju could see this from within the Forbidden City. The Great Bear was beginning to feel a grudging respect for the Scorpion. If he gauged the action in Otosan Uchi correctly, the Scorpion forces had only just relinquished control of the main city. They started fires as they fell back to the inner gates of the imperial compound. From there, they could fight a defensive battle for weeks or months. The walls were tougher and harder to breach than even the Carpenter's Wall.

If I were in there, Kisada thought, with my own men to guard the walls, no one would ever take the throne. Perhaps Bayushi is strong enough to run the empire. Perhaps he does deserve the support of the Crab.

The Great Bear's thoughts were interrupted. A single rider approached his retinue. It was a Scorpion samurai with the imperial mon flying from a banner strapped to his back. The scuffs and tears in his armor and kimono told of the fight he had to get through the enemy lines. He rode straight up to Kisada, dismounted, and lay down on the ground in the deep bow reserved for only the most honored dignitaries.

"My lord, Kisada-sama," said the Scorpion, panting, "I am Tetsuo, cousin to the emperor."

"Get off the ground, you crawling insect!" Kisada growled.

"Hai! Hai!" Tetsuo rose to his feet but did not look Kisada in the eyes. Instead the Scorpion remained bent over double in an extended bow.

Kisada disliked this behavior in anyone. The only superiority that mattered was the strength of a samurai's sword arm, not the station one held. He especially distrusted groveling from a Scorpion. If he could not see a Scorpion's eyes, the sneaky bug must be lying to him!

Clearly, this Tetsuo would not look the Great Bear in the eyes.

"What is your message, 'Cousin'?"

Tetsuo bowed a little deeper. "My lord, the first Emperor Bayushi sends his compliments to the Lord of the Crab. He expresses his admiration at your having made the journey from your homeland so quickly. No samurai other than the Crab have the heart to perform such a feat, and no man other the Hida Kisada could lead such a daring enterprise."

Kisada grunted in a way that meant get to the point!

"Emperor Bayushi is pleased to see you and extends an invitation for you and all your men to stay within the Forbidden City. The imperial forces there are having some difficulties with upstart members of several other clans. Your aid in quelling this rebellion would be most appreciated and looked upon with great favor."

Before Tetsuo even finished, Kisada spat on the ground at his feet. He waved his arm forward and marched by the Scorpion as if he were not there.

"W-what shall I tell my master?" stammered Tetsuo, standing and leading his horse after Kisada.

The Great Bear whirled around, his glare stopping the Scorpion in his tracks.

"Tell your sniveling cousin that I will never side with a weakling like him. I almost did. Looking over that ridge I thought that perhaps Bayushi had some courage in him after all. It certainly took some guts to kill Hantei. Slaying an emperor is a brave undertaking no matter how stealthily one plans it. I thought perhaps your cousin had strength enough to take the throne and hold it. That kind of strength I respect. But to kill an old man, loot his home, then call for help to keep what you've taken? That is the height of weakness. It may indeed be time for a new imperial line, but your 'Emperor Bayushi' stands alone—and he will be a line of one!"

The Scorpion ceased to exist for Kisada. There was only Otosan Uchi and the weak usurper who locked himself within the walls of the Forbidden City.

Tetsuo mounted his horse and rode back toward the city, shame etched on his face. He would have to fight his way through the other clans to get back and report this failure to Bayushi. Kisada hoped Tetsuo found his reward on the blade of Shoju's sword.

That would be the Great Bear's punishment for failing such an important order, but Kisada would never have shown the weakness the Scorpion did. He would stand his ground and die defending what he had taken through force of might. He would never ask for help.

▲▲▲▲▲▲▲▲

Kisada led his troops directly toward the High Gate. Although the Crane, Lion, and Dragon armies ranged along the way, none of the other daimyo sent messengers or runners out. They simply stood back to watch what exactly it was the Great Bear had planned.

The Crab army marched up to the gate and stopped in unison— nearly two thousand strong, and they all moved at one man's command.

The Great Bear took the army's standard from his herald and planted it in the ground beside the banner marking the entrance to the Lion Clan camp.

A cheer went up from all the clan camps. The noise reverberated off the cracked and conquered walls of Otosan Uchi. It rolled out among gouts of flame and belches of dark smoke rising from the capital. It shook the very foundation of the Forbidden City, and the confidence of its residents as well.

▲▲▲▲▲▲▲▲

"Saving the city from fire is futile while the Scorpion holds the Forbidden City," Kisada interrupted. He sat in a pavilion with the daimyo of the other clans.

For the past ten minutes Doji Hoturi, the Crane daimyo, had been going on about the need to put out the fires the enemy set as they retreated. He was worried about saving the outer city while the venomous Scorpion still controlled its heart.

"That bastard Shoju can wait," Hoturi said. "He has no place left to run."

Typical! All prim and proper etiquette, these Cranes, but they had not even a basic instinct for how to win a war.

Matsu Tsuko agreed with Kisada. The acting head of the Lion Clan wanted to force the Scorpion out and do it *now*. No one was sure where Akodo Toturi, the true Lion Champion, was—he disappeared several weeks before the coup. Most people had given him up as the victim of another Scorpion assassination, but Kisada knew Toturi too well to believe that. He was too strong-willed and vigilant to be taken in by a Scorpion plot.

"Better a city of ash than a city of Scorpions," Kisada grumbled.

Most everyone agreed. Even Shinjo Yokatsu, daimyo of the Unicorn Clan, concurred that it was most important to pry the Scorpion forces out of their hiding place before they managed to escape.

The daimyo might not all be in complete accord, but it was agreed. The next morning they would storm the Forbidden City.

▲▲▲▲▲▲▲▲

No plan ever survives contact with the enemy, but Kisada was used to plans remaining fixed until the armies were on the battlefield. Still, he found himself back in the same pavilion two hours before the attack because something had changed—something key.

Akodo Toturi had returned!

The Great Bear marveled at how the other daimyo responded to Toturi. If anyone should lay claim to the Emerald Throne when this brutality was done, clearly it was Toturi.

Still, the Lion Champion's plan did not sit well with Kisada. He called for them to use the same tactics the Scorpion favored— divert the enemy's attention with a fruitless attack while another force crept up and took the Scorpion by surprise. He would have the Crab begin a frontal assault of the Forbidden City's Fudotaki

Gate, then break off the attack in order to sneak through the River Gate in the dead of night. The very thought made Kisada's skin crawl.

"Acting like the Scorpion would bring dishonor to my clan!" he said and glared at Toturi meaningfully.

The Lion leaned toward him and casually said, "Then *you* can stay and storm Fudotaki Gate until we sneak in and open it for you."

"Yosh!" Kisada nodded with approval. "Just do not take too long, or we might break the gate down on your heads!"

▲ ▲ ▲ ▲ ▲ ▲ ▲ ▲

"*This* is what we came here for!" Yakamo shouted. "There is only one way into the Forbidden City, and it is through these gates!"

At the head of the first wave of samurai, Yakamo looked at the Fudotaki Gate towering above him. The barrier surrounding the Forbidden City wasn't nearly as tall as the Kaiu Wall, but it was impressive. This was the first time Crab bushi had ever laid siege to such a structure—they usually defended one. It was a daunting prospect.

"We know the advantage of standing on a wall. We know the power that comes from high ground and a home to defend. But we know one thing more. We know that no wall is equal to our fury, and no army—particularly the cowardly Scorpion army— can stand against our ancient duty to defend the empire. No Crab army ever has failed in this sacred task, and we will not today! To defend the empire we must free the Forbidden City. To free the city we *must* take this gate!"

With a sound that caused the very earth to tremble, the Crab army surged forward. Yakamo and his samurai hefted a great battering ram and ran at full speed toward the gate.

Above them, Scorpion officers gave the order for archers to "skewer the dogs!" A rain of arrows poured around them.

A second regiment ran alongside Yakamo's, holding large wooden hoardings above their brothers carrying the battering ram. Arrows sank deep into the wood, some getting through un-blocked. One bearer bit back a howl of pain as a Scorpion missile pierced his hoarding *and* the arm he used to support it. Still he stood his ground. Three of the bushi in his regiment fell, but the rest of Yakamo's warriors continued on.

Howling like a typhoon up the coastline, the warriors reached the gate. The ram struck hard, harder than anything had struck this gate in living memory. It shook the structure from the ram-parts to the foundation—but left no real measurable effect.

"Again!" shouted Yakamo.

In one fluid motion they rocked back and leaned into their target again, striking even harder than before. Though small chips of ancient wood flew through the air, the Fudotaki Gate did not groan or give.

Yakamo stood there at the very head of the assault, driving the ram again and again against the gate. Arrows, burning oil, and magic spells came down like rain in the planting season. No mat-ter how hard they hit, no matter how many good Crab samurai gave their lives in the effort, the enchanted gate held firm.

Yakamo had no idea how long this went on, but during all the hammering Lord Moon replaced Lady Sun in the center of the sky. To Yakamo, all things other than the Wall and the massive weapon in his hands had ceased to exist. His uncle, Hida Tsuru, came and insisted that the young man fall back to rest. Yakamo wanted to stay. He was about to object, but he knew that if he stayed the remaining samurai under his command would stay as well, and they all looked nearly dead on their feet.

"You have done well!" Tsuru said. "My regiment and I will take your place."

"Hai," Yakamo said wearily, and motioned for his troops to hand off their positions on the battering ram and follow him.

They sat against the wall of a soba shop, eating bowls of the proprietor's best udon noodles. It really wasn't much, particu-larly for someone as large as Yakamo, but it was all he had the stomach for. They slurped the hot soup and thick, chewy strands of flour absently as they watched their comrades continue the assault. The night seemed more like dusk because of the fires raging in various quarters of Otosan Uchi. Spells cast by both sides occasionally lit it up bright as midday.

Yakamo led his troops to a dark courtyard where they could get some fresh air. He ordered them to rest, but sleep eluded him. Sitting against a tree, he looked out at the Forbidden City and thought of the usurper Bayushi on the Emerald Throne. He narrowed his eyes and growled.

Just then, a line of samurai marched past—Akodo Toturi at their lead. To anyone on the wall they would look like more troops coming in to bolster the Crab assault on the Fudotaki Gate. But Toturi led his men deceptively away from the fighting.

Yakamo rose to his feet and stared after them. Toturi was a good commander and as honorable and trustworthy a samurai as any Crab. Yakamo could understand why the other clans respected him so, and he would make a fine emperor when this madness came to an end. But he still could not hold a candle to the Great Bear.

"So it is now," Yakamo said as he watched Toturi's troops angle closer to the unguarded River Gate.

"Yes!" a woman's voice replied. "After ten years it is *now* time to avenge my brother!"

From out of the darkness charged a Dragon samurai-ko dressed in full battle armor. She had her katana raised over her head and a murderous look in her eye. She howled a sharp "kiii-aiiii!" and swung at Yakamo's head. When he stepped to the left, she instantly pivoted and struck again. This time her blade struck his chest.

Sparks flew from the impact of the blow, but Yakamo's breastplate did not fail him.

"Mirumoto Hitomi," the Yakamo said with a dark smile. "Are these the actions of an 'honorable and civilized samurai?'" He reached down and grabbed his tetsubo.

Her answer was to howl again and strike with slashes to the throat, stomach, and knees in quick succession.

Yakamo ducked the first one and blocked the second two with his great club.

His samurai snapped out of their fitful slumber and rose to their commander's defense. Yakamo waved them back.

"Let the little Dragon have her fun," he said. "I spared your life last time, Hitomi. I will not be so kind tonight."

She came at him with a series of blows too fast for the eye to see. Yakamo was not looking at her sword. He was looking in her eyes. She was so filled with anger that he could see her attacks before she moved a single muscle. Every time Hitomi struck, her blade hit only his tetsubo. When her onslaught ended, Yakamo slid his weight onto his right foot and slammed his left into the Dragon's stomach.

Hitomi took five steps backward, but she did not fall or even stumble. She never took her eyes off her enemy.

She raised her katana above her head and lunged forward, but six arms held her back.

Three Dragon bushi, who had been among Toturi's troops, had stepped up to restrain the samurai-ko.

"Hitomi-sama," one said, "what are you doing?"

"Toturi has given the signal," another one told her. "The assault on the Scorpion has begun."

"The assault started this afternoon," Yakamo grunted.

"Of course," the third Dragon samurai said looking briefly over his shoulder. It was obvious he considered the Crab attack to be foolhardy. "Your diversion is what makes Toturi's plan work."

Hitomi struggled against her brethren, but their hold was too strong. Suddenly the light of reason returned to her eyes.

"Toturi has ordered the attack?" she asked.

"Just now," said the first Dragon.

Hitomi paused for a moment, considering her possibilities.

"Let's go," she finally muttered.

"Leaving so soon?" Yakamo called after her. "Is our fight over so quickly?"

Hitomi whirled in place. The other Dragon samurai started to reach for her, afraid she had succumbed to her hatred again. But she did not attack the Crab. She merely pointed a single finger at him.

"This fight is not over," she said. "And it will not *be* over until I have my revenge."

"Or you are dead," Yakamo growled.

"I'll be back, Hida Yakamo," Hitomi called as she turned and followed her comrades toward the River Gate.

"You still know where to find me," he called back. Then he turned to his stunned troops and said, "Come on! We're not getting any rest anyway. Let's go breech that gate before they can finish their swim!"

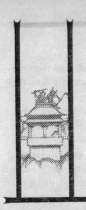

9 THE LADY SCORPION

"All this for nothing!" Kisada spat on the floor, heedless of the fact that he was in one of the most sacred rooms in all of Rokugan. The Great Bear stood at a wood-slatted window in the imperial throne room.

Behind him, the chamber swirled with activity. Courtiers fawned over the new emperor.

Kisada paid them no notice. Instead he stared through the slats at the night sky. There were no stars. The air above the capital was thick with black smoke, lit underneath by orange flames.

Though the coup had concluded three days before, Otosan Uchi still burned. Soldiers from all the clans worked to put out the flames. The aftermath was almost worse than the coup.

Bayushi Shoju was dead, slain by Akodo Toturi's own hand. The Emerald Throne—symbol of the beauty and unity of the empire—had been sundered in the fight. Most assumed it was Shoju's final act of defiance, that if he could not rule Rokugan no one would. Others whispered that Toturi's sword had carved the cleft. Toturi declined to say exactly how the damage was done.

Whoever did the actual deed, this was a sign so powerful that even Kisada had to admit the significance. The coup was over, but the empire remained divided.

In a strange twist of fate, while the Scorpion did kill Hantei the 38th, courtiers had spirited the emperor's son away before any harm could come to him. Already Hantei the 39th had returned to the Forbidden City. On the surface, this seemed a perfect ending—the rightful heir would simply ascend to the throne, and everything would go back to the way it was. However, after Toturi had defeated Bayushi Shoju, he had declared himself the new emperor.

A samurai steeped in tradition and pride, Toturi immediately stepped aside once he learned that the heir lived. There was no question in anyone's mind that Toturi was better suited to rule than this sixteen-year-old boy, but it was a matter not of suitability. It was a matter of honor.

Right away, Hantei the 39th began showing his lack of experience and wisdom. Rather than calling for the immediate death of the usurper's wife Kachiko, he announced that he would marry the witch. Then the new emperor ordered Akodo Toturi stripped of his rank and name. The single most revered samurai in Rokugan became a ronin. Masterless and nameless, Toturi was sent to wander.

"A fine way to reward someone for giving up a throne he could have kept!" muttered Kisada.

"How sad that Toturi was so rash in his ascension," said a cool, feminine voice from behind the Great Bear.

Kisada turned.

Bayushi Kachiko, the Lady Scorpion, silently moved to his side. She wore a scarlet kimono—a vestige of her now-outlawed clan. Her hair was pulled back into an intricate knot. She wore a mask, as all Scorpions did, but hers was more natural than most. She had a delicate, vaguely butterfly-shaped lattice of crimson paint and lavender lace affixed around each eye. It made Kachiko seem as though she could see all things at once, and that was not far from the truth.

The Scorpion Clan was well known for its information network—they had spies everywhere and raised the social skills of flattery and polite gossip to art forms. No one trusted a Scorpion, yet everyone spoke to them. And the most cunning, most sweetly engaging, most subtly seductive Scorpion of all was Bayushi Kachiko.

In spite of himself, Kisada found Kachiko's presence at his elbow both distracting and welcome.

"Toturi did what was in the empire's best interest!" The Great Bear shook his head and focused on the discussion rather than Kachiko's intoxicating perfume. "He believed—we *all* believed—that Shoju slew the young Hantei. Toturi knew that the throne could not sit vacant long and, if he did not take it, a new fight would break out between the clans. He knew that *he* was the one person we would all support as the new emperor. He claimed the throne for the sake of Rokugan, not to fulfill some personal ambition."

Kachiko raised her eyebrows as if scandalized.

Another mask, thought Kisada. Kachiko changed moods to suit her situation. She could appear demure and chaste one moment and lascivious the next. Under it all she was as cold and calculating as a trained assassin.

"Of course Toturi did what he thought was best," she said and flashed a smile. "But if he was willing to make that sacrifice, he should have been willing to do what was necessary to keep the throne. Particularly from the weakling son of the former emperor."

"Th-that man is to be your husband!" Kisada could barely stammer out the words. He looked over his shoulder to see the young Hantei the 39th complaining that the cleft throne hurt his delicate behind. Kisada would have laughed if not for the dire consequences this unproven ruler spelled for the empire.

"How can you slander him so?"

Kachiko leaned very close. Whether this was so that no one could possibly overhear her or so that her soft warm body would rub against the Great Bear, Kisada would never know.

"I have done what I needed to survive," the Lady Scorpion whispered. "I have saved myself from the execution that should have been my punishment for my late husband's crimes. This does not mean that I am blind to the fact that my future husband is a weak-willed, easily manipulated little boy."

How boldly she laid out her plan, thought Kisada. Surely she means to become the power behind the throne, pulling the boy's emotions and planting ideas in his head so that he acted at her accord. The Scorpion had won the throne after all.

"That is not what is best for Rokugan!" Kachiko continued. "Toturi would have made a better emperor. If he had decided to kill the young Hantei, or even deny his claim to the throne, who would have opposed him? Certainly not the Crab Clan."

Kisada shifted uncomfortably but said nothing.

"Clearly the empire needs a strong leader. Clearly my fiancé is not that. What will it mean? Can things go back to the way they were when so many men of action have come within a whisker's length of claiming greatness? Somehow, I doubt it. We are doomed to live in turbulent times until someone of conviction, power, and respect claims the Emerald Throne for himself."

"Or herself," Kisada said slyly.

Kachiko looked at him with mock disbelief. "A woman on the throne?" she said. "You know that would never happen."

"Perhaps not," agreed the Great Bear, "but even a demur wife has subtle control over a dominating husband. How much more power can a calculating wife wield over a hapless husband?"

Kachiko smiled gently, as if acknowledging his point. Very few people expected such keen insights from the Crab daimyo. "True, but how much *more* power would such a woman hold if she had a *strong* husband?"

"Are you shopping for a third husband even before your second honeymoon?"

Kachiko's smile only deepened.

"I know that my husband is not well liked or respected," she said becoming deadly serious again. "Neither of these conditions is likely to change in the coming months. You are right in assuming that I want what is best for me, Kisada-sama. But you do me a grave disservice if you think that I am not also interested in the health of the empire.

"You have done me the 'honor' of being straight to the point. I will offer you the same 'courtesy.'" She clearly was unimpressed with the Great Bear's lack of subtlety. "It is only a matter of time until the new Hantei meets the same fate as his father. This time no one will have the 'unscrupulous Scorpion Clan' to blame it on. This time it will be a clan of honor, one that believes in upholding the code of bushido and strengthening the bonds of tradition—so long as it puts them in power. *I* say that the empire would be much better served by a man of power and military vision—an emperor who can repair the damage done by an Imperial Palace filled with bureaucrats, not warriors.

"You are such a man, if rumors are true. With the support of the empress, you could repair this divided throne."

Kisada looked away from the Lady Scorpion. He gazed again at the capital in flames. So much had gone wrong in the last week. So many twisted and weak people were vying for power. The Great Bear longed to be back at the Kaiu Wall.

Then he remembered the oni's words.

Two voices, neither trustworthy, urged him to seize power. Why would the Shadowlands and the last remaining Scorpion want him on the throne? Was it possible to turn the machinations of evil against itself? Was it possible that he indeed was the best choice to repair the recently rent Emerald Throne?

"I will think upon what you've said, Lady Kachiko. Please ask no more of me."

She honored his plea, but as the Lady Scorpion turned to walk to her young husband's side, she suppressed a triumphant grin.

10 AT WHAT PRICE, WAR?

"This is like old times again, my friend!" Kisada barked in the midst of a fight atop the Wall.

Hearing a new foe, he turned and swung his tetsubo furiously at eye level. If his opponent had been human, the blow would have crushed his skull. Unfortunately, Kisada faced an ogre, head and shoulders taller than he. His blow slammed into the creature's ribs but had little effect.

"If you say so, my lord," said Hiruma Waka. "But in the old days these beasts fell much quicker!"

His no-dachi flashed through the swarm of goblins and other terrible creatures. The nearly seven feet of its blade decapitated one foe and injured four more. The no-dachi was usually a young man's weapon, requiring brawn more than brains. Waka's arms no longer had the strength they did in the days when he and Kisada raided into the Shadowlands for the sheer joy of battle, but Waka used the gigantic sword with cunning. Whirling strokes staved off several attackers while cutting a single target into pieces.

"Time is our enemy, Waka," Kisada said.

He thrust the broad flat head of the club into the ogre's midsection, hoping to steal its breath. The ogre's stomach proved as resilient as its side. The tetsubo pushed the monster back a few steps but didn't knock the wind from its lungs.

Now, the ogre had room to swing its tree trunk-sized arms to swat the Crab daimyo off the Wall.

"That's funny," Waka muttered. He swung his no-dachi in a double circle, once over his head and once at knee level. "I thought the Shadowlands were our enemy." Three legless goblins fell screaming to the stone walkway atop the Carpenter's Wall. An ogre clutched its hands to its now-blind eyes.

"You know what I mean!" Kisada dived over the ogre's arm as it swung in a deadly arc toward his neck. He rolled up behind the ogre, leaving the creature with an almost comical look on its face as it tried to find the Great Bear. "Nothing ever changes! The Wall is the same. The battle is the same. Even the enemy is the same. For all we know, we will fight these very same creatures again after the Shadowlands sorcerers raise them into undeath.

"The only thing that changes is *us*! We age. Our vision fades. Our reflexes slow. Eventually we weaken to the point where we can no longer adequately defend ourselves, and we do not return from the next battle. A noble death to be sure, but then the whole work of our lives, everything we fought for, goes unfinished."

The ogre found its target and turned.

Kisada swung his tetsubo in an upward arc.

The creature set its shoulders and gritted its teeth, anticipating a strike to the chin.

Kisada struck between the ogre's legs.

The creature howled piteously and fell to its knees.

"What are you saying, Kisada-kun?" Waka was an old enough warrior and friend to speak to the daimyo in such a casual manner. "That you don't want to fight anymore? That you want to retire before you fall one step short? That does not sound like the Great Bear! Not at all!"

"Of course that's not what I mean!" Kisada twisted his waist all the way to the right and uncurled himself in a powerful but dangerously off-balance swing. He struck the ogre across the cheek. The mighty blow broke the creature's spine. When the ogre fell lifeless to the ground its head faced the wrong direction.

"I meant that, like you, I am beginning to think about fighting like an old man. I'm considering very carefully who the real enemy is. I could fight the creatures of the Shadowlands for the rest of my life and three lifetimes more, and I could not really protect the empire. For every monster I slay, two more will rise to take its place. This border will never be secure."

"So who would you fight? Even the Great Bear cannot have a battle without an enemy."

Kisada caught his balance and looked around. For the moment the only enemies were the goblins that ringed Waka. Kisada engaged three of them.

"My duty is to protect the empire, and Rokugan has more enemies now than ever. But the greatest threats come from *within*. It has been two years since our emperor took the Emerald Throne, and the empire is no more stable than it was the day he stripped Toturi of his name."

Two years? Had it really been two years? Kisada marveled again at how time worked against them all.

"So what?" Waka blurted. The constant barrage of foes was beginning to steal his breath. "Nothing is different—not for the Crab. Whether it is one Hantei or another, Scorpion or Lion sitting on the throne, we still must defend the border. What concern is it of yours how the emperor runs his court?"

Kisada pondered the question as he crushed the first goblin's skull. How could he tell his friend of the opportunity he'd passed up—twice? The Great Bear knew that if he had taken the Emerald Throne, the empire would not be in the weakened condition it was now.

Hantei the 39th had turned eighteen, but he had not become a man. Shortly after ascending the throne, he contracted a plague—the same plague that now ravaged the countryside, a plague for which no healer or shugenja could find a cure. Some said the illness was caused by Shadowlands curses. Others said the kami punished the foolish child for marrying the Scorpion Lady. All Kisada knew was that the young Hantei was rarely well enough to tend to matters of state. Kachiko did most of the governing—Kachiko, who had urged the Great Bear to claim the throne. Whether by her own hand or not, she'd certainly gained the power she craved without Kisada's cooperation.

Now he wondered if he had refused out of honor or cowardice.

A new wave of goblins spilled over the ramparts. Like floodwaters they were suddenly everywhere, with barely a moment's warning. They chewed on Kisada's legs, hung off his arms, and tried to pry off his helmet.

Sometimes, he mused, the best thing about battle is that it keeps you from having to think about the tough questions.

▲ ▲ ▲ ▲ ▲ ▲ ▲ ▲

"The Great Bear is finally coming out of his cave!" Kuni Yori cackled to himself as he stared into the scrying pool.

Whenever Hida Kisada went off to fight on the Wall, the shugenja retired to his private sanctum and cast a spying enchantment. In battle, Kisada felt comfortable. He let his guard down and allowed his true feelings to come out. From the things the daimyo said to Waka, Yori knew his scheming and nudging were having their intended effect.

The shugenja seemed tall and powerful in the dark, tiny room—at least he would have if anyone could see him. There were plenty of dead eyes in this place—the shiny eyes of stuffed creatures dangling on wires, the empty sockets of skulls that lined the shelves, even the eyes floating in jars of brine. To them, Yori seemed tall and powerful. The only light in the room came from the image in Yori's magical pool. It played across his painted face in odd flashes of color.

Yori was a patient man. He knew that the only way to accomplish great things was to take them one small step at a time. He had been waiting for two full years for this first sign that his work on Kisada was beginning to bear fruit.

"You fought well and hard, my lord," he said to the warrior in his scrying pool. "And left to your own devices I think it would still be years until you came around to see the truth. The empire might not be dead, but with the weakling Hantei on the throne its heart has been removed. You know it. I know it. And the other clans certainly know it. Tensions rise between them, and open hostility is a near certainty. How can you protect an empire that is tearing itself apart? What Rokugan needs now is a strong emperor."

Yori's spell showed Kisada beating savagely at the goblins that engulfed him. Every shrug of his massive shoulders sent two or three of the creatures flying, but four more took their place.

"Yes, the Emerald Throne, Kisada," Yori continued. "That is your karma. You are destined to be emperor, whether you want to or not. I will not see you deny that destiny. I will not miss the chance to become the power behind the throne. All it takes is patience. The Bayushi woman knows that better than anyone, and look where it got her."

The shugenja leaned forward to decipher the chaos displayed in his pool. The tips of his dangling thin moustache nearly brushed the water. Still he could not make out Kisada's form under the mass of Shadowlands creatures.

"This will not do," he muttered. It would be unfortunate if the Great Bear actually fell in battle just when Yori started making real progress. Of course, not everything would be lost. The shugenja had already begun to work his influence over Kisada's heir, Yakamo. The boy had the Great Bear's powerful physique, and he owned the respect of the rank and file of the Crab army. He also had the eminently exploitable weakness of high ambition. Yakamo thought the Crab was intrinsically better than the Lion, Crane, and other clans. He believed that it was his clan's destiny to rule all the others.

Yori sometimes considered the work he did softening Kisada's resolve as a means of gaining absolute control over Yakamo. The more the daimyo listened to Yori, the more his heir accepted the shugenja's word as holy truth. In the end, it might well be in Kuni Yori's best interest if Kisada fell before the swarm of goblins—for he surely would hold even tighter sway over a Crab Clan headed by young Yakamo.

The only Hida that Yori could not dupe was Sukune. The daimyo's second son seemed to see right through every ploy and misdirection the shugenja used. Thankfully, the Great Bear was blinded by the boy's frail body—he never paid Sukune the attention he deserved.

"No," muttered Yori as he pulled the hood of his black velvet robes lower across his brow. "I still have need of you, Great Bear. You have influence in quarters your son has not yet reached. Besides, I can see that I've already won this battle—I just have to wait for the cracks in your sanctimonious armor to spread. Then you'll be doing my bidding and believing it's all of your own accord."

In the scrying pool, a goblin wielding a nage-yari got free behind Kisada and was about to thrust the javelin between the Great Bear's ribs.

Kuni Yori reached deep into his robes and pulled out a strip of silk as black as midnight. He held it over the scrying pool and said, "No, minions of darkness! We need Kisada alive—for now!"

The shugenja squeezed the silk. An oily bead of liquid dribbled out between his fingers and dropped into the scrying pool.

The goblin stopped in midstab. A glazed look came over its eyes. Instead of skewering the unprotected Kisada, it turned the nage-yari around. Placing the blade against its ridged breastbone and wedging the bottom in a seam in the tower's floor, the creature threw itself down against the javelin. The first blow did not crack its thick ribcage, so it pulled itself off the nage-yari and thrust down again and again until at last the blade passed all the way through and came out the other side.

▲ ▲ ▲ ▲ ▲ ▲ ▲ ▲

I cannot move my arms, Kisada calmly thought to himself. I cannot feel my feet.

The goblins' chipped fingernails jabbed under the seams of his armor. Viciously pointed teeth broke the skin on his legs and shoulders. The weight of so many opponents kept his arms pinned to his body, preventing the Crab daimyo from using his tremendous tetsubo.

The thought of death held no terror for Kisada. Novice warriors lost nerve in battle for fear of life and limb. They came ready to kill, but never considered that they might die. Overcautious, they often lost their lives, dying because they were not willing to risk themselves completely.

All Crab samurai were trained to enter each battle with a "dead body"—the sense that they were already dead—and fight as though they were trying to steal enough life essence from each enemy to allow them to walk away from the battle. This made them more vicious and unpredictable than any other army in Rokugan. In battle, their minds were not focused on staying alive but solely on crushing as many enemies as possible.

Though Kisada had admirably mastered the technique of entering battle with a dead body, he never truly entertained the possibility that he would *not* kill enough opponents to earn his way back to the land of the living. Now, for the first time, he faced that demon.

As soon as that possibility became real to him, the goblins atop him fell off. Most likely Waka had given the monsters reason to fear for their lives. Kisada's arms were free again, and he peeled the last of the goblins off his helmet.

Waka stood nearby, blinking. All the samurai were looking around in the same confusion. The goblins were in full retreat, though the Crab forces had done nothing to force such a withdrawal.

Kisada was certainly going to take advantage of it. "We have them on the run!" the Great Bear snarled. "Press the attack!"

He raced to the edge of the Wall, shouldering his tetsubo while drawing his yumi and nocking an arrow. He would not take aim. With the Shadowlands hordes barreling down the wall in such a rush, all he had to do was let a flesh-rending arrow fly—he was sure to hit something.

Kisada leaned over the wall and looked directly into a fist the size of a hog careening in his direction. It impacted with the sound of a giant oak being felled. Kisada's whole body snapped backward, and he flew through the air. He crashed onto the parapet with such force that he felt as if he'd been struck a second time. There was no air in his lungs, and the world tilted and rolled despite the fact that he lay on cold, solid stone.

The hand that struck the blow gripped the rampart as though it were a rail. Another hand, even bigger than the first, did the same. A creature that was all chest, arms, and shoulders raised itself up onto the Wall. Its spindly legs seemed incapable of actually moving the creature around, but they kept the torso steady as it raised its mighty hand to crush Kisada.

"No!" screamed Hiruma Waka.

He dropped his no-dachi and flung himself onto the arm, trying to pin it back through sheer force of will. Drawing his wakizashi, he stabbed where the beast's head should have been. This only enraged the creature.

The beast reached its other arm around and closed its whole hand over the top of Waka's head and upper torso. With less effort than a man might use to flick an ant from his arm, the creature lifted Waka high in the air. One mighty twist of its wrist cracked the Crab's spine in three places.

Waka went immediately and completely limp.

The monster slung the lifeless body over its massive shoulder. It made a motion as though it might go back after Kisada but then flung itself over the wall to fall in with the retreating goblins.

"No!" screamed Kisada. He launched himself forward.

It took six samurai to restrain the daimyo, but eventually he collapsed against the Wall, his face drained of emotion. Death had come for him today, and he had not flinched. But the thought of one of his oldest friends dying in his place sapped the strength from the Great Bear's limbs.

Eventually, he rose and leaned on his tetsubo as he gazed out into the Shadowlands. The other samurai stood far enough away to give their leader a moment of privacy but near enough to grab him should his grief overwhelm him again.

"I am brave enough to face the endless hordes of the Shadowlands every day of my life," he said to the friend who was no longer there and never would be again. "I am willing—even glad—to give my life defending this wall. Dying is easy. You showed us that, old friend. But the empire does not need another dead samurai—it needs a leader.

"The question remains—am I brave enough to seek peace by sitting on the Emerald Throne?"

11   IDLE HANDS

"**B**y all the minions of Fu Leng, what does she want *now?*" Kisada stood on the tatami dais at the rear of his makeshift courtyard.

At Kuni Yori's advice, he had decided to receive the imperial runner in this setting—a deliberate attempt to undercut whatever order the missive contained. Kisada knew it must be a dictate of some sort. All normal correspondence went to the command center at Shiro Kuni and was eventually funneled to the Great Bear's attention if warranted. This runner, however, came directly to Kisada's mobile headquarters, bearing a message that she was ordered to release *only* into the daimyo's hand.

Yori had once again proven to be correct. By adopting this maddeningly formal posture Kisada made the runner feel uncomfortable. He had seen this particular runner before. Her name was Chiya, one of only three or four runners entrusted with hand-written messages from the emperor. She carried herself with the pride of a Crane sword master. Chiya usually stood her ground and held the Great Bear's gaze, despite the fact that Kisada physically loomed above her like the Carpenter's Wall over the Shadowlands plains, Chiya usually stood her ground and held the Great Bear's gaze. Today, though, she knelt and bowed politely, never looking him straight in the eye.

"I do not know, Kisada-sama," Chiya said, using her most formal and deferential voice. "I only deliver my lady's word. It is not my place to question, only to serve."

Kisada knew, of course, that the runner would have no knowledge of the missive's contents, but he was enjoying this change in her attitude and wanted to take full advantage of it.

The message read:

Kisada-san,

The emperor and I request your presence, or that of a duly designated representative, in the Imperial Palace to attend an imperial proclamation of momentous import. We have instructed the messenger not to return until you or your representative departs for Otosan Uchi. Until that time, please treat her with all the respect and courtesy you would extend the emperor himself.

Her Imperial Majesty
Empress Kachiko

The words were pretty, but the message was clear: come to the capital—*now*!

Kisada shook with fury. The nerve of the Lady Scorpion! Was the emperor so ill that he could no longer write his own correspondence, or was Kachiko beginning to craft imperial policy by herself? Either way, it didn't matter. The Crab Champion had no choice but to send someone to Otosan Uchi immediately. The line about treating Chiya the way he would the emperor saw to that. No one would deign lavish such luxury on a simple runner—to do so would make a mockery of the daimyo's hospitality. Not to do so, though, would be to invite imperial discipline for failing to follow direct orders.

"Should I prepare to leave immediately, Kisada-sama?" Chiya asked.

"No!" spat Kisada. "My representatives will not be ready until nightfall. Until that time, you are afforded the most luxurious accommodations I have to offer—this open-air reception hall. Make yourself comfortable."

The Great Bear rose without further preamble and strode through the silken entryway. Chiya could hear his feet stomping menacingly toward the command tent.

"Yori! Bring my sons to me!" The order was as clear as if the daimyo was still in the courtyard.

▲▲▲▲▲▲▲▲

"You're sending Sukune! Why must *I* go, too?" Yakamo would never question his father's orders in front of other soldiers. But the command tent was empty except for Kisada, Yakamo, Sukune, and Yori, so he spoke his mind.

"Because one day you will have to go to court to represent the Crab." Kisada understood how his son felt, so he chose to explain his order. "When you become daimyo you will not always have the luxury of sending a representative, even one as noble as your brother."

"Bah!" Yakamo wanted to spit on the ground, but he knew that his father would brook no more dissention. "You sent us both last time."

"And as I recall," Sukune chimed in, "you antagonized the Dragon Clan representative and spat on the imperial floor."

Yakamo growled at his brother. It was a feral sound from deep in his throat.

"I have made my decision!" Kisada barked. "You will ride out of camp at sunset."

The three others looked at the daimyo confusedly.

"Why wait so long, my lord?" asked Kuni Yori.

"We can be ready to go before the sun reaches its peak. Why lose so many hours?" Yakamo asked.

"It is a message I am sending back with the runner." Kisada actually smiled.

Sukune smiled too. "A message about power and how to wield it, if I am not mistaken."

"Hai!" the Great Bear laughed raucously. "Now go 'prepare' for your trip."

Yakamo and Sukune withdrew, each eyeing the other antagonistically. Kuni Yori lingered, watching the daimyo.

"Though they look so different, they *are* brothers—that is for certain!" Kisada shook his head.

"If I may be so bold," Yori said after an interval, "why are you sending your sons in your stead? The empress seems to have something very special planned. One would guess the other daimyo will come themselves. Do you not wish to take this opportunity to meet with your peers? You all gather so rarely these days."

Kisada frowned.

"I . . ." he began, then thought for a moment. "I have my reasons for not wanting to travel to the capital at this time."

Within the shadows of his black velvet hood Kuni Yori grinned. You do not wish to go to Otosan Uchi, he thought. You're afraid that if you even *see* the emperor or the Emerald Throne, you will be tempted to depose him. You have come so far, Kisada—and you've only a little farther to go.

"In that case, may I humbly offer to accompany your sons on this portentous journey?" Yori bowed formally as he spoke. "I understand your distrust of the empress. I personally would not put it out of her capability to call this meeting to ensorcell the daimyo in order to add to her own power. As counsel to your sons, my presence would be unobtrusive, and I could serve as a safeguard against magical influence."

The Great Bear thought about this and grumbled. "I do not like the emperor, and I do not trust the Lady Scorpion. But even I have trouble seeing this as a threat to my sons."

Yori approached Kisada. "I am certain," he whispered, "that Hantei the 38th said the same about Bayushi Shoju's final visit."

▲▲▲▲▲▲▲▲

"What a load of dung!" Yakamo threw his hands in the air.

"For ten days you've been blathering on about how playing the role of the 'proper guest' is a tactical decision that will help you win the war of politics!" He glared at Sukune. "And *nothing* you've said even begins to convince me that you're doing *anything* other than playing a stupid game. A game whose ridiculous, pompous, self-important rules were invented by imperial courtiers so that they are the only ones who can win!"

"It is a long-term strategy," said Sukune for about the twentieth time that day. "You do not want to win this 'game' quickly—the only way to do that is to follow the path of the Scorpion."

Kuni Yori rode between the two brothers but said nothing. In fact, with his hood pulled close over his painted face, neither Hida could tell whether he was paying the least attention.

"If you play the game for too long, your opponent has won," Yakamo said adamantly. "The minute you switch your tactics in hopes of gaining the approval of bureaucrats, you've lost any chance of making the changes you really want. If you want to reform the Imperial Court, you must tear it down. There *is* no way to rebuild it piecemeal."

"So you favor overthrowing the emperor?" Yori's voice startled the brothers.

"N-no," said Yakamo. "Not necessarily. I think that simply ignoring the Imperial Court is a much better solution. If they want their borders secure, they will not interfere with Crab decisions."

"But if they insist on regulating our comings and goings?" Yori played Yakamo the way a geisha played a shamisen—subtly but with great power.

"If they cannot see what is in their own best interest, they deserve whoever's wrath they incur." That was as close to sedition as the elder Hida was prepared to go.

They rode on in silence. It might well have lasted the rest of the day if not for the appearance on the horizon of Otosan Uchi. The capital city gleamed like a jewel at the seaside. Its broad walls stood proudly silhouetted against shimmering waves. In the midst of thousands of rooftops rose the Forbidden

City, a white citadel with a white waterfall. It was their destination, home of the emperor.

"One thing I can say for polite hospitality," muttered Yakamo, "is that the emperor will offer us food and drink no matter how much he wishes we would go away."

Sukune laughed.

"Still," the younger Hida said, "we'd do well not to arrive like ravenous vagabonds. We don't want the other clans to think we are incapable of feeding ourselves."

Yakamo grunted his agreement.

About an hour later they rode through the gates. Just beyond the entrance, a small city of tents and shacks beckoned to travelers, offering basic supplies, spiritual guidance, and food in abundance.

The trio rode up to a soba shop. A nice bowl of cold noodles would fill their bellies but allow them to get back on the road quickly.

"It has been a while since I saw your dueling form, Hida Yakamo," said a samurai-ko who sat in the shade, loudly slurping her noodles as they approached. It was Mirumoto Hitomi. "Why don't you climb down off that horse and finish what we began two years ago?"

To answer the challenge in any way would be unwise. If Yakamo refused, he would seem afraid to fight. If he agreed, he would have to fight a duel to the death. Yakamo looked at her with utter disdain but said nothing. He glanced meaningfully at his brother, as if to say: See? I can hold my tongue when the moment is right.

Yakamo dismounted and entered the shop without even looking in Hitomi's direction. Sukune and Yori followed him. Both made a point of watching the Dragon in case she planned some treachery. Inside, they each ordered a bowl of cold buckwheat noodles and sake, and then came back out to find a bench where they could sit in the shade, hopefully far from Hitomi. Thankfully, the samurai-ko was gone by the time they returned.

Soon the group was happily slurping their noodles and clearing the dust from their throats with delicious, if watered down, sake. It was a fine meal on a hot afternoon.

"All fed and watered now, Crab?" Hitomi had returned, but this time she had brought a retinue of Dragon samurai with her.

"Mirumoto-san," said Sukune, "under normal circumstance my brother and I would be glad to invite you to join us and our counselor in a midafternoon tea ceremony to honor the fates for bringing us together again. However, we are bound for the Forbidden City on a most urgent matter, and we will have to take our leave of you immediately. I apologize."

The younger Hida proved again what a brilliant tactician he was. There were no flaws in his speech. Any further challenge or antagonism on Hitomi's part would reflect very badly on the Dragon Clan.

"I too am bound for the Forbidden City," said Hitomi, "and I say your brother can spare the time to indulge me in a duel to see if his skills outrank those of the Mirumoto School. Unless of course he would be willing to concede the point."

The other Dragon samurai's mouths dropped. The only ruder thing Hitomi could have done would be to draw her katana and attack the man. The look in her eyes spoke that very desire.

Yakamo looked coolly at the samurai-ko—the way he might look at a noisy dragonfly that disturbed the quiet of the afternoon. He stood, reminding everyone of just *how* much larger he was than the Dragon, used his tongue to pick some noodles from between his back teeth, and turned toward his horse.

"Come, Brother, we need to be on our way," Yakamo said lazily.

Kuni Yori spent the whole time standing behind Sukune. The opposing samurai would interpret this position as fearful. In truth the shugenja clutched his black silk, preparing to draw on its power should the Dragon retinue become more than verbally belligerent.

"You arrogant bastard!" Hitomi's fists were clenched, and her hair seemed to bristle. "Do you think that you can kill my brother and completely ignore the rest of the Mirumoto family? Do you have so little respect for the man you murdered that you deny me the right to revenge?"

Yakamo stopped. He slowly looked back over his shoulder.

"It is out of respect for your brother that I do not kill you as well, little Dragon," he said through clenched teeth. "Your behavior when last we dueled was scandalous enough that I am surprised you have the nerve to talk about *anyone's* cowardice. Attacking an ally is not a practice for an honorable samurai. I understand how overwhelming bloodlust can be. I was willing to forgive your transgression, given that you Dragons so rarely see *real* battles."

"Our battle never reached a resolution. Any *honorable* samurai would have sought me out when the siege was done. Or perhaps you are merely the same bullying coward as your father—willing to fight only when you know you can win."

Yakamo glared at her silently. When he finally spoke, his voice was as quiet and sharp as an assassin's blade. "Your grief is great, Hitomi, and I am willing to overlook your slights against me. But my patience is not endless, and I will not allow you to slander my daimyo."

Hitomi smiled. At last she'd found the right nerve to tug.

"Your father needs no words from me to slander his name. All it takes is his own selfish disinterest in the empire," the samurai-ko said these words clearly and distinctly so as to heighten their impact. "At a time when the empire needs warriors, he stays on his wall and turns his back on the rest of us. What kind of bravery is that? No, Hida Kisada is a coward—and you are his mirror image. Too afraid to accept a fair fight, even within sight of the emperor's protection."

Yakamo turned and took three tremendous steps toward Hitomi.

"Very well," he said. His voice was calm but an undertone of menace ran through it. "You may have your match. But if we fight I will not take pity on you for being such a fool. *You* are the one who has asked for this, and you are the one upon whom all the consequences fall."

Hitomi laughed. "Spare me your threats, Crab," she said. "I know who I'm facing. I know what you're capable of. And before we even start, I already know the outcome."

Yakamo grunted.

The two turned and stalked side by side toward a nearby dueling school, where a legal, honorable, and highly public match could be arranged.

Students of every ability level practiced in the large courtyard. The younger students performed their kata in long, neatly aligned rows. The intermediary students fought mock battles where every blow was choreographed like a Noh drama. Along the periphery the advanced students gathered around dueling pits, small arenas where two of their fellows fought one on one, using bokken.

The Crab and Dragon samurai followed them over to one of the pits. Yakamo and Hitomi's faces were set with grim determination. The others wore worried expressions. This was clearly more than a simple duel. Yakamo and Hitomi approached a group of sensei, explained their challenge, and asked to make use of the dueling arena.

The eldest of sensei agreed, with the provision that he and his colleagues act as referees for the match. He could see the burning hate in both combatants' eyes. This would be a match to first blood, not to the death.

Hitomi and Yakamo agreed, but each knew the first hit would be deadly.

Word spread quickly through the streets of Otosan Uchi. Before long, students, teachers, and visitors alike crowded around the pit. They stood five and six deep, craning their necks to see the combatants as they prepared for their duel.

Mirumoto Hitomi knelt in one corner, her head bowed in meditation. She had her katana drawn and laid across her lap.

At the other end of the pit, Hida Yakamo stomped around and shook his head like a caged animal. He swung his tetsubo through the air in great arcs that passed frighteningly close to the first row of the crowd.

"Is it wise to allow this to go on?" Sukune whispered to Yori.

"Do you know of a way to stop it?" the shugenja returned.

The young Hida leaned his head to the left as he thought, then simply shook it.

"There is a tension between these two that *must* be released," Yori said. "Their karma has been intertwined for many years. This day was unavoidable. What's more, this may not be the end of it."

Mirumoto Hitomi stood and faced her opponent.

"Come," she said, "let this battle—the same battle we began here at Otosan Uchi during the Scorpion Coup—be finished here and now!"

Yakamo spat at her feet.

At the sensei's direction, they both took their stances. Hitomi adopted a classic dueling pose. Yakamo held his tetsubo over his head as though he were going to bring it crashing down on the referee.

"Remember," the sensei said, "this fight is to first blood only. May your actions bring honor to your clans."

Both contestants grunted.

"You may begin."

Hitomi stood still, studying her opponent. She looked for a point of weakness, a chink in his defense.

Yakamo snarled. He did not anticipate this kind of thoughtful fight from the Dragon. She was so angry and belligerent, he expected her to come right out and charge him the way she had last time. But apparently the young Mirumoto remembered what happened when her brother used that tactic in his final duel.

The Crab stomped one tremendous foot as though he would make the first charge. He pulled back and lowered his tetsubo. Standing with the weapon poised overhead would only tire his arms and slow his defenses.

Some of the novice students whistled and called for the pair to "stop dancing and start fighting!" Wiser members of the audience avidly watched the tension and drama unfold.

Both Hitomi and Yakamo made subtle shifts in their posture, testing the other's reaction. Hitomi dropped her left elbow and turned her katana perpendicular to the ground. Yakamo held his tetsubo directly in front of his body, pointing down at the Dragon's feet. Yakamo began to swing his club in looping figure-eights. Hitomi stood with her sword inverted directly over her head so the blade tip pointed at the bridge of the Crab's nose.

The moment lasted long.

Yakamo swung at Hitomi's midsection. She pivoted on her heel, spun, and lashed out, narrowly missing Yakamo's forearm. Some would argue later that the samurai-ko could easily have nicked the Crab then and there, ending the duel. For these combatants, though, merely winning was not enough. They wanted only the complete destruction of their foe.

Hitomi launched the next volley. She took two steps toward her opponent and nimbly ducked under his tetsubo. It whizzed where her head had just been. Doing a forward tumble, she rose within inches of Yakamo and struck directly up with her katana.

The crowed gasped.

The gigantic samurai thrust himself into a backward somersault, avoiding the deadly blow and coming up in a swinging stance.

He feinted for Hitomi's head, then swung down and across her body, hoping to clip her shoulder or knee—but missed entirely. The swing left his neck exposed, and he hoped the samurai-ko would take the bait. All it would take was one step toward her and a pivot of his hips to send her flying out of the pit and three rows deep into the spectators.

Hitomi's blade flashed in the sun, slicing toward the Crab's unprotected neck.

Yakamo stepped toward his foe and began his pivot.

She, too, changed targets. Instead of following through on her attack at his neck, Hitomi leapt into the air, spun to face him dead-on, and struck at his left arm.

Yakamo heard a faint, moist sound that thrilled and repulsed him.

The audience took a single deep breath and groaned.

Yakamo had no idea what happened until he tried to follow through with his pivoting blow. His right arm brought the tetsubo up toward Hitomi, but his left provided no support. The club slipped from his grip and fell to the ground. He reached down to regain his weapon but came up holding something warm and wet.

Glancing down, he realized he held his own severed left hand.

The world ceased to exist for Yakamo. He did not hear sensei yelling that the match was over. Nor did he see Hitomi spinning in preparation for another strike—this one to separate the Crab's head from his shoulders. Yakamo stared blankly at his lost hand as a group of ten strong samurai grabbed Hitomi and struggled to drag her away. He did not recognize his brother Sukune when he slid to a halt with Kuni Yori close behind, both trying to find a way to stanch the bleeding. He knew nothing until he threw his head back and howled. Then the world came back into focus.

"I'm not done with you yet, Hida," snarled Hitomi as her own samurai pulled her away. "Your life is mine! I will be back to claim it!"

Yakamo tried to go after the Dragon samurai-ko, but his legs would not support him. He tried to yell after her—that even with one hand he was still three times the warrior she ever could be—but his voice only came out as a baleful growl.

Kuni Yori placed three fingers on Yakamo's brow and whispered an arcane phrase. The injured Crab slipped into unconsciousness.

"What will we do?" asked Sukune.

"You must continue on to the Forbidden City," Yori told him. "Nothing that happened here today changes the fact that the emperor awaits the Crab envoy."

"But Yakamo—" Sukune disagreed with his brother, even disliked him on many occasions, but he could not leave Yakamo in this condition.

"Between my spells and the city's healers, we will make him well enough to ride back to the Crab lands," Yori assured Sukune. "Once there, I may be able to do something to alleviate the problem."

Sukune nodded. "You must help him, Yori-san. You must!"

"And *you* must go to the Forbidden City. Focus on the task before you. You know what your father would say."

"Yes," Sukune agreed. "'No matter how many battles you have won or lost, the only one that matters is the one you are *in!*'"

The dueling school's healers came running up to Yakamo's side.

Elsewhere, the school's sensei argued with a representative of the Dragon Clan. Half the sensei were considering banning Mirumoto from setting foot in the academy ever again. The others demanded compensatory payment for the shame Hitomi brought by not following the agreed-upon rules and attempting to kill her opponent after the match was done. No talk was given at all to recompensing Yakamo for his loss.

As he turned toward the Forbidden City, high and white above the clustered rooftops, Sukune could only think of what Kuni Yori's had said: "This day was unavoidable. What's more, this may not be the end of it."

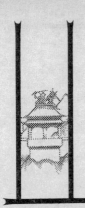

12 THE CALL OF KARMA

I have bled all my blood . . . I have no more. I must be dead."

"You are not dead, Yakamo-san," said Kuni Yori. "But you *are* delirious." Between a substantial loss of blood, pain-killing herbs, and Yori's own spells, Yakamo felt no pain. Unfortunately, he was also quite insensible.

"No blood, no blood, I'm an empty shell, a Crab without a claw." Yakamo said in a childish lilt. "I fought and fought, but I lost my hand to the tiny Dragon's maw."

Traveling was difficult with Yakamo in such condition. The samurai could hardly stay balanced on his horse. He needed to stop to rest at least four times per day. It had been six days since they began their return journey to Crab lands. The stump of Yakamo's left wrist, which they'd cauterized with white-hot steel, was healing acceptably. It now only oozed, and Yori was certain it would not become infected as long as he changed the bandage every day.

But no more of the herbs remained, and it would take at least a day to reach the Great Wall of Kaiu. Yori feared what would happen when the herbs ran out—not because of the pain. The shugenja worried how Yakamo would act when he finally regained his senses.

When Yakamo's mind was whole again, he might insist on turning his horse around and riding after Mirumoto Hitomi to seek revenge. Even in this weakened state, Yakamo could overcome any resistance Yori put up. But fighting the Dragon samurai-ko again in this condition would be suicide. Of course, seppuku was another possible reaction Yakamo might have.

The problem with bushi, Yori thought, is that they are too willing to throw away their lives needlessly. The shugenja still had plans for the young Hida, and they would be dashed if Yakamo decided he had been so dishonored he could not go on living.

The reaction Kuni Yori hoped for was that Yakamo would remain in a state of shock. Often a trauma such as this could induce a condition that resembled sleepwalking. This would have the advantage of permitting the young man to ride a little more strenuously without thinking clearly. With any luck, the shock would last until Yori got him safely back to Kisada's camp. The Great Bear would surely be able to talk sense into his wounded son.

"You are not the man you seem, Yori-kun," Yakamo shouted, though he rode no more than ten feet away.

"What do you mean, Yakamo-san?" Yori was intrigued.

"You paint your face like a geisha—making a new one you think is more pleasing," bellowed Yakamo. "But underneath you are just the same as you always have been. Your mask does not scare me."

"Why should it?" asked the shugenja nervously. Did Yakamo actually have a clue about his machinations and intrigues?

"That is what you want. I can tell. You want to be feared," Yakamo now began to mumble. "You paint your face and hide it beneath a velvet hood. You peer out with narrowed eyes, as white as death. You want to be feared, Kuni-san, but the truth is that you are my best friend." Yakamo slid in his saddle and nearly fell off the horse.

"I think it is time for you to rest again," Yori said, reaching over and reigning both horses to a stop.

"No, it's true," Yakamo insisted. "I lost my hand, and my own brother abandoned me. My father will certainly disown me for being such a failure. I can't even ride a horse right, and *you* are the only one who will take care of me."

Within the folds of his cloak, Kuni Yori smiled.

"I am glad you recognize that, my lord," he said as he lay Yakamo down on the roadside grass to sleep.

▲▲▲▲▲▲▲▲

"We're nearly there, Yakamo-sama, but we must make a short stop at my tower before we complete our journey."

Yakamo merely grumbled in response.

It was nearly two days later, and he had been without the pain-killing herbs for most of that time. He had not fallen into shock, as Yori had hoped. Instead, Yakamo emerged fully cognizant of what had happened but completely withdrawn. He seemed to feel nothing about the matter. The sharp throbbing at the end of his left arm kept him focused on the task of riding. Unfortunately, it had also made it impossible for him to sleep for the past two nights.

They'd reached the Wall an hour ago and were now riding north toward Hida Kisada's camp. The sky was a metallic gray. The ground was covered in a thin layer of mist that seemed to pass straight through the Wall.

Yakamo felt as if he was riding through a nightmare. If only he could awake to find the sun shining and his missing hand restored. But he knew that this world, as bizarre as it seemed to his sleepy eyes, was the real one.

The Wall looked exactly the same as it did anywhere along its expanse—tall, crenellated lengths connecting blocky towers set exactly fifty yards apart. Regular. Predictable. Safe.

Something irregular loomed out of the mists. About three hundred yards ahead there seemed to be a station where *two* towers were built, one behind the other. The second tower was only half as tall as all the others, plus it was not actually connected to the Wall but sat four or five hundred yards removed like a tiny reflection. At first the young samurai thought he might be hallucinating. Then he remembered that Kuni Yori had this tower constructed to house his personal residence and magical library.

More than the tower's size distinguished it from the rest of the Kaiu construction. Rather than the gray, cold stones that made up the Wall, Yori's Tower was built of dark stones. Yakamo could not be sure whether they were black or an extraordinarily deep red. They seemed to breathe in and out in a ragged rhythm. The entire building appeared to be alive.

"So this is the 'cursed tower of Kuni Yori,' " said Yakamo. "Some of the bravest warriors I've ever fought beside tell me they are afraid to step within a hundred yards of your home."

Yori chuckled.

"It is good, sometimes, to cultivate a bad reputation," he said over his shoulder. "It makes the neighbors less likely to bother you at inopportune times."

Both riders dismounted and walked their steeds to the building's only entry—a large stone arch. The only other exit was a single window on what must have been the topmost floor.

"I'll admit, your home has a certain . . . sinister feel to it," Yakamo said. "But it's hardly anything to shake the nerves of a battle-tested samurai."

Just then, the air was split by an ear-piercing scream. It lasted about ten seconds, then faded into silence. It was not quite a human scream, but neither did it seem wholly bestial.

"Wh-what was that?" asked Yakamo, clutching his injured arm tightly to his body.

The shugenja laughed. "*That* was something to shake the nerves of battle-tested samurai."

As they entered the tower, it was too dark for Yakamo to see farther than fifteen feet in any direction—strange for midday even with an overcast sky. He couldn't see the ceiling. In fact, when he looked up Yakamo couldn't see anything other than an impenetrable inky veil that might go on forever.

Next to the door, wooden stairs were built into the wall. They led up into the darkness above. At a wave of Yori's hand, torches flared to life in sconces up and down the walls. The young Hida could now see that the structure was completely hollow. The stairs ran up to a platform about fifty feet above his head. Cages hung from hooks at various heights on the wall. Most of them were empty or held skeletons of misshapen creatures Yakamo could only guess had once been goblins. One cage very near the platform swayed back and forth slightly, and Yakamo thought he could see motion within. It seemed very likely the tortured creature had made the disturbing noises he had heard while approaching the tower.

In the center of the floor Yori had built a house. In fact, if it had been surrounded by maple trees and a rock garden, the small building would have been cozy, even peaceful. But sitting here at the center of a dimly lit, dank tower on the edge of the Crab lands, the building looked wrong—perhaps even malevolent.

Yori stepped up onto the raised wooden walkway that surrounded the house.

"Please wait out here, Hida-sama," he said to Yakamo as he slid open the shoji. "I will be only a moment, and you will be quite pleased with what I bring out."

Yori slipped off his sandals and backed into the house. The shugenja knelt, bowed, and slid the rice-paper door closed. The shoji was so thin that Yakamo could still make out Yori's shape as he rose and moved deeper into the home. He heard the shugenja open another set of shoji and begin rummaging around with heavy, wooden objects.

A pitiful whimper drifted down from the cage near the ceiling. Yakamo wondered if the creature was part of an experiment, was being tortured for information, or simply served as entertainment for Yori—and a warning to others.

The shoji behind him slid open again. Yakamo turned to see the shugenja sliding his feet back into his sandals. Yori was carrying a box about the correct length to hold a matching katana and wakizashi. However it was much too wide and heavy to be home to a simple dai-sho. The wood was so black that at first Yakamo thought it was ornamentally lacquered. As he looked closer, he could tell it was raw, unstained, gnarled wood with large ugly splinters sticking out on all sides.

"What is in there?" asked the samurai.

Yori just smiled.

"Soon enough, you will see," he said. "But I must discuss the contents with your father before I reveal them to you."

Yakamo was growing more and more frustrated with Yori's mysterious ways.

"Very well, then. Let's ride. We can be at the daimyo's camp by nightfall."

▲▲▲▲▲▲▲▲

"Why? Why didn't they let her kill him? At least there would have been *some* honor in that!" Pacing the tatami floor of his courtyard dais, Kisada seemed very much like his namesake—a great bear trapped in a cage. Kuni Yori knelt on a mat directly before the daimyo. Yakamo knelt off to the side, his forehead bowed to the ground.

"Tono."

The word literally meant "lord," but it had a familiar feel to it. Yori called Kisada that only when he wanted to make a personal point, to show his daimyo that he was more than just an advisor— he was a friend.

"Tono, your son was willing to give his life to defend not just his honor, but yours as well. He has not shamed himself or you in his loss—or his survival."

"Shame?" Kisada roared. "Of course he has brought us no shame!"

He stepped off the dais and into the gravel without donning any sandals and walked over to where Yakamo bowed in supplication.

"Yakamo—my firstborn, my chosen heir—Yori is correct. You have nothing to be ashamed of. If anything, you have had a grave wrong thrust upon you. It was your right to die in that contest, and they denied you the ending you deserved and were prepared for. If you died like the warrior you are, they gained nothing, but by leaving you this way the Dragon has cast doubt upon your spirit and your devotion. They insult the entire Crab Clan!"

Yakamo looked up, his eyes as dry as bones but somehow filled with passion.

"I will avenge myself upon them," he said so softly that Yori barely heard.

"I believe," the shugenja said, "that I may be of some help in that regard."

The two Hidas looked at him unconvinced.

"This is matter for the sword and the heart, Yori," said the Great Bear, "not magic and the brain."

"Yes," Yakamo agreed. "I must earn my revenge in glorious battle, not have it handed to me through a spell cast by my father's adviser."

"I have no intention of robbing you of your rightful and personal revenge," Yori said smiling. He clapped his hands twice, and two servants carried in the black box he'd retrieved from his tower. "I simply want to help make you capable of achieving it sooner."

The samurai stared at him in confusion.

"Mirumoto Hitomi stole from you the dominance and power that are your birthright. She made it so that your body can no longer keep pace with your warrior's heart. Within this box I have something that can reverse this setback—something that can make you even more powerful than you were before."

"What is it?" asked Yakamo. He had the look of a starving man staring at a pot of rice that was not quite at a boil.

"And what is the price of this power?" asked Kisada.

Yori answered neither question, but simply undid the latch on the black box and raised the lid. It was filled with straw, but the two samurai could see a large, black object below the topmost layer.

Kisada brushed aside the straw, stood back, and gasped.

"What is it?" Yakamo repeated.

They were looking at an ungainly contraption made of

hinged metal, lacquered leather, and thick strands of silk. It looked very much like a giant crab claw covered in deadly spikes. The metal and leather were stained flat black, except along the hinges and the interior of the claw itself, which were plated with brass—presumably to make them operate more smoothly. At the back of the claw, the leather strips bore a passing resemblance to arm guards from a suit of heavy armor—clearly this *thing* was meant to be strapped to one's arm.

"If I am to wear a false arm, it will be that of a man—not an animal!" Yakamo said firmly and turned away.

"You misunderstand, Yakamo-sama," said Yori. "This is more than a decoration. With a few simple incantations it will respond to your thoughts just the way your natural limbs do. It will become a part of you—and more, it will become the most powerful part of your arsenal. This claw can crush tempered steel as easily as you snap a pair of chopsticks. A man with strong enough determination could draw on the claw to fill his entire body with more raw power than he could ever summon before."

Yakamo was transfixed.

Kisada was leery.

"Where did you get such a wondrous item?" he asked suspiciously.

Yori shrugged. "I removed it from one of the prisoners I examined about a year ago," he said. "Since then I have been testing its properties."

Yakamo's mind went back to the tower and the pitiful creature locked in the cage. He swallowed hard. Could this claw have been removed from that tortured beast? Or perhaps Yori "tested the properties" on that particular captive. None of these ideas bothered the young samurai in the abstract. After all, the Shadowlands were the enemy, and they would do worse things to any Crab they dragged back to their unholy dens. But the thought of actually wearing such a thing—taking it as a part of himself—gave him pause.

"A product of the Shadowlands?" the Great Bear roared. "You suggest that my son, heir to the Crab daimyo, should strap to his arm a device that looks like it came off an oni? That he should walk around for the rest of his days wearing a machine forged by our hated enemy?"

"I suggest," Yori said carefully, "that we use materials at hand to our best advantage. I suggest that it makes no difference who made the claw as long as your son uses it for the greater glory of the Crab Clan. I suggest that we have a way to take two terrible wrongs and turn them into a powerful weapon in our war to protect the empire."

"No!" Kisada loomed over Yori. The shugenja had to lean so far back to look in his daimyo's eyes that his hood fell off, revealing his painted face and thin eyes. "There are some lines that are not to be crossed, and attaching the arm of an enemy to my son is one of them. You know as well as I do that too much exposure to the Shadowlands can warp a man—taint him with the mark of corruption. If this happens from standing too close to the abyss, what do you think the result of wearing a slice of evil on your arm will be?"

"The taint is not a result of proximity to the Shadowlands," Yori answered calmly. This was a dangerous argument he could not afford to lose. "It is a sign that your heart and spirit have given in to the call of the Dark God. You know that, Tono. Are you saying your firstborn son doesn't have the character to remain true to himself and his heritage?"

"Of course I'm not saying that, and don't try to turn this argument around on me. The point is not the danger, the point is the principle."

"Father," Yakamo said, his voice cool and level. "The point is winning the war. If you do not allow Kuni Yori to attach this claw, I will never be able to walk into battle again. I will never be able to stand on the Wall and fight by your side. I will become just what my brother is—a great bundle of wasted potential."

"Tono, the Crab have lost one of our finest warriors," Yori agreed. "Only *you* are more respected by the soldiers on the Wall. It would be a great blow to morale if Yakamo-sama could never fight again—a blow that is rendered unnecessary by this device."

Yakamo looked his father square in the eye. "We have a chance to use the Shadowlands' own magic against them. You yourself always say to me, 'We must use every weapon within reach. We must take advantage of every opportunity. We must win at *any* cost, for if we fail, the empire falls.'

"Well, I have already paid the cost, Father," Yakamo said holding up the stump of his left arm. "Will we allow this opportunity to slip through what fingers I have left?"

Kisada lowered his eyes. "Yakamo, my son and my heir, is there no honor in accepting your karma and leading the clan through the force of your character? You have nothing left to prove."

"I have to prove that I am not a coward," Yakamo replied. "I have to prove that when confronted with opposition I will not back up and find some way around it. No, I will gather my strength and meet it head-on using every weapon at my disposal. I must prove that I am a Crab!"

The Great Bear turned his back to Yakamo and Yori and looked toward the sky. Where, he wondered, did honor and reason part company? Was every sensible answer wrong and the insane perversion of his son's flesh really the correct solution? No answers were written on the gray tableau above.

Finally Kisada turned around. He carried himself in his usual commanding demeanor, but somehow he looked melancholy.

"Very well," was all he said.

13   IMPERIAL DECREE

You're not nearly as offensive as your father or brother! In fact, I would say you're actually quite pleasant."

Hida Sukune turned to his right and stared blankly at the Unicorn Clan diplomat sitting there, smiling brightly.

"I was unaware that bald-faced insults were in fashion this season," he finally answered. It was the only thing he could think to do other than kill the man where he sat.

"I always thought that the Crab appreciated honesty above all else," the Unicorn said. "I was merely trying to accommodate your tastes."

The Unicorn Clan had spent many long centuries in the barbaric world beyond the Emerald Empire. Although they had returned to Rokugan two hundred years ago, they still occasionally had trouble in polite society. In fact, the Unicorn were considered by many to be even *more* uncultured than the Crab. After all, the Crab might be rude, but at least they *knew* when they were breaking the rules.

"If you have nothing honest *and* nice to say, you should say nothing." In spite of himself, Sukune found he liked his neighbor. The man was obviously being sincere, and he had complimented the youngest Hida—in a backward sort of way. "How do you know my family?"

"It was my honor to meet both the daimyo and his son here in the Forbidden City about a year before Hantei the 38th was assassinated," the Unicorn said. "They both went on at length telling me what they thought of my clan's—how did they put it?—'two-century holiday.' It seems they felt our efforts would have been better spent fighting the Shadowlands."

Sukune chuckled. "No doubt their opinions were bolstered by the emperor's sake."

"Indeed," said the Unicorn smiling. "By the way, I am Utaku Hentai, special envoy for Shinjo Yokatsu."

"I am Hida Sukune," he said bowing. "Though it seems that my reputation has preceded me."

"You *are* the only Crab in attendance," Hentai pointed out.

Sukune looked around the audience chamber. The Crane had sent the most representatives—an entourage of nearly twenty—while several small clans, like the Hornet and the Dragonfly, sent merely three. The Crab was the only clan to deign to send only one envoy.

"So I am," Sukune said noncommittally.

This place was arranged similarly to Kisada's courtyard. A slightly raised dais covered with tatami mats stood at one end of the large open room. The main space was all hardwood floor with three rows of square, flat pillows lined up along the side walls. The attendees sat cross-legged on these cushions. It was considered impolite to require guests to kneel during long announcements. The envoys faced one another across an open aisle. Anyone who had to address the speaker would come to the center of the room and kneel for the duration of his or her exchange.

At the back of the dais stood an artistically fashioned suit of heavy armor. In the center was a large, soft pillow where the emperor's representative—probably a chamberlain or general—

would sit to address the gathered envoys. Clearly the emperor did not intend to make the announcement, whatever it was, himself. If he had, the diplomats would have been shown into the throne room.

The room fell silent as a shoji at the rear of the dais slid open. A servant knelt on the other side and bowed her head to the wooden hallway floor. The imperial representative entered— Empress Kachiko herself.

In an audience such as this one, the guests usually remained completely silent until the speaker invited comment. When the clan representatives realized they were about to be addressed by Empress Kachiko, though, a muffled chatter arose. Some clans seemed upset. Others were impressed and flattered.

Sukune was mostly worried. What matter, he wondered, was delicate enough to call for a direct audience with the Lady Scorpion, but not important enough to warrant the emperor appearing at her side?

At first, Kachiko seemed every inch the empress, carrying herself with regal authority and poise. Her long hair was raised in a conservative style and wrapped in a loose knot at the back of her head. Kachiko wore a double-layered kimono, traditional for members of the imperial family at important functions. Two handmaidens lifted her heavy silk train as she entered the room. But the pattern on the cloth was anything but traditional. Instead of the usual imperial purple and gold, her outer kimono was dyed crimson and black. Rather than the traditional floral decoration, the kimono bore an abstract pattern that contained dozens of scorpions hidden in the design.

Many of the guests shifted uncomfortably and whispered to one another. How could the empress be so crass as to draw attention to her unfortunate past? What did this mean?

Sukune sat calmly. If anything truly bothered him, it was the reaction of the other guests. Kachiko was still the same manipulative, unprincipled, beguiling woman she always had been. Sukune refused to give the Lady Scorpion the satisfaction of reacting to her clothing. That was what she wanted. The only way to beat her at her own game was to identify what she wanted and deny it.

Kachiko smiled demurely, then bowed her head and came up with as serious a look as Sukune had ever seen. Her face truly was the ultimate mask. It showed the world just what she wanted it to see and never revealed her inner thoughts.

"Honored guests," Kachiko began, "I thank you for attending this meeting on such short notice. I bring the emperor's most humble apologies for not greeting you himself. As you know, Hantei the 39th suffers from the debilitating plague that has swept across the empire, making it difficult for him to attend the gatherings he would ordinarily enjoy."

Sukune smirked to himself. The message must be pretty controversial if Kachiko was opening with such a blatant bid for sympathy.

"Ironically, the topic my august husband wished to discuss with you was his illness," the Lady Scorpion continued. "He has been ill for well over a year now, and his healers present no guarantee—or even reasonable hope—that his condition will improve. In fact, the healers say that if our emperor's health has not begun to improve by now, it likely never will."

Everyone in the room gasped. Such things were simply *not* talked about—especially when they had to do with the emperor. As the message sank in, Sukune saw every diplomat come to the same realization. Kachiko was saying that the emperor was deathly ill and never would recover.

"I can tell you are beginning to see the real problem here," Kachiko said with a tinge of mean-spiritedness. "For the last few months the emperor and I have been working as hard as his fragile health will allow to provide an heir to the empire—a fortieth Hantei to fill the unimaginable void that would be left when . . . *if* my husband succumbs. However, so far the emperor has been unable to produce an heir."

Sukune marveled at the Lady Scorpion's speaking skills. She could easily have broached this subject without using such blatant terms. The representatives of the "polite" clans would be so disturbed by the announcement's form—by the fact that she was talking openly about illness, death, and sexuality—that they would be taken unawares by its intent. In truth, Sukune sensed that Kachiko had not yet come to the real point of this gathering.

"My husband has given long consideration to his duty to provide the empire with a continuous line of leadership. He remembers quite vividly the covetous actions of the traitor Toturi in the wake of his father's demise. He does not wish to see the empire thrown into such chaos again."

How convenient, Sukune thought, for Kachiko to omit her own part in the coup that forced the chaos to begin with.

"And so, in the event that we continue to be unable to produce an heir, the emperor has decided to name a successor. Rather, he will name a clan to succeed the Hantei should he in fact be the last of that noble family."

The room fairly broke into chaos. All the assembled diplomats, politicians, and dignitaries began guessing which clan would be chosen and, if it was not their own, why the decision was ill-advised. Finally, the senior representative of the Crane Clan—an eighty-year-old man who rose only with support from both a walking stick and a younger assistant—asked on which clan the emperor would bestow such an honor.

"That has yet to be decided," Kachiko said slowly, savoring the murmurs that ran through the crowd. She pulled out a scroll, unraveled it, and read, "The emperor issues the following decree on the matter:

> "For reasons already described to you, I am considering the matter of which Rokugani clan to task with the unenviable responsibility of caring for and leading the Emerald Empire from the day of my death onward. This is a decision of the utmost gravity, and one to which I devote all my available faculties.
>
> "Every clan offers several valuable and unmatchable services to the empire. The Crane have long served the Hantei as loyal advisors and guardians. The Lion too have provided generations of military support and advice. The empire owes no debt larger than the one earned by the Crab, who defend our borders from the army of the Dark God. But our abilities in the mystic arts would be nearly nothing if not for the efforts of the Dragon Clan, and our understanding of the elements would be woefully incomplete were it

not for the Phoenix Clan. And we would still wallow in ignorance of the world beyond our borders except for the Unicorn's centuries long travel."

As Kachiko read, the representatives gave vocal recognition of the particular duties their clans gave. Sukune, being the lone Crab, grunted loudly and banged the floor in his best imitation of his father.

"Since it is impossible to choose the most deserving clan based on past service, we issue this imperial decree to say that our decision will be based on which clan can prove itself most capable of leading and governing the entire empire in our absence. We will watch the military, political, and cultural activities of all the clans over the coming months, and when one proves itself to be the superior of all the others, that is the clan to which we will entrust Rokugan's future.

"Let your victories prove your merit, and your defeats show your true value."

With that, Kachiko rolled up the scroll, bowed demurely, and rose, completely ignoring the bickering confusion that reigned among the delegates. Her handmaidens tended the hem of her kimono. The servant in the hall once again slid the shoji open, allowing the empress to exit.

Sukune shook his head ruefully.

The Crane delegation was nearly at blows with the Lion representatives. The Dragon and Phoenix envoys seemed ready to summon their sorceries. Loud disagreements, sounding more like drunken arguments than civilized debate, erupted all over the room.

Sukune knew this was only the beginning. How could any clan *prove* it was better or worthier than another except by defeating its rival? How could a clan prove its military dominance except by war?

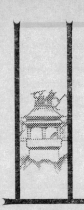

14 THE LAST STRAW

This will be the end of the empire." It was not the first time Hida Kisada had spoken those words, nor the first time he believed them. But something was different this time. Today, as the setting sun threw the shadow of the Great Wall across the daimyo's command tent, everyone within believed the Great Bear was correct.

"Already there are reports of skirmishes between various clans," Sukune said. He looked unwell, as though he might pass out. After the meeting with Empress Kachiko, he had leaped on his horse and ridden hard for Crab lands, stopping only when he had to for food and rest. It took him not quite a week to make the trip but, Kisada noted, any other Crab samurai would have done it in half that time and would not have stopped for anything.

"They are testing themselves," Kisada mused, "and seeing how prepared their neighbors are for war."

It was unthinkable. Certainly, throughout Rokugan's history, there had been conflicts between clans—some that led to bloodshed. Never before had the entire empire seemed poised on the edge of full-scale war.

Sukune staggered but caught himself.

The Great Bear grunted in disapproval. "Go get some food and sleep," he told his son disgustedly.

"I-I'm all right—" Sukune began.

"No, you're not!" Kisada said more harshly than he wanted. "You can barely stand, let alone give me useful analysis or advice. Go rest and come back at sunrise. Bring your brother and Kuni Yori with you when you return!"

"Hai!" There was no point arguing. The young samurai bowed and backed into the twilight outside the command tent.

When Sukune was gone, Kisada sighed and removed his helmet. He'd worn his full armor every day for so long that it had become like a second skin to him. He hardly even noticed it and was able to sleep comfortably in his shell of wood, metal, and leather.

Right now the helmet seemed too heavy to bear. It pressed down on the back of his neck and dragged his chin toward the ground. He ran his hand through the short-cropped mass of black and gray hair and found it slick with sweat. It had been a hot day, to be sure—the summer heat refused to break even though autumn was just a few weeks away—but the sweat was cold and smelled of fear.

Hida Kisada, the Great Bear, daimyo of the Crab Clan was afraid.

Rokugan stood on the brink of a conflict so terrible that the empire might never recover. This was the fault of one person, and one alone—Bayushi Kachiko. She orchestrated it step by step, smoothly guided the ailing emperor into just the right decisions, and manipulated every man, woman, and child in every clan into doing exactly what she wanted. The question remained, *why?*

What did the Lady Scorpion gain by setting the clans against each other? She was already the empress. If she wanted to, she could have arranged for the emperor to declare *her* the heir to the throne. People would complain, but in the end no one would be able to do anything about it. What motivated her to start a civil war?

Could Kachiko be so self-absorbed, so petty, that she did all this in revenge for the death of her husband? Did she love Bayushi Shoju so deeply that she would lay the entirety of the Emerald Empire as an offering on the altar before his grave?

Or perhaps she truly was evil. Perhaps it was *Kachiko's* influence that turned the Scorpion Clan from deceptive tricksters into cold-blooded assassins. Perhaps the Lady Scorpion had formed an alliance with the Dark God, Fu Leng. Perhaps she was his agent, fomenting trouble within Rokugan to weaken the empire and make it an easier target.

In the end only Kachiko knew why she did what she did. The most the Great Bear could hope for was to see his way through the coming days with honor and grace.

The problem was, none of the other clans liked the Crab. In fact, very nearly all of them felt slighted in one way or another by his clan or himself personally. If the other daimyo had to pick which clan to attack based on pure antagonism, Kisada was certain his would be the favored target.

The Crab had the largest standing army but were spread thin along the length of the Great Wall of Kaiu. A large army could sweep over a third of the Crab positions before the rest of the Crab gathered in force. The Crab would be caught fighting a two-front battle, for the Shadowlands would certainly not curtail their assaults.

As the last slivers of sunlight dropped behind the Wall, Kisada's thoughts plunged into darkness. He pondered again the lesson of the first Crab: You are only as strong as your weakest point; plan a strategy around that weakness, and you can never be defeated.

▲▲▲▲▲▲▲▲

Sukune awoke ten hours later, feeling rested but not refreshed. Too many things weighed on his mind and spirit. He knew the

Crab would make an inviting target. He had seen it in the delegates' eyes as he'd left. They'd watched him, the lone Crab, scuttle away. They'd mumbled and plotted and wondered if after all these years on the Wall, the clan was not standing on its last legs.

Of course, the same delegates had been asking the same questions about all the other clans. Each sought the opponent against which it had the best chance for success.

Sukune rose and straightened his kimono. It was nearly time to get his brother and return to the command tent. He remembered Yakamo's terrible defeat. He had been so worried about the impending civil war that he'd forgotten to see how his brother was dealing with his loss.

The young samurai tucked his katana and wakizashi into his belt. It was still an hour before sunrise. He could visit with Yakamo for a while before they met with their father.

Sukune walked across the compound toward Yakamo's tent. Yakamo must feel like someone asked to walk blindfolded through a familiar room—sure of the obstacles but unsure how to avoid them. The loss of his hand would require Yakamo to re-examine everything in his life. He would have to learn to see the world in a different, somewhat diminished light.

Sukune could offer his brother words of advice and encouragement. No one knew better than Sukune the pain of living with a body that could not keep up with the dictates of his mind—or the expectations of his spirit. He doubted Yakamo would want to hear such things yet, but eventually this incident could bring them closer. The brothers would finally and forever have something in common.

"Oy!" Sukune said just outside the flap to Yakamo's tent. It was a gruff greeting, one the younger Hida used only with his brother. It established that, despite their obvious physical disparity, Sukune was not going to allow Yakamo to bully him. "Yakamo-kun! I'm coming in!"

"Well then come in already!" came the answer, much more robust than Sukune had expected.

"How are you, Brother?" Sukune asked as he pushed through the flap. He halted when he saw Yakamo lifting a gigantic claw from a wooden box. Both the claw and the crate were so black they looked as though they'd been pulled half-burnt from a fire.

"What is that?"

"A claw! What does it look like?" Yakamo sneered. "And people say *you're* the smart one."

"Where did it come from?" Sukune asked, refusing to be baited. "It took our blacksmiths months to fashion my armor. How did they make this claw so quickly?" Like his brother and father, Sukune wore a suit of heavy armor when he went into battle. To compensate for his unimposing presence, he'd had the smithies forge his armor in the shape of a gigantic crab. Sukune did not merely wear the clan mon—he actually *became* a walking, fighting crab.

The claw twitched in Yakamo's hand. Though it was made of leather and iron, it moved with a life of its own. The center hinge opened and closed with a rhythmic pulse.

"By the kami!" Sukune jumped back and reached for his katana. "It is cursed!"

Yakamo laughed.

As the first rays of the sun pierced the veil of night, Sukune began to see.

"Y-you knew about this?" he asked suspiciously.

"Not at first," Yakamo chuckled. "I damn near threw the thing in the fire when it first moved. But then Kuni Yori explained to me that the claw was enchanted. That is what will make it so useful to me when I strap it on permanently. It will respond to my thoughts the way my own hand once did."

"Kuni Yori," muttered Sukune. "I should have known. That man is not to be trusted."

"Our father trusts him!" Yakamo returned. "Counsel that is good enough for our daimyo is good enough for *me*!"

"Brother," Sukune said reasonably. "Even Father does not trust Yori completely. He picks and chooses when to accept or reject his twisted advice."

"True enough!" Yakamo countered. "And in this matter, Father sides with me."

"H-he agreed to this madness?" Sukune stammered in disbelief.

"Of course! This claw is my salvation!" Yakamo said proudly. He held the device aloft and marveled at it. "It is a weapon and a tool. Once it is attached, it will crush and block and do anything I ask it to, and it cannot be taken from me—*ever*!"

"It is an abomination!" Sukune could not believe that his brother would allow such a monstrosity to be attached to him or that his father would countenance such a thing. It was clearly wrong in every sense of the word. Had they all gone mad?

"Do you really want me to sit around and plan while others fight?" Yakamo asked boldly. "To spend the rest of my life a weakling like you?"

"Who are you to challenge your karma? Things happen for a reason, Brother. You should walk this path awhile. You may learn something from the experience. Your destiny may hinge on these lessons."

"Bah!" Yakamo spat. "Do not talk to me about destiny. It is my destiny to be the most feared warrior in all of Rokugan! And I will not allow that Dragon bitch to rob me of it!"

Sukune looked at him seriously. "Do not let pride and ambition cloud your judgment," he said quietly. "Take the clay that life gives you and make the best sculpture you can with it."

"I have taken life's opportunity! Do you think I went out looking for this thing?" The claw wriggled in Yakamo's grip, apparently displeased at being spoken of with such disregard. "No! Kuni Yori presented me with an opportunity, and I grabbed it!"

The younger Hida frowned. "Yori presented you with a temptation, and you succumbed!"

"We are Crab!" Yakamo roared. "We fight with whatever weapons are available. We use any tactics we can think of. All that matters is that we win! We cannot lose or the empire falls!"

The claw opened and closed sharply, a soft, clacking applause punctuating Yakamo's outburst.

"Yes, but only when we stay true to our mission, Brother. We are just as capable of making mistakes as anyone else."

"Our mission is to protect the empire! Our destiny is to protect all of Rokugan from the forces of Fu Leng!"

Sunlight crept over the Wall and shone on the tent wall behind Sukune. He seemed to be enveloped by a golden halo as he shook his head ruefully.

"No man knows his own destiny," he said. "Anyone who claims otherwise is a dangerous fool."

▲▲▲▲▲▲▲▲

"It is my destiny to rule the empire!"

Sukune could not believe what his father was saying. Still, he knew better than to challenge Kisada.

The sun stood a full hand-width above the Wall, but the sky had grown overcast. Thick mists from the Shadowlands seemed to roll right through the Wall. Only faint light passed through the thick canvas of Kisada's command tent, making it hard for Sukune to see anything clearly. His father, brother, and Kuni Yori were mere silhouettes—shadow-puppets acting out a strange, unthinkable play.

"Can you explain that again?" Sukune asked. "I was so moved by your speech that—"

"Do not play etiquette games with me!" Kisada interrupted. "You think I have lost my mind, and you want to examine the root of my 'madness,' don't you?"

Sukune nodded. He saw no profit in denying his shock. His father would respect his honesty.

"Very well!" Kisada took a deep breath, preparing to launch into his reasoning again. "It is clear that Kachiko's decree was intended to have one effect—to set the clans against each other in a civil war unlike any Rokugan has ever known."

"Which apparently is already happening," said Yakamo. He clutched the stump of his left hand across his chest, *almost* managing to look casual, but Sukune knew him too well. His brother was obviously consumed with thoughts of his new "hand," and impatient to perform the required rituals to attach it permanently.

"Yes," Kisada continued. "Our clan's reputation and immobility make us a likely first target for nearly all the other clans. We must prepare to defend ourselves from attack. It will come, if not this fall, then certainly next spring."

"Hai!" said Sukune. So far he agreed with his father.

"If we must defend ourselves, and the weakest point of our defense is the fact that our army is immobile, we must choose a strategy that counters that weakness. We must not fight a defensive battle in the coming civil war—we must strike first, fast, and hardest."

This was where Sukune's support wavered. "I fail to see that as our only option," he said, hoping to lead into a more reasonable line of thinking.

Kisada burst back in. "There is another choice—to simply lay down our weapons and surrender like cowardly dogs! That is no choice! And it does the empire no good." His tone softened. "However, you are correct that we do not have to fight the other clans. Kachiko has made one mistake, and we will make her pay for it.

"In order for the clans to attack us or fight one another, they must move their armies back and forth across the empire. But the Spine of the World stands in their way. The only place it is convenient to move large numbers of troops across those mountains is Beiden Pass. If we control the pass, we can stop this war before it starts."

"A most brilliant plan, Tono," said Kuni Yori from behind the daimyo.

It seemed to Sukune as though his father and brother and the shugenja had formed a strategic alliance to deny his sensible objections. He felt like the Crab Clan itself—wanting only a sane path through these turbulent times but beset on all sides by unreasonable opponents.

"So we take and hold Beiden Pass," Sukune said slowly. "This will impress the emperor so much that he will name the Crab heirs to the Emerald Throne? Is that your plan?"

"This is not about gaining the emperor's blessing!" said Kisada. "We know that this whole directive is based on the Lady Scorpion's planning. She has no intention of allowing any clan to reach a position of power. She will find some way to make our efforts seem sinister and aggressive."

Sukune wondered how *else* the other clans ought to view the Crab leaving their positions on the Wall to seize control of Beiden Pass. It was a blatantly aggressive act.

"She will try to rally them to drive us out of the pass so that blood can spill in every corner of the empire. But we are the Crab! If we've held this wall for centuries against the inhuman onslaught of the Shadowlands, we can hold Beiden Pass for a thousand years! By controlling the pass I will control the empire!"

Yakamo and Yori both stomped their feet and hooted loudly.

"Eventually the other clans will see that we are not fomenting war or attempting to overthrow the emperor. We are merely enforcing peace. Then they will join us, and we can remove the Lady Scorpion—and if she has poisoned his brain beyond recovery, the emperor, too. But we will do it together, as a united empire!"

Sukune still did not share his father's enthusiasm or the sense that this was the surest way to victory. He did, however, agree that with the threat of all-out civil war, this might well be the least bloody and quickest way to save the empire.

"What about the Shadowlands?" Sukune asked. "I agree that our army could hold Beiden Pass indefinitely. But even we do not have enough troops to hold both the Wall and the pass at the same time. Can we give up our centuries-long duty to hold back the forces of Fu Leng?"

"Certainly not!" Kisada snapped. "Protecting the empire from the Dark God is our *most* important duty."

Sukune was relieved to hear his father say that. He was not shirking his responsibility as Crab daimyo. He was still the level-headed commander he had always been.

"That is why I am going to visit the oni we captured two years ago. I intend to take it up on its offer."

15 THE DEMON YOU KNOW

Lightning flashed in the dark gray clouds above, but no bolts flew down to earth—at least none Kisada could see. Though the autumn was warmer than usual, this wasn't heat lightning. Thunder rumbled low and resonant in the air. It felt as if the daimyo stood too close to someone pounding on a tremendous taiko drum.

As near as Kisada could tell, he and his samurai were the only living things for miles around—very strange so deep in the Shadowlands. He brought many of the same warriors who had accompanied him the last time—two years ago when they rode out to retrieve his lost tetsubo.

"Are you certain the oni is still where we left it?" The Great Bear turned in his saddle to face Kuni Yori. The shugenja rode a respectful dozen feet or so behind his daimyo.

"As I told you, Tono," Yori's words were muffled. Despite the heat, he wore the heavy hood of his black velvet robe up completely covering his face. "My spell of containment has not been shattered. Unless the creature found a way to escape without disturbing the walls of its prison, it is there yet."

Yakamo chuckled. "Not the guarantee I was hoping for." The young Hida rode next to his father and looked back at the shugenja with open contempt. Although Yori had supplied the claw that would replace his lost hand, the shugenja had not yet completed preparations for the ritual to attach the mechanism.

"Life offers few guarantees other than death," Yori replied and said no more.

They rode on for another few miles in silence. Although they would be hard pressed to point out any landmarks to prove it, all the samurai were sure they grew near to the site of their previous battle.

A hot wind swirled the mist at their feet, then blew it away entirely as Kisada's horse strode onto a large, open plateau.

"Have you changed your mind so soon, Lord of the Crab Clan? I know you humans are fickle, but it has been less than a decade since you laughed so uproariously at my proposal."

The oni sat right where Kisada had seen it last, hunched uncomfortably in a sphere of translucent white light. While it had a vaguely human shape, the fact that the creature had no features made it hard for Kisada to tell whether or not it was mocking him. The ropy tendrils that made up its body were a deeper color now—closer to purple than red—and its eyes were a darker shade of yellow, but it still made the same straining and popping noises as it shifted within its tiny cell.

Kisada dismounted but made a sign for the others to stay as they were. He paced slowly toward the prison and stopped just as he went completely out of the beast's view. The oni to had to shift uncomfortably within the cramped sphere in order to meet Kisada's eye.

"At the time it struck me as an arrangement I would never have use for," the Great Bear said. There was no use being evasive.

"It would seem that 'never' has come!" The oni stretched its face into a broad grin and made a grating noise the samurai could only assume was laughter. "Are you ready to seek the Emerald Throne, Kisada?"

"You continue to read me wrong, oni," Kisada said. "The throne is no place for a warrior like me. I belong on the battlefield, not at the Imperial Court."

"Then why have you come back?" the creature asked. "To mock me? I thought even you Crab were above that."

The Great Bear bristled, but he did not allow the oni to bait him. He was here for a reason, and allowing himself to be cajoled into a fight would not accomplish anything.

"Many things have changed in the empire since last we talked," Kisada said. "Many more things are about to change."

The oni grunted. "Things are always changing in your world. Your lives are so short there is no continuity. Just as soon as one of you begins to accomplish a measurable task, he dies, and the next generation undoes all he worked for. Or, worse, they ignore the lessons he learned and make the same mistakes over again. I am not afraid that the world will pass me by while I sit here in this prison your shugenja conjured." The oni tapped absently against the inside of the sphere, sending tiny arcs of lightning across its surface. "I know that in a thousand years, when this spell finally fades away, you humans will still be making the same mistakes you are today, guarding the same wall and fighting the same feuds. And if you're not, it will be because my master the Dark God has crushed you once and for all."

"Then why offer to help me seek the throne?" asked the Great Bear.

"Because I am bored," the oni said with a sinew-popping shrug. "I was bored two years ago when I decided to participate in that assault on your wall, and I'm doubly bored now."

"Don't waste my time with lies!"

The oni stared at Kisada with its pale yellow eyes and threw its head back in raucous laughter.

"Very well," it said. "The truth is my master cares not a whit for me or my soldiers. We are only a part of his grand plan for revenge against the Hantei, and a small part at that. If we all died on Crab blades, it would make no difference to Fu Leng."

It leaned closer, the tendrils of its nose sizzling as they pressed against the magical sphere. "I place a higher value on my life."

Kisada laughed. "Your great plan to save your own life is to strike a bargain with your age-old enemy?"

The oni shrugged again. "My master has made no promise of my safety—that is something I would demand of you before I lent you my aid."

"What makes you think I wouldn't accept your help, then order you and your army slaughtered the moment I reach my goal?"

"Over the years you have proven to be reliable, Kisada—violent and aggressive, but reliable. You will keep your word. You always do. In you I see a chance to forge my own destiny. It may be generations before I find another Rokugani who warrants the respect and trust I have for you."

Kisada grunted, a sound even gruffer and deeper than the monster's. "I understand," he said reluctantly. "It is rare to find an enemy that you can revere at the same time you attempt to take his head. However, the fact remains: I will not seek the throne for myself, and I certainly will not do so for you. I *do*, however, offer you a counterproposal."

The ropy segments of the oni's forehead twitched and rose in an expression of curiosity.

"What is this counterproposal, oh mighty Crab?"

"Order your army to cease its attack on the Wall for one year."

"And why should I do that?"

The Great Bear leaned forward like a father whispering to his son. The oni pressed its face and hands against the sphere.

"A civil war threatens the empire. Empress Kachiko has set the clans against one another, vying for the Emerald Throne."

"I know *that!*" thundered the oni. "I foresaw these events before we had our first meeting! Why do you think I have *any* interest in who sits on my enemy's throne? "

"Ah, but it isn't the throne in which you should be interested." Kisada paused and raised his eyebrows imitating a particularly annoying expression of Kuni Yori's—one that presaged a particularly insightful comment.

The oni leaned back and considered, his expression similar to the one Kisada wore in such situations—half disbelief and half curiosity.

"Sitting on the throne is no guarantee of control. The emperor cannot master his own wife, let alone the ambitions of the clans. Taking the throne wouldn't give me unquestioned authority over anyone.

"But I can rule the country—control the movement of troops. You want me to assure that the Rokugani forces will not wage war against your troops. I cannot guarantee that even *I* could do that from Otosan Uchi," Kisada paused dramatically. "But I *can* promise that when I seize control of Beiden Pass!"

"The pass?" croaked the oni. It scratched its chin with a finger made of entwined tentacles. "You will not move against an emperor you know to be weak and unable to rule, but you will make a military maneuver that will bring you in conflict with every other clan in your empire?"

Kisada threw his head back and laughed. "After fighting the Crab for so long, I'd have thought you'd understand us better! My duty is to protect the empire, whether from unholy monstrosities or from honorless dogs. If other clans cannot see that civil war is a threat to the empire, I have no compunction about teaching them with steel and blood."

The oni nodded. "You truly are a man of vision, Crab Lord."

Kisada waited. So far the oni had agreed to nothing.

"I cannot accept this proposal. The taking and holding of a mountain pass is a temporary thing. What you win today, you could lose tomorrow. If anything goes wrong for you, my army's inaction will bring Fu Leng's wrath down on us all."

"What is the difference?" demanded the Great Bear. "Could I not just as easily lose the throne, if I decided to make it mine?"

The oni laughed that terrible, grating laugh. "Any warrior can kill a foe or take a pass—but it takes a legend to kill an emperor!"

"So you reject my offer?" Kisada was obviously displeased.

"As I said," the oni continued, "I cannot completely hold off our attacks based on your plan. However, I can offer you two things: a reduction in aggression against your position, and support in your efforts to take the pass, if not the throne."

The Great Bear blinked several times.

"Support?" said Kisada. "What do you mean support? And how severely would you curtail your assault on the Wall?"

The oni smiled so broadly that several tendrils snapped and whipped around at the side of the creature's maw.

"I offer support in the form of troops. I will send as many of my warriors with you as you like. Our mission is to invade Rokugan—Fu Leng never said anything about waging war against the Crab in order to do so."

Kisada cocked his eyebrow and tilted his head slightly. "You will place your troops under my command?"

"No," the oni looked aghast. "They will not fight for your cause. But they *will* march by your side and bolster the apparent size of your army. Your army will seem an unstoppable force. Tell me how many troops you wish to take. Every goblin, ogre, and zombie that follows you is one more creature who will not be assaulting your precious wall in your absence."

Kisada sat as still as a decorative suit of armor. For a very long time he said nothing. "You want me to march my army off to war alongside an army of our greatest enemies? How can we possibly trust that your warriors will not turn on us the minute we lie down to sleep? How can I be sure that you will not order your beasts to wait until we are engaged in battle with our enemy, then attack us from our exposed flanks?"

"And how do *I* know, Hida Kisada, that you will not march my subjects into the heart of enemy territory and slay them where they stand? Trust, you see, cannot always be earned. Sometimes mutual suspicion is enough. I respect you, Crab Lord. I do not trust you. This proposal is so perilous for both of us that we cannot enter into it with duplicity in our hearts. We have no choice but to be true to one another."

▲▲▲▲▲▲▲▲

From their vantage at the plateau's edge, Yakamo and Yori could make out most of what the oni said. Its voice resonated low and clear and seemed to travel through the very ground itself. However, they could not hear a word said by the Great Bear.

"How can he accept such a proposal?" Yakamo said.

"Your father is a cunning general," replied Yori, though he knew the question was rhetorical. "He knows that sometimes the most strategic tactic is not the most likely to succeed. The one your enemy least expects is."

Yakamo looked at the shugenja.

"If he does agree," Yakamo said, this time specifically to the shugenja, "what does that mean for the Crab? For a thousand years we have defined ourselves by our fight against the Shadowlands. If we march into battle with those creatures at our sides, what do we stand for?"

Yori smiled underneath his hood. He had been waiting for Yakamo to ask this question, and now he needed to be careful in answering it. He had to let the silence hang for just the right amount of time, and he himself had to appear to struggle with the matter. The shugenja raised a hand to his long mustache and stroked it pensively. This was the art of manipulation. This was the moment when years of planning came together.

"History is replete with tales of enemies who became the closest of allies," he finally said in his practiced, faraway voice— the one that made it seem he was drawing on some mystical store of knowledge. "If Kisada succeeds in bridging this gulf, he may well be remembered as the greatest leader in the history of the empire."

Yakamo grunted in agreement. As far as he was concerned, his father already deserved that accolade.

"Savor this moment, Yakamo-san," Yori continued. "It is one that history will remember for centuries to come. Make yourself a part of it. Use it to improve your own karma."

Yakamo became still, his eyes never leaving his father's yet-silent figure.

🔺🔺🔺🔺🔺🔺🔺🔺

"Very well," Kisada finally answered. "I will take two thousand of your troops to march alongside mine."

The oni clapped its tremendous hands together once.

"So it shall be," the creature said. "They will report to your Wall at first light tomorrow. Remember, they will follow you and take your marching orders, but they will not fight for you."

Kisada smiled wryly. "But they *will*, I think, defend themselves if attacked by other forces."

"Without a doubt."

Both Kisada and the oni burst into laughter, but not at each other. For the first time, the two ancient enemies laughed together.

"Now have your shugenja release me, and we will drink a toast to our new alliance."

Kisada grew deathly quiet.

"We are not allies," he said. "And you are not leaving that prison."

"What?" roared the oni.

"Let's call it 'insurance,'" the Great Bear said. "I need some guarantee that your soldiers here will behave themselves while my army is divided. I suspect that even depleted by two thousand, your army could continue to throw their lives away on our blades for weeks before we noticed a slack in your attacks."

"You are indeed clever—and quite correct," replied the oni. "But the fact is that my army poses a greater threat to your position if I am imprisoned and cannot punish them for disobeying my orders, which they do with alarming frequency."

Kisada considered this. "So what I need is a way to put you back in command of your forces and still maintain the position of strength I have while you're my prisoner."

"I know how you can accomplish such a thing," said a figure who had not been there a moment before. It was small and thin, and its face was hidden beneath a black velvet hood.

"Yori!" Kisada snapped.

"I humbly apologize for disobeying your orders, Tono," the shugenja said, bowing deeply. "But I believe I know how to overcome your current conundrum."

"Yes?"

"Give the oni a name," Yori said. His voice had a musical lilt, as though he was explaining some incredibly obvious fact to a young child.

"A name?" Kisada asked.

"A name," said the oni. "My Dark Lord and master does not allow his minions such luxuries."

Kisada stared wide-eyed. He could not begin to fathom an existence without an identity—particularly with a life as long as an oni's.

"Fu Leng knows the power of a name, the fear it can instill and the devotion it can inspire," the creature continued. "He forbids us from having or taking names. Only the children of the other kami may name us."

"More correctly," Yori said, "someone can share his name with the oni and thus control it. When a human gives his name to a creature of darkness, the two are inextricably linked. If the person is sufficiently resolute, he will control the oni."

"And if the person is less strong-willed?" asked the Crab daimyo.

"Then I would control him," answered the oni.

"Essentially, yes," agreed Yori.

The Great Bear straightened his armor and raised himself to his full height.

"Give the creature *my* name," Kisada said.

"No!"

Yakamo came running up to the group. He stopped nose-to-nose with his father and placed himself directly between the Great Bear and the imprisoned oni.

"You are clearly the best choice, Father," he said. "No one can match your courage, determination, or strength. But in the coming days you will be responsible for overseeing the single most important military campaign in Rokugan's history. The strain of controlling so forceful a creature as this," he looked over his shoulder, "would jeopardize the entire operation." Yakamo bowed deeply. "I humbly ask to be given this terrible responsibility."

Kisada's first reaction was to deny Yakamo's request. The young man had all ready been through so much, and would be going through even more in the weeks ahead.

Kuni Yori stepped up and whispered in Kisada's ear.

"Who better than the heir to the Crab daimyo?" the shugenja hissed. "His reputation will be secured not only among our clan but among all the others as well—the man who tamed an oni. Tono, you may be disliked in some quarters, but no one doubts your capabilities. Yakamo must be given the chance to prove himself for all the world to see. This is the stuff from which legends are made!"

Kisada ground his teeth—a sound like the one made when the oni smiled. "Very well. You have my consent."

"The containment spell will have to come down," Yori said. "I will need to lay my hands on both parties. The naming ritual is perfunctory, but accuracy is required."

The Great Bear grunted assent, then shot the oni a glare warning it against trying to escape.

The beast nodded solemnly.

With a simple snap of Yori's fingers, the glowing white sphere winked out of existence. The oni, though, did not tumble to the ground in a heap. Instead it nimbly rolled in midair and landed softly in a three-point stance, like a runner preparing to sprint. Rather than burst away, the oni stood tall, and then sat on its haunches.

Both Yakamo and the oni held out their right hands.

Kuni Yori clutched Yakamo's wrist and wrapped his hand around one ropelike tendril of the oni's thumb. He closed his eyes and began to mumble in an ancient tongue remembered only by sorcerers. He called to the elements, as he had to forge the prison. His body began to shiver as though someone even larger and stronger than Kisada stood behind the shugenja, shaking him vigorously.

Yakamo began to shake as well, his armor rattling like an army of Shadowlands skeletons climbing the Wall. He began mumbling in the same language as Yori, echoing the shugenja's words mere seconds after he spoke them. The oni too began to shiver. Every tendril on the creature twitched individually, and Kisada feared it might fly into a thousand pieces.

The three of them stayed that way, connected and shuddering, for a full minute.

Yori's eyes shot open. The hood flew off his painted face as though an invisible hand tugged it. All three participants

threw their heads back and howled one word to the heavens—
"Yakamooooooooooo!"

That name rolled out like a word of power, bringing the shuddering trance to an end. The contact between oni and shugenja and samurai broke.

Yori pulled his hood low over his face and hid his hands inside his sleeves. He stood stock still for a very long time.

Yakamo slumped momentarily, then stood upright. He shook his head as if slightly disoriented.

The oni stood proud and tall, its attitude even more human than before. However, the tendrils covering its body continued to writhe and pop. Parts of the creature's head and arms seemed to be bulking up—it was metamorphosing before Kisada's eyes.

"I have a name!" the oni cried. Its voice had less of the unnatural popping and grating than before; it was even beginning to sound more human. Raising both hands to the overcast sky, it threw its head back and laughed long and loud.

"You have your freedom, Yakamo no Oni," Kisada said calmly. "Will you order your minions to lessen their assaults against my positions?"

Yakamo no Oni looked at the Great Bear and smiled. Something about the shape the creature was taking felt disturbingly familiar.

"So long as my samurai travel with you in peace, I order that aggression against the Crab wall cease," Yakamo no Oni said with a gracious bow.

"Will your troops be ready to depart in the morning?" asked Kisada. He would never acknowledge the Shadowlands forces as samurai.

"Hai!" said the creature.

Kisada grunted and nodded. Without further ceremony, he spun on his heel, returned to his horse, mounted, and urged it back in the direction of the Wall.

"One more thing, Kisada."

The daimyo stopped but did not turn to face the oni.

"We have taken a historic first step today," said the creature, "but there is so much more we could do for each other. My previous offer remains open, should you decide a mountain pass is not enough for you."

"Beiden Pass is not a mere mountain pass. It is the heart of the empire."

"Still," Yakamo no Oni said. "If you give me one life, one innocent life, I will put you on the Emerald Throne."

"Get on your horses," the Great Bear barked at his son and adviser. "It is time to save the empire."

16   PRELUDE TO WAR

Are you Crab samurai, or whining children afraid of the shadows cast on your wall?"

The assembled generals shuffled uncomfortably. At some point in their careers every one of them had been reprimanded by Hida Kisada for some transgression, but before now he had never called any of his soldiers cowards. Of course, the day was filled with things that had never happened before.

In the past, Kisada had always met with his generals in the privacy of his command tent. Though the commander issued orders, the atmosphere had been casual. As much as Kisada was daimyo, he was also one of them—a soldier who had earned his position by serving on the Wall. Today, though, the Great Bear made them stand at attention in his courtyard while he sat imperiously on the tatami dais and issued commands.

Those commands were the greatest surprise of all. How could the daimyo berate them for balking at the idea of marching into battle side by side with creatures from the Shadowlands?

The generals looked to Hida Tsuru, Kisada's brother. As a rule, the other generals did not like Tsuru. He had all the worst aspects of the Hida family—the perfectionism, the demand for absolute obedience, and, most of all, the temper—but few of their finer qualities. Although he was an accomplished warrior, he did not have his brother's (or even his nephew's) leadership skills; his men followed him because they *had* to, and because he was a deadly fighter. His samurai held their commander in more fear than awe. Still, if anyone could talk sense to the Great Bear, it was Tsuru.

"It is not that we are afraid, Kisada-sama," Tsuru ventured. "Our entire lives have been spent slaying these creatures—we have nothing for them in our hearts but contempt. You cannot expect samurai to fight alongside their most hated enemy."

The other generals nodded and murmured their agreement.

"Brother, you are a fine general, and as skilled a warrior as I've ever seen," Kisada's voice was flat and even, but it contained an edge of anger sharper than any blade in the Crab armies. As he spoke he stepped closer and closer to Tsuru until the face-plate of his helmet was flush against the younger officer's nose. "But you know less than nothing about the matters at hand! As we prepare for this campaign I would rather take the advice of your horse! At least it will do what it is told and not waste time balking!"

Tsuru's cheeks flushed, and his hands clenched but did not flinch as his brother's breath and spit flew from the helmet.

Kisada whirled to face the rest of the generals.

"I have ruled this clan for more than twenty years. In all that time have you ever known me to do anything that was not in the best interest of the Crab?"

"Iie!" the generals said as one, Tsuru more loudly than any three others.

"Have I *ever* put my personal interest above any samurai under my command?"

"Iie!"

"Do you understand the ramifications of the empress's declaration? Do you see that civil war is about to tear the empire to pieces?"

"Hai!"

"And do any of you—*any* of you—have even the beginnings of a plan that will stop the dissolution of the empire, prevent the clan from being destroyed by our own supposed allies, rip power away from the treacherous Lady Scorpion, and prevent the Shadowlands from overrunning Rokugan?"

Silence.

The Great Bear waited.

"Anyone?"

Someone coughed nervously.

"Well then," Kisada continued, his voice calmer, "I expect you all to go back to your posts and prepare your men for the upcoming campaign. They will be fighting an enemy unlike any they have ever faced—Rokugani samurai! Our purpose is not to win a war but to prevent one. It is the same battle we Crab have fought for a thousand years, and I expect nothing less than absolute success!"

"Hai!" answered the generals as they bowed and backed out of the courtyard.

"That could have gone better," said Sukune from the corner where he stood next to Yakamo.

Before the audience had begun, Kisada asked both his sons to stand off to the side and say nothing. "Just wear the sternest face you can, and growl when I do," he'd said. They had no idea what he was going to tell the generals. Still they did as their father ordered, staring down the generals with a look of contempt that Kisada taught them the day they finished their training and became full fledged samurai. The look was surprisingly effective, even on older or higher-ranking officers.

"Nonsense!" said Kisada. He rose from the tatami, walked to the command tent, and entered. His sons followed. "I expect no less from my generals. I do not want them to be spineless toadies afraid to trust their own judgment. I do not want them to be like the other clans' generals, following meaningless or moronic orders simply because they come from a famous mouth. I expect my generals to question orders that seem strange or offensive." He paused and smiled cruelly. "But after I explain myself, I expect them to shut their mouths and do as they're told."

The silk entrance parted, and Kuni Yori entered, the sounds of chaos coming in behind him. Even under the shadow of his hood and the white paint that masked his features, it was clear the shugenja was exasperated and exhausted.

"The goblin commander wishes to know when we will be departing," Yori said wearily. "He says the scent of a human camp is driving his soldiers into a frenzy. If they don't have something physical to do soon he is afraid that rioting may break out."

All three Hidas chuckled darkly.

"Go back and loudly tell the little monstrosity that we will leave when I give the order. Any aggressions made by his so-called soldiers would violate the orders of Yakamo no Oni, thus freeing our samurai to slice them into little pieces."

"B-but *that* wasn't part of the agreement," said Yori.

Kisada winked and smiled at the shugenja. "When the rest of the goblins break into panicked squeals, tell the goblin commander to prepare half his forces to leave at midday, and the other half tomorrow morning." The smile fell from the Great Bear's face. "And tell him that if he ever loses control of even one goblin, zombie, or skeleton I will personally separate his head from his shoulders."

Yori smiled and bowed.

"When you're done with that, come back here, and I will tell you *your* orders for the first part of our campaign."

"Hai, Tono!" Neither the shugenja nor the makeshift silk door made any noise as he left.

Kisada waited a few moments. Kuni Yori was his most trusted adviser, but the daimyo knew that he was not above lingering outside the courtyard to hear what was being discussed in his absence.

"We have the largest standing army in all of Rokugan," Kisada finally said. "But the plan I have in mind will tax even our manpower. We will split our forces into thirds. One-third will remain on the Wall to protect against treachery from our Shadowlands supporter. The second third will leave for Beiden Pass today and march at double-time the whole way. The final third will leave to-morrow morning, but march at a slower pace."

"You wish it to appear that the group that leaves first is heading for one of the other conflicts!" In his excitement, Sukune's voice rose even higher than usual. His father's cunning was impressive.

"Yes," chuckled the Great Bear. "There have been skirmishes along the Lion-Dragon border. Each side will likely view our advance as a move to support their enemy. The Crane have Beiden Pass only lightly defended—they do not want to appear to be asserting control over so important a junction. We will relieve them of that duty and take control of the pass ourselves. Our force will be small enough that the Crane will not see it as a threat to their homeland, but it will be more than enough to take that one position. Before the Crane can get reinforcements, the trailing group will arrive and fortify our position."

"A brilliant plan, Father!" said Yakamo. "I will prepare to leave at midday. It is a shame that you will miss the real action again, Brother, but—"

"I want Sukune to lead the first group," Kisada interrupted.

Neither brother knew what to say. They both assumed that Yakamo would lead the army that was to take Beiden Pass and Sukune would lead the support troops. The younger Hida was never given command of important assignments.

"But, Father!" Yakamo began to complain.

Kisada raised his hand. "Taking the pass should pose little challenge, even to a less-seasoned commander," the Great Bear said. Sukune bore the implied insult without a sound. "Unless the Crane have secretly increased their guard. If that *is* the case, I want my more experienced commander leading the secondary forces so that we are certain to crush all opposition. If we do not take Beiden Pass on the first try, the Crane reinforcements will make it so that we never will."

This seemed to satisfy Yakamo's pride as well as Sukune's desire for a chance to distinguish himself.

"Each of you will take half the Shadowlands armies on your march," Kisada continued. "Remember, they will go where you tell them to, but they will not fight except to defend themselves. Use them as you see fit, but never make the mistake of *trusting* them."

"Yes, Father," both sons said in unison.

Kisada reached inside his armor and pulled out two scrolls. Handing one to Yakamo and the other to Sukune he said, "Unless something goes terribly wrong, you should secure the pass several days before I arrive. Only after the enemy is routed and you've merged your forces, read these scrolls. They will tell you what I expect you to do while you wait for me."

"But where will you be, Father?" asked Sukune.

"Are you afraid to be out in the field alone for so long?" teased Yakamo.

Sukune refused to be taunted. "I merely wonder what other matter could deserve more attention than the taking of Beiden Pass," he said.

"I play the battlefield the way a master plays a go board. Every action sets up the final victory. You will know more when the time is right," Kisada said. "Now go. Some of your troops will meet you on the road to the pass. You want them to have to work to keep up. A good commander never lets his troops appear to be more prepared than he."

"Hai!" said Sukune as he bowed and backed out of the tent.

"Are you certain I should not lead the first force?" asked Yakamo.

"Your chance for battle will come, Yakamo. This will not be as easy an operation as I make it sound. The other clans will put up more than token resistance. If we do this correctly, though, even their combined might will not be able to pry us from Beiden Pass. Now go prepare your own troops—you don't have much more time than your brother."

Yakamo bowed and turned to leave.

"On your way out, tell Kuni Yori to stop lurking around the tent flap and come inside. I've got plans for him as well."

The shugenja lifted the silken door and entered, making a show of looking nonchalant. He bowed to Yakamo as the brothers exited.

"Hai, Tono," Yori said. "You wished to see me."

"Yes," Kisada said slowly. Obviously there was something on

his mind. "I have put Sukune in charge of the army that is to take and hold the pass."

Yori looked shocked in spite of himself. Recovering quickly, he said, "I am certain he will shower honor upon himself and the entire clan." In this case, honor meant nothing less than absolute victory.

Kisada paced the length of the dais twice before he said, "I certainly hope so. I've given Yakamo and Sukune different orders. Yakamo's are the more difficult, but Sukune's are the more important. If he fails in his tasks, my entire plan may fall apart. Part of Yakamo's orders are to keep an eye on his brother's command, and never allow Beiden Pass to be taken from us once we control it."

"I understand," said Yori.

"Yakamo will judge his brother harshly," the Great Bear muttered. "I want you to go with Sukune's forces. Act as advisor to my son, but your real job is to be my eyes and ears. I want you to be the final judge of whether or not Sukune is bringing honor to the Hida name."

"I am humbled by your request." Yori bowed deeply.

"If my youngest child brings shame to our clan," Kisada continued. "If Yakamo does indeed have to relieve him of his command, I leave you with an even greater task. You must see to it that Sukune does the right thing. You must make sure that he does not return from the campaign."

"Tono?" Yori looked troubled by the order.

"If he fails so utterly—and if he is a true samurai—Sukune will commit seppuku to save face. But he so often acts in strange ways. If he fails to follow honor's dictates, I want you to kill him." Kisada took a long breath. "I cannot be more plain than that. Do not make me say it again."

Kuni Yori stared mutely at the Great Bear. All he could do was nod in agreement.

"Very well," Kisada said looking relieved that the matter was done. "Now go prepare. Sukune's troops leave at midday."

"And where will *you* be during this opening skirmish in your war to prevent a war?" Yori allowed a hint of contempt to creep into his voice.

"I will be preparing for the worst," said the Great Bear. He looked at the entrance, and then back to Yori. "My next visitor awaits, and your battalion leaves in a few hours. I will see you at Beiden Pass, Yori."

"Hai, Tono. You will."

On his way out, Kuni Yori bumped shoulders with a small man of about fifty years. The man's face was covered with wrinkles, and his skin was tough and dark from too many years in the sun. He wore a simple outfit of rough cloth, and on his head sat a wide-brimmed peasant hat. He looked like a man who might serve the daimyo meals, but not one whose opinion the great man might seek.

"Come in Taka, my old friend," Kisada said warmly. "You were going to talk to me about boats. . . ."

17 THE FIRST WAVE

Sukune played his gambit just right. He began by ordering the Shadowlands troops to make camp in a patch of woods about three miles from Beiden Pass—not wanting their presence to alert the Crane forces to his troops' real intentions. Sukune then led the Crab forces toward Beiden Pass at quick time, looking as though they had a long way to go.

"Ho!" the Crane commander called out to Sukune as the Crab forces approached. "You're a long way from your wall."

"Yes, we are!" Sukune answered, motioning his samurai to continue their march while he parleyed with the Crane.

"Off to the Lion lands?"

Sukune grunted—a fair imitation of his brother.

"Say, you're Kisada's youngest, aren't you?" the Crane said when Sukune approached.

If his size and build hadn't given him away, his armor had—it was unlike anyone else's. It had the very look of a crab to it, as though Sukune had a shell strapped to his back and crushing weapons built onto his bracers.

"Hai!" he answered. "I am Hida Sukune, off to seek honor in battle." Certainly a true enough statement, but not one the Crane had any hope of interpreting correctly.

"I am Doji Kenji," the Crane commander said. "I wish you and your men good fortune in your upcoming battle!"

Sukune knew that before the sun set Kenji would regret those words, but the Crab bowed and thanked the Crane all the same. Without another word he spun on his heels and rejoined his marching troops.

▲ ▲ ▲ ▲ ▲ ▲ ▲ ▲

All through the pass Sukune looked up at the rocks above. There were plenty of nooks and ledges where archers could be posted, but the Crane assigned troops only to those near the beginning and end of the trail. They could easily defend themselves from assailants coming from either entrance, but were completely vulnerable to a two-pronged attack from an enemy already within Beiden Pass.

The pass was a thin stone path through the mountains, wide enough for four or five samurai to march abreast. Here and there, rough, thorny brush grew among the inhospitable gray rocks. Though the autumn remained warm throughout the empire, this road traveled so high across Rokugan's spine that Sukune could see his breath even at midday. It was a cold and lonely place made of unforgiving stone, and a day or more's ride from anyone who might offer support in a time of war.

A great shout went up ahead of Sukune. This was the signal that the front of the battle line had reached the far end of the pass—it was the signal to begin the attack.

"Attack!" Sukune cried. He turned and led his troops in a charge toward the backs of the Crane forces.

Sukune had ordered his troops to give the Crane every opportunity to withdraw or surrender, but he knew none would. Crane measured a warrior's worth by the purest interpretations of bushido—the warrior's code. It would come to a fight—and it would be a slaughter.

▲▲▲▲▲▲▲▲

"Traitor!"

Sukune turned at the sound. At first, Sukune did not recognize Doji Kenji. The Crane leader's armor was in tatters. His left shoulder guard had been sliced in two by a Crab blade, and the right one had been torn off entirely. A katana trembled in the man's grip.

"We offered you safe passage through our lands, and *this* is how you repay us?"

Sukune held his katana at the ready. No matter what words were spoken, a final confrontation was at hand.

"Your safe passage is what will doom Rokugan," Sukune said calmly. "We must stop all military traffic until the madness that sweeps the empire can be cured."

"The only madness here is Kisada's," Kenji returned. "The other clans will not allow him to bottle up all travel within Rokugan."

"Are you all in such a great hurry to kill one another?" asked Sukune, but he could tell that the Crane was no longer listening.

Around them the battle ebbed. Crane soldiers lay dead and dying throughout the pass. Only here and there could Sukune see Crab warriors among them. Beiden Pass would belong to the Crab by nightfall. But first Sukune had to deal with the Crane commander.

"I cannot win this day," said Kenji, "but I *can* ensure that you do not live to celebrate this honorless victory."

Sukune tensed, lifting his katana. His battle strategy was to leave his guard down in the places where his armor offered extra defense, drawing the enemy's attack. So many samurai were trained to react instantly to any weakness, the young Crab was usually able to dupe them into striking just where he wanted them to. Still, Cranes were master duelists.

With a crisp shout, the Crane struck at Sukune's neck. The blow was easily blocked, but its force staggered Sukune, driving him back two steps. Kenji pressed the attack with a triple slash across the chest and abdomen—a maneuver the Crane called Three Winds on the Plain. Sukune deflected the first two blows. The third slid across the belly of his armor, gouging it deeply but not getting through to his flesh.

Sukune desperately slashed back at his opponent. He aimed for Kenji's right shoulder. His katana was neatly blocked by the follow-through from the Crane's successful attack. The sword slipped in Sukune's hands, and he almost dropped it. Recovering his grip cost him his balance. He staggered to a stop turned three-quarters away from his opponent. He tried to spin back but couldn't move fast enough.

Kenji brought his blade down directly at Sukune's back. There was no force under the sun that could prevent the blow from landing.

A loud clang filled the air. Instead of sliding through the light armor most samurai had on their backs, the Crane's blade bounced off Sukune's reinforced armor.

The blow sent shivers of pain shooting through Kenji's arms and even snapped a chip out of the middle of his katana.

Perhaps these Crane are not as experienced as they think, mused Sukune. Sometimes pride is a powerful disadvantage.

Sukune continued to turn toward his opponent, whose last strike left a hopelessly overextended ribcage for a target. Sukune's katana bit deeply into the Crane's skin.

The stroke seemed to last for minutes.

Sukune led with his elbow, pulled with his wrists, and drew the blade through, severing Kenji's armor, ribs, and everything beneath. It was only after the katana emerged on the other side with a wet sound that time seemed to resume its normal pace.

Blood sprayed from the Crane's chest. Sukune felt it warm and wet, dripping down his face and across his chest—his blow had cut Kenji's heart in two.

"Now you look like a Hida!" said Kuni Yori in mock appreciation. The shugenja appeared as if from nowhere.

Sukune glared at him. It was the withering stare his father had taught him, but it seemed to have no effect on the shugenja—

probably from so many years weathering the same look from Kisada himself.

Looking around, Sukune could see that the battle was finally over. No Crane remained.

"Tell the generals to take their samurai to the locations we discussed last night," Sukune told Yori. "My brother's troops will be here by nightfall tomorrow. In that time I want this entire corridor secured. Beiden Pass is ours—let's make sure it stays that way."

▲▲▲▲▲▲▲▲

"You bungle your way to success and call it victory?"

Sukune had not expected his brother to be overflowing with praise, but he likewise never expected Yakamo to call him inept. After all, he took Beiden Pass in less than an afternoon. Granted, he had overwhelming numbers on his side, but the reason their father wanted the pass in the first place was that it was so easily defended. A well-organized and prepared force could hold off an army ten times its own size if they used the cliffs and narrow mountain trails to their best advantage.

"I call it achieving my goal with minimal casualties," Sukune said trying not to sound petulant. "We lost only sixteen bushi in the assault, and killed more than fifty of the enemy. How can you call that bungling?"

This might not have been the most efficient operation in the history of Crab warfare, but it certainly was not a debacle. Abundant campfires lit the granite walls of Beiden Pass—a warming reminder that his force had come through practically unscathed.

Yakamo bent down so that he was eye to eye with his brother. They stood in one of the darkened stretches between camps, but the distant firelight danced across his helmet and shone in his eyes.

"When you have a force of completely expendable Shadowlands creatures at your command, I call any losses unacceptable. If you sent the goblins into the pass ahead of you, they would certainly have come under attack by the Crane and fought tooth and claw to defend themselves. They clearly could have taken the pass on their own—after all, *you* did."

Sukune ignored the jibe. Clearly Yakamo still felt threatened by the fact that he had not been chosen to take the pass. The rivalry between the brothers ran deep, but only Yakamo had any sense that it was for a purpose. Sukune knew how his father felt about him. No matter how many foes he slew or military victories he commanded, he would always be "the weakling" to Kisada.

Yakamo, however, needed to prove his superiority, if only by denigrating any shred of success Sukune achieved. It was perhaps the greatest fault of Yakamo and Kisada's mindset—measuring self worth by conquest. Holding the Wall against the forces of Fu Leng ceased to be enough to satisfy their insecurities. Now they protected the empire from itself. Would that prove to be enough, or would they need to seek a greater victory after this campaign? How many greater victories remained? What would they do when there *was* nothing bigger to be achieved?

"I refuse to honor only the letter of our agreement with the creature to whom you gave your name," Sukune said stiffly. The decision to link himself with an oni was just another in the growing list of poor choices Yakamo had made in recent days. "There is no honor in putting these creatures in harm's way."

"Honor?" cried Yakamo. "Honor? These are goblins and worse! Half the forces are undead zombies! They have no honor!"

"Yes, but we do. This is our fight. Father may have made the right decision in negotiating this truce, but that does not mean the Shadowlands army is ours to throw away."

"I cannot believe that there is *any* circumstance under which you would give up the life of a single Crab samurai instead of a dozen Shadowlands monstrosities!" Yakamo emphasized his point by poking Sukune in the chest with each significant word.

"Once again, we see that there is simply a fundamental difference between us," Sukune said calmly. "Please, use the creatures under your command as you see fit. But allow me the same latitude."

Yakamo grunted. "It is time to open our orders."

They reached under their armor and pulled out the scrolls Kisada had given them five days earlier. They held them out at arm's length, never taking their eyes off one another—staring intently into each other's soul—each trying to prove by force of will that he was in the right in this argument.

Simultaneously, they broke both eye contact and the seals on their scrolls. A minute later they lowered the scrolls and looked at one another again. This time they were trying to guess the contents of the other's scroll.

"It seems you will have to defend this pass without my aid," said Yakamo slowly.

"Something I have been prepared to do from the beginning," answered Sukune. He held the scroll up again and read, " 'Deploy your troops along the pass, and prepare to hold it through the coming winter. You must prepare a safe haven for Yakamo and his troops, for they will return with enemies close on their heels. We should only face strong opposition for the first month or so. After that you will have only the Crane to worry about. The approaching snows will drive the other clans back to their homelands until spring.' "

Yakamo nodded and smiled.

"You have another objective. One that will bring you great glory."

"Indeed, I do," the elder brother said. "Mine says, 'To hold the pass over the winter, Sukune's troops will need two things: supplies and protection from the local Crane forces. You must get both by leading your troops to the north and taking the fortress Kyuden Kakita. Rout the Crane stationed there. They will fight to delay you, to hold you off until reinforcements can arrive. Do not allow them to succeed in this. Crush the castle's defenses, then destroy the building itself. Take their stores and rejoin Sukune at Beiden Pass. That is where we shall winter, and from there we shall save all of Rokugan.' "

The brothers stared at one another for a long while, neither saying a word. Finally they were interrupted when Kuni Yori stepped from the shadows—neither Sukune nor Yakamo had seen him approach.

"Is there a dispute I can help settle?" asked the shugenja, although the smile on his face hinted that he was well aware of what was *really* going on.

"My troops and I leave again in the morning," said Yakamo. "We were just saying farewell."

"And wishing one another luck," Sukune continued. "Despite our differences we all fight for the same thing."

"The glory of the Crab Clan."

"The safety of the empire."

18 THE OTHER HAND

The chill autumn wind was a thief, sneaking through Beiden Pass and stealing the warmth from the dying campfires. No tent flap or blanket or animal hide was proof against its icy fingers.

While Sukune's guards watched either end of the pass, Yakamo's samurai slept soundly between. He had expressly forbidden a guard. Every samurai would need his or her strength for the coming battles.

A lone figure emerged silently from his tent, lifted a large wooden crate, and walked away from the rest. He climbed a narrow, nearly invisible trail up the north wall of Beiden Pass. The moonless night made his going even more difficult, but he managed it without once stumbling or making a sound. Toward the top of the wall, he followed a trail back away from the pass until he came to a flat, open space. He laid the box on the ground and waited, though not for long.

"All is prepared," a shrill voice said from the darkness.

"It is well past time! Now give me some light."

A sharp sound filled the air. It might have been fingers snapping or a dried bone being broken in two. Torches flared to life in a large circle at the plateau's center.

Standing within the circle was Kuni Yori, dressed in heavy velvet robes, the hood pulled tight around his head. Instead of his usual black robes, he wore deep crimson garments covered with the kanji for "crab" and "victory" as well as several pictographs. The shugenja's face was painted differently, too. His usual pallid mask was splattered with odd red shapes, particularly around eyes and mouth. The two ends of his long, thin mustache were braided under his chin. As cold as the night was, no steam escaped the hood. Either Yori's breath was as cold as the air itself, or he wasn't breathing at all.

The torches cast a flickering light on Yakamo and the black box he'd carried all this way.

"Let's get this over with."

"No!" said a third voice. It came from the trail that Yakamo had just traversed. "Brother, I implore you: Do not do this thing. A warrior is measured by the strength of his heart, not his arm."

"Of course *you* would say that!" Yakamo spat, turning to see Sukune's pale face in the dim light. "Your arms are weak—*you* are weak. But I am not. I have always been strong. If I cannot fight, I am nothing."

"If that is what you believe," Sukune said, "you already are nothing."

Yakamo growled an unintelligible reply.

"Sukune-san," Yori said. "I appreciate your concern, but I warn you that interfering with the ritual once it is in progress will only make matters worse. Perhaps you should go back to your tent."

"No," Sukune replied. "I may think he's a fool, but I will not let my brother go through this alone."

▲ ▲ ▲ ▲ ▲ ▲ ▲ ▲

Yakamo lay on the cold ground within a large circle of rice sprinkled on the nearly flat rock of the plateau. Yori stood over him, his feet outside the circle, but his head and arms leaning in.

Suddenly, despite the cold and windy night, despite the chilling mission that brought them here, Sukune found the air hot, damp, and close. Standing on an open plain atop the tallest mountains in the region, he felt crowded and watched.

Kuni Yori actually looked concerned—as if he knew how wrong he was to perform this act.

"This will hurt," Yori said, "quite a bit, actually. I just thought you should know."

"I am not afraid of pain!" grumbled Yakamo.

The shugenja looked at him quizzically.

"I didn't think you were," he said. "But you must be sure not to twitch about. If you *or* the claw break the circle, things will become even more unpleasant—and I won't be able to do anything to help."

Sukune stepped forward, but Yori placed his hand on the young man's chest.

"You cannot break the circle either," he said in a tone that made it clear that this was an order, not a suggestion. Then he wandered away mumbling to himself.

The two brothers stared at one another. Sukune wanted to say something, anything to bridge the emotional gap between them. The look in Yakamo's eyes was as cold and hard as the mountain on which he lay.

Yori came back holding the claw. It seemed huge in his hands, and it snapped at Sukune as the shugenja passed near.

"It is time to begin."

Yori reached into the rice circle again and fastened the claw to Yakamo's left arm. It was exactly the same procedure as the young samurai used to go through every morning when dressing for battle, except that the claw was as cold as the night and caused his arm to stand in goose bumps.

When the claw's laces were securely tied, Yori sat cross-legged on the ground next to the circle, closed his eyes, and pressed his palms flat together, directly in front of his nose. He began chanting in a low voice, speaking very quickly in a language only shugenja could fathom. Yori's body began to glow a menacing blue.

Sukune took a step back but never let his eyes wander from his brother. As he watched, Yakamo began to glow blue as well. The color, which seemed to be flowing from Yori's stomach, leaped at Yakamo violently. Each time a bolt of blue attached itself to his body, the samurai twitched and grimaced slightly.

Yori's chanting grew louder and more emphatic. He seemed to be arguing with or yelling at something that no one else could see or hear. Finally his eyes, which had remained tightly shut, flew open. He shouted a short, guttural word, and a ball of blue light shot from his mouth.

It circled the plateau with amazing speed. Higher and higher it went, filling the space below with its unnatural radiance. Finally, the ball flew so high it nearly became lost among the stars. It hung there for a moment, then, without warning, dived directly down at Yakamo.

When the ball hit Yakamo in the chest, his whole body convulsed. He snapped his head back and raised his chest directly into the air, gasping for breath. He held his arms as still as he could, but the claw twitched closer and closer to the edge of the rice circle. It seemed to want to cross that line.

Lightning arced between Yori and Yakamo, striking viscously, causing muscles to spasm and contract. With each strike, the claw's movements grew more and more responsive to Yakamo's. It twitched in time with Yakamo's pain.

A blue lightning bolt shot from Yakamo's body straight up into the sky. Then went another, and another. Finally a single, blood-red bolt leaped from the claw and exploded in the air above them with a deafening crash.

"It is done," said Kuni Yori, his voice shaky and weak.

▲ ▲ ▲ ▲ ▲ ▲ ▲ ▲

"Why won't it work?" Yakamo sat in his tent staring at the claw on the end of his left arm. It still twitched of its own accord. Indeed, now the young man's own upper arm twitched with the same rhythm, but neither responded to his mental commands.

"You must give your body a chance to become familiar with this new addition," Kuni Yori said smoothly. "It will take a little time."

"I have only so much time," Yakamo growled. "I am about to ride off to lead my troops into battle."

"Trust me, Yakamo-san, you be ready when the time comes."

The samurai stared down at his still-useless arm.

"I had better be!"

He grabbed a cloak from his belongings and wrapped it tightly around his broad shoulders. Normally Yakamo did not wear such over garments—he preferred the chill of the air on his skin—but he could not let his samurai see him walking around with the claw hanging like a dead weight on his arm. He cinched the cloak so that it would hold his arm across his chest, the way he would if he'd dislocated his shoulder. Better to look injured than weak, he thought.

Yakamo strode from the dark seclusion of his tent into a world filled with white, wispy clouds. Autumn in the mountains meant fog, thick fog that often took half a day to burn off. The young Hida couldn't see more than a dozen feet in any direction.

So much for seeming weak in front of his troops, he thought. The only one who would see him was his cousin Hida Amoro, his second in command.

This was the first time Yakamo was in charge of a large force of soldiers. He had led a battalion once, and more combat units than he could count, but he'd never before led an army. After careful consideration, he'd chosen Amoro to ride at his side.

In his heart he knew what to do. There was no room for self-doubt in Yakamo's world. However, now that a thousand men were marching at his orders, ready to fight to the death at a single word of his, Yakamo found that he wanted to seek the opinion of a trusted ally. For years he had wondered why his father kept Kuni Yori around. Surely the Great Bear did not need to consult with a shugenja before every major decision. Now Yakamo understood. Kisada did not need Yori—he just needed someone to talk to.

"Let's ride."

"I don't like this. You can't see anything!" Amoro waved his hand in front of his eyes.

That was the first time Yakamo had ever heard Hida Amoro say he didn't relish the possibility of battle. Side by side they rode into the deep fog, at the head of their marching army.

"What would you like to see, Cousin?" Yakamo teased. In truth, he agreed with Amoro. He could barely make out the man's shape five feet away. But he learned from his father that to keep troops calm under difficult conditions, a commander should act as though the situation at hand was exactly what he desired.

"Anything!" answered Amoro. "Anything but this cursed fog. The entire Crane army could be out there, and we'd never know."

Yakamo chuckled.

"If the Crane were out there, they'd certainly not be so impolite as to attack us without warning."

They laughed.

"No," Amoro returned. "That would be dishonorable. We know that the Crane would not want to take unfair advantage of an enemy marching to sack their outpost."

Without warning, Yakamo sat up tall in his saddle and raised his hand. The samurai behind him stopped, spreading the sign back through the ranks. In moments, the entire army, even the soldiers a mile down the line, halted and waited.

The air was still. Not a bird or frog or even the rustle of the wind could be heard. But there was a sound. A faint sound to be sure, but it was there, wafting through the midmorning fog.

Yakamo knew that fog played tricks with sound. It took noises and shuffled them around like a child's puzzle. He could never tell if a sound came from right next to his shoulder or a hundred yards down the road.

Whatever this sound was and wherever it came from, it made Yakamo nervous. The more he listened, the more it sounded like voices whispering.

Yakamo dropped his own voice to the barest whisper. "Amoro, get ten foot soldiers and come with me. Tell the rest of the column to wait here. We're going to see who's up there."

Amoro came back with six men and four women, most of whom Yakamo knew from his days on the Wall. It felt good to be surrounded by his old comrades. He dismounted and addressed them.

"Do nothing unless I tell you to," Yakamo told them. "This isn't like the fighting we're used to. These could be farmers, or merchants, or even one of Sukune's scouting parties that got turned around in the fog. If it is an enemy, I want them to be more surprised than we are."

They all nodded, even Amoro, but Yakamo could see the bloodlust building behind his cousin's eyes. This was the one reason he hesitated before naming Amoro as his aide. Once a battle began, he would slip away below his "red curtain" and become useless for anything other than killing. In fact, near this berserker was probably the worst place for the army's leader. Yakamo suddenly realized how difficult it was to choose a proper aide. He appreciated Kuni Yori all the more and wished the shugenja had not been ordered to remain with Sukune.

The twelve samurai crept through the fog, stopping every few yards to listen for telltale sounds. They carried their weapons drawn, but not at the immediate ready. It would not do to walk sword-point first into a tree or a rock. Yakamo held a tetsubo—not as large as the one he'd used before he lost his hand but still bigger than most samurai would be able to wield. He was prepared to use his favorite weapon one-handed if necessary, but he counted on Kuni Yori's promise—that the claw would be ready when he needed it.

In the hours since Yori attached the claw, the numbness had fled. Now there was a dull ache down the length of his left arm, but he still could feel nothing below the wrist. Where it lay against his chest, he could feel the claw opening and closing reflexively.

Yakamo stopped and listened again.

Nothing.

Then one word came floating through the mist: "Toturi."

Before Yakamo could even begin to consider why the banished ronin was being discussed, a cool wind crossed his cheek and created a rift in the fog. Where once there had been nothing but an impenetrable wall of clouds, Yakamo could now see a small glade with a campfire and ten samurai sitting around it— Dragons by the look of them. But what were they doing here in the Crane lands?

The Dragon leader looked at Yakamo with a confidence that bordered on arrogance. "So the Phoenix were right. The Crab *have* finally been turned by the Shadowlands. But what did you think you could do with such a tiny band?"

Yakamo did not answer. In fact he was about to ask questions of his own, such as what the Phoenix Clan had to do with this. Just then two more Dragons burst from the fog and into the clearing.

"There's an army of Crab!" one shouted.

"Hundreds of them, maybe thousands!" cried the other.

"We stumbled across them on our patrol," continued the first.

"They slew Yoshi, but we escaped. We must warn the Crane and get word to Toturi!" the second gasped.

The Dragon leaped to his feet and looked Yakamo square in the eye.

"Scatter into the fog!" he ordered. "Don't worry about anything other than getting this information back to Lady Mirumoto. She'll get word back to Kyuden Kakita, then to Toturi!"

Lady Mirumoto, thought Yakamo. Hitomi?

"After them, all of you!" Yakamo snapped. "If any of them reaches the Crane stronghold, we might as well send gold foil announcements of our arrival."

A dozen Dragon samurai disappeared into the fog with an equal number of Crab hot on their tails. Yakamo followed the Dragon leader, whose shadowy form moved through the mists with surprisingly surefooted strides.

Yakamo nearly lost his footing with every step. The rocky landscape was covered with loose stones and sand.

To his left the Crab leader heard sounds of steel on steel. At least one of his samurai had found the enemy.

Behind him he heard another battle. This one ended quickly with a swift slicing noise and a muffled cry. But whose cry?

Yakamo returned his attention to his quarry, but the Dragon's silhouette was gone.

Damn!

He slowed his pace and walked cautiously forward. Maybe the Dragon had fallen off a ledge or stumbled on the uncertain terrain. It wouldn't do for Yakamo to follow him in such a fate. The Crab took another few steps and stopped to listen again.

No sound came at all.

His foe had escaped or was lying unconscious somewhere just ahead.

Or, Yakamo thought just in time, he is lying in ambush.

From out of the fog to his left the Dragon commander stepped forward, katana raised for a lethal blow. Yakamo could not possibly raise his tetsubo quickly enough. He braced himself for the strike, hoping his armor would deflect enough of it so that he would be able to fight back.

Without thinking, Yakamo raised his left hand and looked away.

There was a solid clang as the blade crashed against the black claw strapped to Yakamo's arm. What's more, the young Crab felt—actually *felt*—the blow land. There was no pain, just a feeling of solid strength.

With a grunt of triumph, he pushed against the Dragon's sword, sending the man a few steps backward. Yakamo whirled his tetsubo into an offensive position.

He flipped the giant club forward and back, making passing attacks at the Dragon's head. He never pulled the weapon back into a defensive posture. Every time his opponent tried a counterstrike, Yakamo's left hand (for such was how he immediately began to think of the claw) reached out and stopped it.

The look on the Dragon samurai's face went from rage to perplexity and finally to panic.

"What is that thing?" he asked in a desperate voice. "What are *you*?"

Yakamo swung his tetsubo in an arc at about chest height, knocking the katana from the Dragon's hand. He then stepped forward and placed his left hand around the man's throat.

"I am Hida Yakamo," he said tersely. With a single, easy motion of his left arm he lifted the Dragon off the ground, gripping his neck tighter. "And I am your death."

A warm breeze swirled the fog around them so that Yakamo could barely make out his foe's form at arm's length. But he could feel the man's soft skin give way beneath the metal of his hand. He could feel the warm blood trickle down his arm as the Dragon squirmed in his grip.

With a single snap the man's neck broke, and Yakamo let him fall to the ground.

The warm breeze blew across his face again, and he could feel the first of the sun's rays. The fog began to thin. Within a few minutes he could again see the glade around him and even more.

Over a mutilated foe stood Amoro, slowly coming back to his senses. Seven other Crab samurai stood over fallen enemies at various points across the landscape. Three Crab lay dead, defeated by opponents who had disappeared into the fog, presumably on their way to raise the alarm at Kyuden Kakita.

Yakamo grunted and called back to the column of samurai who were now visible less than five hundred yards away.

"What are you waiting for? Let's move! Let's kill the messengers, then kill the Crane!"

19 RUMORS OF TOTURI

Steam rose from still-warm blood as it ran across the rocks of Beiden Pass. The day had turned crisp and cold, but the fighting was hot. Wispy clouds flew quickly across the deep blue sky overhead—the wind above the rock walls blew at a frightful speed. Down in the pass, though, the air was still as death.

Yakamo struck a Dragon samurai to his right. His tetsubo caught the man under the chin, lifting him clear off his feet with the sound of shattering bone. No other opponents presented themselves immediately, so he took the opportunity to glance around. His samurai fought with wild abandon. Heedless of their own safety, they launched themselves against groups of Dragons two and three times more numerous than their own battle units.

This was the Crab army he knew.

"Yakamo!" a tortured voice howled above the din of battle. "I know you are here! Show yourself, son of Kisada!"

He knew the voice. It filled him with lust and desire—bloodlust and the desire to silence the speaker forever.

Yakamo waded through the fighting, shoving past enemy and ally alike. He kicked a goblin out of his way and shouldered past a Crab samurai, nearly impaling the man on his enemy's weapon. Confronted by a mounted Dragon, Yakamo grabbed the reins just below the bit and pulled down as hard as he could. At the same time he clubbed the samurai-ko with his claw, knocking her from the saddle. She landed in an awkward position, and he could easily have finished her off if not for the fact that he'd already moved on—searching desperately for the source of the voice.

Finally, he pushed through a battle between an ogre and five Dragon samurai to see a small but powerful female figure standing over the form of a fallen Crab. She put her foot on the corpse and pulled her katana free.

"Mirumoto Hitomi!"

She looked up and smiled evilly.

"So you heard my call?" she said. "I knew you were here, but I wondered if you were brave enough to face me."

Yakamo laughed.

"I have been looking for you, little Dragon," he said. "This time your Dragon clan mates won't be able to save you. You will *pay* for what you did to me."

"A one-handed samurai is like a toothless bear," she mocked. "Your roar is great, but you are a trifle."

"Oh, but I have a second hand," he said, raising his claw for her to see. "A better one in fact. Come closer and I will show you how it works."

The claw opened and quickly snapped shut three times in succession. The sound it made was mostly metallic, but it echoed with the sound of bones being ground to dust.

"It quite becomes you," Hitomi said. "What a shame I will have to remove it as well. But do not worry. This time you won't live long enough to fret about finding a replacement."

Yakamo laughed. "You are more than welcome to try. But you'll find I've grown quite attached to this hand—and it to me."

The Crab struck at Hitomi, but *not* with his tetsubo. Yakamo launched an offhanded attack using only the claw. Swinging his arm in large figure-eights aimed at the samurai-ko's head, he slid closer.

Hitomi chuckled at the absurdity and swung her blade in a path to sever the claw at the leather strap—just where she'd taken the Crab's original hand. Her blade clanged off as if it had struck solid rock.

"How is this possible?" she cried. "This is the ancestral blade of the Dragon! It has never failed to cut through *anything*."

"Well, by all means," Yakamo said switching attacks and swinging his tetsubo at Hitomi's head, "try again. I wouldn't want to ruin the reputation of the mighty Dragon's ancestral weapon with my simple arm."

Hitomi struck. Again the blade bounced off the leather as though it was made of stone.

Yakamo swung his claw in a backhanded arc that caught Hitomi across the face. She went flying but landed on her feet ready to return the favor.

The Dragon raised her sword and charged at her Crab foe, shouting a wordless oath. Bloodlust filled her eyes. Fury rang in her voice. She swung a mighty blow designed to cut Yakamo from the tip of his right shoulder all the way down to his left hip.

He seemed to offer no defense, but at the last minute he raised his left arm. With a flick of his wrist, the claw deflected the blow and sent Hitomi lunging forward hopelessly off balance. Yakamo stepped in close to her body, moving in tandem with her—a deadly dance. He placed his right hand on her elbow and twisted, throwing her off her feet. He landed atop her, pinning her. She lay there helpless, his faceplate rubbing against her jaw.

"And now, my young Dragon," he whispered, locking her eyes with his own. "We see that what goes around always, *always* comes around."

Yakamo opened the claw and placed it around Hitomi's wrist.

She spat on his faceplate but did not struggle. She knew she could not break his grip.

Hitomi did not scream. She did not make a sound as Yakamo slowly closed the claw, crushing every bone in the samurai-ko's hand. She held his eyes the entire time and even narrowed her gaze as he finished the job with a distinctly self-satisfying snap.

The heavy, wet sound of her severed hand landing on the stone was accented by two distinctly metallic clanks. She looked down.

Finally Hitomi did scream.

Yakamo had not just maimed her—he also snapped the blade of the Dragon's ancestral sword in half. The sword that represented the honor and pride of one hundred generations of Mirumoto lay broken beside her.

Yakamo threw his head back and laughed. It was a cruel, cold sound—one his father and brother would not recognize. Throughout the pass, the samurai who heard it assumed that one of the Shadowlands creatures was howling like the soulless animal it was.

Yakamo looked down at the helpless Hitomi.

"Now, I will spare you the torture you inflicted on me," he said, his voice filled with hate. Sitting up, Yakamo stretched his right arm behind his head, aiming his tetsubo at the samurai-ko's ear. He would end her life—end this rivalry—here and now. The Crab visualized his tetsubo impacting behind her ear and crushing her head beyond all recognition.

He smiled.

Just as Yakamo began his strike, another wave of enemy samurai crashed against the Crab forces. A hulking Dragon wielding a no-dachi threw his shoulder into Yakamo's chest and knocked him ten paces back.

Enraged, Yakamo swung his tetsubo with his good right arm, which was filled with power unlike any he'd known before. The Dragon samurai had a comical look of surprise on his face as the iron-spiked club crushed his skull with a sickening sound.

Yakamo stepped forward to finish Hitomi, but she was gone—probably spirited off by her samurai.

"Hitomi!" Yakamo screamed. But there was no answer.

Blind with rage, Yakamo stood reeling for a moment. If Hitomi was gone, he would take out his anger on Kyuden

Kakita. Lifting his hand high, he summoned his troops to him. "Break through! On to Kyuden Kakita!"

▲▲▲▲▲▲▲▲

"Be sure to lay in enough arrows, and have each samurai carry *two* extra bows." Sukune stood in a notch at the top of a ridge overlooking the north end of Beiden Pass.

Three days had passed since Yakamo left to lay siege to Kyuden Kakita. If everything went as planned, he would return in another week with tales of how easily the Crane were defeated—and with enough supplies to last the winter. If everything went poorly, he had already met major opposition on the road to the castle, and a force of Crane samurai were even now marching toward this position, intent on retaking the pass.

He looked down at the point where the wide plain funneled into the narrow slip of a road that led through the mountains. Only four or five foot soldiers could walk through the pass at a time, and no more than two samurai on horseback.

This spot in particular would be very useful. It provided archers with a broad view of an incoming force, but was situated so that the enemy would have a hard time firing back. The ledge fell away at odd angles below the perch, preventing attacks from the canyon floor. Other nearby ridges would not interfere with an archer's aim but afforded great protection from return fire.

"From this spot alone we could hold off an army!" said Hida O-Ushi.

"Yes, that's what the Crane thought, too," Sukune answered. "Unlike them, we must be sure to use this place to its best advantage."

Like Yakamo, Sukune chose a member of his army to serve as an advisor and confidant. His father had sent Kuni Yori to serve that purpose, but Sukune did not trust the shugenja. Whenever he could, Sukune left Yori out of his planning and brought his sister along instead.

Hida O-Ushi was the Great Bear's third child. In truth she was his *second* child, being three years older than Sukune, but the fact that she was a woman completely disqualified O-Ushi from running the clan—at least in Kisada's eyes. Sukune continually pointed out to his father that samurai-ko in other clans rose as high as their ambition and skill allowed—Mirumoto Hitomi was proof of that—but Kisada would not listen. He allowed his daughter to be raised as a warrior and taught her all the same lessons he did his sons, but when it came to the responsibilities of leading the clan, O-Ushi was completely shut out.

This did not seem to bother his sister terribly. She reveled in the thrill of the battle as much as, if not more than, Yakamo. Kisada's unusual child-rearing technique allowed her to act and speak in ways that most Rokugani women would never dream of. O-Ushi used that freedom to taste life through a progressively more intense series of visceral experiences. She fought, ate, drank, and even engaged in the pleasures of the flesh as though she might die at any moment, just like any other Crab samurai. Not surprisingly, though she had many lovers, O-Ushi never had a single proposal of marriage. Kisada could not shackle his only daughter with a marriage of convenience with some noble from another clan. She would probably *kill* any "proper" husband who tried to tame her.

As they walked back to the main camp, brother and sister discussed the strategies the army would use when the Crane arrived. The Crab forces were well trained at defending a location from invaders. That, in fact, was all they had done for a thousand years. But defending Beiden Pass was much different than holding the Carpenter's Wall. Their tremendous numbers were not as great an advantage here. Like the enemy, they could only move soldiers up a few at a time. On the Wall every samurai fought at the same time. Here they would have to lay in wait, or worse, stand in line before they could be part of the action.

As they neared the command tent, Sukune could see Kuni Yori waiting for him.

"Thank you, Sister," he said to O-Ushi. "I believe I must now deal with whatever worries the 'painted man.'"

O-Ushi laughed raucously. She shared Sukune's distrust of Yori and often pointed out that the shugenja's habit of painting his face made him more like a geisha than a samurai. She continued to chuckle as she left to rejoin her troops.

Sukune approached Yori with a warm smile.

"What news today, my father's most trusted aide?"

"One of your scouts has returned, Sukune-san, with some most disturbing news," answered Yori. For once he seemed genuinely upset. "He says that the lands surrounding the pass are also being combed by another clan's scouts."

"The Crane?" asked Sukune."

"No," Yori replied. "They were not Crane—they were Dragon forces."

"Dragon?" Sukune exclaimed. "I thought Yakamo finished off that little band. What are more Dragon doing this far south?"

"According to the scout, they talked about being taken from their usual commander and placed under the control of the ronin Toturi."

"Toturi!" the young Hida gasped.

Since his banishment Toturi had been seen traveling throughout the empire. There were constant rumors that he was trying to raise an army for the purpose of taking the throne. Of course, there were also rumors that he was trying to raise an army for the purpose of defending the emperor. Either way, Toturi's presence near Beiden Pass posed a serious threat to the Crab plans. If anyone could outthink and outfight Kisada and his army, it was Toturi.

"Send word to my father," Sukune told Yori. "I'm certain *you* know how he may be reached." This was a point of some contention between the two since Sukune still knew nothing about Kisada's whereabouts or actions.

"Indeed I do," the shugenja said with a wry smile. "Do you really think Toturi is leading the Dragon army?"

"No," Sukune said firmly. He didn't feel nearly as confident as he sounded. "But it scarcely matters. All our plans hang on my brother's attack at Kyuden Kakita."

The Crane stronghold was much too far away to see, but the young commander looked to the north anyway. An autumn storm rolled over the mountains, and thunder rumbled in the distance.

20 THE FALL OF THE HOUSE OF KAKITA

f you laugh at me one more time, you misshapen little monster, treaty or no, I'll cut you in half!"

Tempers were wearing thin. The army was less than a day's march from Kyuden Kakita, but they had spent the last two days in the Kakita woods felling trees and building battering rams and simple siege engines. Only the humans, though, were doing this backbreaking work. The goblins and other creatures sat huddled in groups, as unsettled by greenery and wildlife as humans were by the lifeless wastes of the Shadowlands. Occasionally one or two of the braver goblins came over to mock and taunt the humans as they worked.

Crab samurai, who were leery about traveling with the Shadowlands forces to begin with, were nearly ready to forget their upcoming attack on Kyuden Kakita just for the satisfying familiarity of killing goblins, zombies, and other creatures of darkness.

"Oy!" Yakamo barked at Kuni Toshio, the man who just issued the threat. He spoke loudly to make it clear that this message was for all the Crab. "You will not raise hand or blade against our guests—no matter how bad their manners are."

The troops laughed. They'd never heard Yakamo call someone *else* rude.

A goblin sitting on a moss-covered log laughed, too. It then stuck a purple tongue out at Toshio and made a disgusting noise. Yakamo snapped his hand out, grabbed the tongue in a gloved fist, and pulled the creature closer.

"And you stop bothering my men," he said with an ocean of menace. "You're a long way from home, little goblin. And a lot of 'accidents' can happen that do not break our treaty with your master." Yakamo smiled menacingly, the yellow-white of his teeth shining behind his helmet. Then he released the goblin's tongue and shoved the creature.

The goblin and its cronies crawled off the log, turned, and ran to rejoin their troops.

The assembled Crab laughed loudly at their retreating backs. None laughed louder than Yakamo.

"Tono," Toshio asked Yakamo, "why do those monstrosities lounge about like Crane courtiers while *we* do all this work? If they're our allies, why don't they share in the work?"

Yakamo turned a measured glare at the young foot soldier.

"These creatures are *not* our allies," he said in a low voice. "Never forget that. They are tools the Great Bear has given us to use in our great work." Yakamo made a point, when addressing the troops, to refer to his father by one of his titles.

"W-well if we cannot use them to do even menial labor, what part are they to play?" asked another samurai, who stood naked to the waist and drenched in sweat despite the autumn chill in the air.

"Trust me," Yakamo said with a sly grin. "The part I have planned for our guests is much more horrible than the work you've done these past two days. Now hurry up! At sunset we march on Kyuden Kakita!"

▲▲▲▲▲▲▲▲

By the time Yakamo's army arrived at the Crane stronghold, stars filled the sky. The moon was a mere sliver in the sky, but the Crab samurai could see the great plain approaching Kyuden Kakita, and the castle itself was awash in torchlight. They could see tiny figures coming to the battlements to try to get a look at the approaching Crab army. Clearly someone had warned the garrison at Kyuden Kakita—they were ready for an attack.

As he led his forces closer, Yakamo saw that the fog seemed to have worked in his favor. The figures on the wall scurried here and there pointing at the Crab troops. Indistinct voices rose in argument. The Crane appeared to have no idea how large Yakamo's army was.

"Make rows of camps by platoons!" Yakamo called out. "Cavalry farthest back, then infantry! Every camp light a fire— I want them to start guessing at how many of us are out here."

Yakamo turned to the leader of the Shadowlands troops, a creature that looked similar to the oni to which he'd given his name but it was less than half that creature's size. "I want your troops to make similar camps too, but I want you closest to the castle."

The creature looked at Yakamo with burning orange eyes and spoke in a gravelly, popping whisper. "We will not fight for you, son of the Bear."

"I know full well what you will and won't do," Yakamo spat at the thing. "I'm not asking you to do so much as draw your weapons—but I am telling you to make your camps at the head of my army!"

The creature ground its teeth, or would have if it had any teeth to grind. Instead it made a soft wet sound as it clenched its ropy jaws.

"As you command."

▲▲▲▲▲▲▲▲

Hida Tsuru rode back and forth in front of the main gate to Kyuden Kakita. The sun had risen two hours before only to be immediately swallowed by gray, menacing clouds. The day was sufficiently warm that it would not snow, but rain waited to burst from the sky.

"Surrender, Crane!" Tsuru called out. At Yakamo's order he offered the Kakita officers an honorable alternative to being over-run. Both men knew the proud Crane would never accept such terms. "Half your garrison is dead from the plague, and the rest are falling down with exhaustion."

In fact, the battlements looked very sparsely manned. Crane samurai stood around in clusters of seven or eight, shaking fists and swords above their heads and hurling curses down at the Crab army.

"We have nearly ten times your number," shouted Tsuru. "There is no chance of defeating us. If you try to hold our armies at bay, you will gain only the slaughter of your men. Give us the palace, and we will allow your troops honorable deaths!"

Tsuru rode just out of arrow range, which happened to be between the front ranks of Crab samurai and the rear ranks of Shadowlands troops. He harangued for half an hour with no response, then guided his horse to the Shadowlands comman-der's camp.

"These are your orders from Yakamo-san," he said holding forth a scroll but making no effort to hide his disdain for the creature.

"I told your leader, we will not fight for you," it said.

"Yes," said Tsuru before the creature even finished its sen-tence. "We know all that. If you bother to read the scroll, you'll see that your orders are to maintain your camps and observe the battle."

The Shadowlands commander blinked its ropy eyes.

"But we are within range of the—"

"Your orders are quite clear—and within the parameter of your master's agreement with Kisada-sama!" Tsuru pulled on the reins and turned to go. Before he nudged his steed, he said over his shoulder, "Personally, I hope you all sit around your campfires and *let* the Crane pepper you with arrows. The Crab have had the pleasure of slaying your kind for so long, it's about time another clan had the same opportunity."

▲▲▲▲▲▲▲▲

"Death to the Crane!"

The cry echoed up and down the ranks of Crab, accompanied by the sound of katanas banged against lacquered wooden breastplates. One or two goblins even got particularly caught up in the heat of the moment and joined in the shouting.

Yakamo ordered the troops to shout, stomp their feet, and make as much noise as possible until the signal was given to commence the attack. Although this seemed strange to many samurai, none questioned their commander. Most had been on only one or two offensive maneuvers, having spent most of their careers defending the Great Kaiu Wall. Yakamo, however, knew the advantage of making his opponents wait and filling their hearts with fear. In duels he always began by swaggering about with an utter lack of concern for his opponent. Shouting was his way of doing so on an epic scale.

The Crane considered the Crab little better than animals because of their coarse and wild ways. Let them see how wild the Crab could be.

"They're probably soiling their kimonos, looking out at all those rows of pointed teeth and scaly skin," Yakamo chuckled.

His generals laughed too, but they also grew impatient.

"When will we launch the attack?" asked Hida Tsuru, just returned from delivering his messages. "Before or after our voices give out?"

Yakamo chuckled again. "If nothing happens in the next five minutes, you can—"

He stopped himself in midsentence. A commotion had begun among the goblins that banged their spears on the ground. A group of Crane archers had responded to all the shouting by firing a round of arrows into the ground in front of the goblins. Naturally, being honorable warriors, they had not actually shot the creatures—just launched a warning shot. The goblins, though, were outraged. They picked up rocks and threw them at the wall, shouted curses in their foul tongue. They even took turns dropping their pants to expose themselves in the Cranes' direction.

"There!" Yakamo said. "That's what we've been waiting for. Hand me that bow."

Tsuru did as he was told.

Yakamo notched an arrow and aimed it on a high, arching path. He looked back down at the goblins, adjusted his aim slightly, and let the arrow fly.

The taunting continued in the Shadowlands camp. One goblin capered in a particularly amusing fashion, waving body parts in unpleasant ways. Suddenly the goblin stopped and stood very still.

At first its companions thought it was merely pausing before an even more impressive bit of mockery. Then they saw the arrow sticking straight out of the top of its head.

The gamboling goblin fell flat onto its face and moved no more.

A shriek went up among the other goblins—a shriek that spread from one Shadowlands camp to the next and soon drowned out the Crab chants. The Crane were attacking *them!*

Yakamo watched as goblins, zombies, ogres, and other monstrosities stopped banging their weapons on the ground and began raising them in anger. The tightly gathered camps broke and became one swelling mass of enraged monsters. With a final shout from their commander—a shout of exasperation rather than anger—the forces of darkness surged toward the walls of Kyuden Kakita.

"*Now* we attack!" Yakamo said smugly.

▲ ▲ ▲ ▲ ▲ ▲ ▲ ▲

"This is torture!" Yakamo grumbled as he paced restlessly.

After two full days of guiding his army from a hillock just west of Kyuden Kakita, he longed to take his tetsubo in hand and fight the Crane himself. For the first time in his military career, he had to stand back and watch while others did his fighting for him. This was the cost of rising to a position of authority. He'd heard his father sometimes wonder whether the price of being daimyo was not greater than he cared to pay. Yakamo never understood what Kisada meant until now.

The army depended on his guidance. He signaled orders to the commanders, telling them to press their assault or fall back and regroup. He judged whether it was better to attack the main gate or batter a hole in the wall. All of this required a full appreciation of everything happening on the field of battle—a perspective gained by observing the ebb and flow of war from a distance.

But when he saw a squad fail to press into an opening or a company being taken by surprise by a countermaneuver, Yakamo wished he could lead the charge himself. He grabbed a runner by the arm and pointed to an area about two hundred yards from Kyuden Kakita's main gate.

"See the formation that just avoided having hot pitch poured on them?" he asked. When the young man nodded, he continued. "That is Hiruma Matsu's brigade. Find Matsu and tell him to keep his samurai up close to the wall and to press forward with their battering ram. Tell him that he must not fall back even if the Crane bring more pitch. He is to press the attack. He will not succeed at breaking through the wall, but we must keep the Crane distracted. Kaiu Utsu's force is about to punch a hole through the wall, and we must draw attention away from him until he does."

The runner started to bolt, but Yakamo placed a tremendous hand on his shoulder and drew him back.

"Once Utsu has broken through, Matsu is to split his troops. He should send half to join Utsu's samurai as they charge the compound and take the other half with their battering ram to join those at the main gate."

The runner nodded and waited.

"That's all! Go!"

The sun stood only a little more than halfway through its journey. The castle would fall well before night.

▲ ▲ ▲ ▲ ▲ ▲ ▲ ▲

"He is a monster! A demon! Get out of his way before—"

Another Crane fell beneath the sweeping strokes of Hida Amoro's no-dachi. It was ironic that—surrounded by zombies, goblins, and ogres—Amoro was the one the enemy feared. Once again wrapped in the crimson haze of his uncontrollable blood-lust, the samurai was clearly the most dangerous opponent to step through the breach.

Cold rain turned the courtyard to mud and made footing treacherous.

Amoro hacked at a fallen samurai until a trio of zombies shambled past on their way to intercept an approaching group of Crane. The other Crab were smart enough to stay out of Amoro's way, but the Shadowlands creatures had no idea that he was as dangerous to them as he was to the Crane. In his berserker rage, Amoro knew nothing other than that a new set of targets had come into view.

He kicked one zombie in the back, knocking it to the ground. Stepping on it, he closed with the second creature and took its unliving head off with one stroke of his massive blade. The third undead warrior knew it was in trouble, though its life-less brain had not yet figured out why. It turned and raised its katana just in time to deflect Amoro's overhead slash.

The first zombie struggled to rise, but Hida Amoro dropped to one knee, landing square on its back. The Shadowlands warrior felt no pain, but a resounding crack filled the air. Amoro had snapped its spine. Its legs stopped scrabbling, but its arms con-tinued to grab its human attacker.

The Crab thrust his no-dachi between the standing zombie's legs. The creature stumbled forward, its katana raised to strike Amoro down. Before it could swing, Amoro pivoted on his knee and drew his blade overhead in a strong pulling motion. The no-dachi cut straight up through the zombie's body, neatly slicing it in two.

Amoro rose, and his hazy eyes looked around for another vic-tim. The zombie below him snatched at his ankle, but all it could do was scratch at the side of his foot.

Without even looking down, Amoro used two hands to swing the flat of his blade hard against the side of the fallen zombie's head. He batted it off the creature's shoulders and sent it skidding to the feet of a pair of goblins, who watched with undisguised awe.

The goblins were beginning to realize that this Crab killing machine was purposely attacking their comrades. What's more, he was looking right at them, bloodlust in his eyes. That wasn't part of the agreement between Hida Kisada and Yakamo no Oni!

Crane samurai converged on Amoro. He shifted his attack to them. The goblins stared in disbelief as the raging Crab fought four Crane to a standstill—and even gained the upper hand.

One goblin looked to the other. They silently agreed that getting far away from this insane Crab was the smartest thing they would ever do.

The ground was littered with dead humans from both clans as well as Shadowlands creatures, but the fighting had moved on. Crane defenders left their posts to battle the forces pouring through the hole in the west wall. Crab battering rams, left relatively unmolested, didn't take long to pound through the weakened main gate. Troops flooded into the courtyard.

The ring of steel on steel and the sound of humans dying drifted out from the main palace. Before the goblins could cross the compound, they saw Crab samurai leaving the castle, carrying sacks of rice, bushels of ground barley, dried and pickled vegetables, and barrels of sake.

"Looting!" one goblin said to the other.

"Quick, let's go before all the good stuff is taken!" replied the other.

It was already too late.

The sound of a horn filled the air. Once, twice, a third long blast—the signal to retreat.

"Take the food! Burn the palace!" called Hida Tsuru from the other side of the shattered gate. "Retreat!"

▲ ▲ ▲ ▲ ▲ ▲ ▲ ▲

Yakamo sat astride his horse and watched flames lick up the walls of Kyuden Kakita. Thick, black smoke poured from its upper floors. The golden cranes at either end of the roof began to melt and warp into twisted mockeries of the clan namesake.

"Glorious . . . simply *glorious!*" he complimented himself.

Hida Tsuru rode up, his face smudged and wet. The rain had stopped, but the entire plain had been churned into cauldron of mud and soot.

"The last of the stores have been removed," Tsuru reported, "and our men are carrying them back to our camps. What's more, the Shadowlands troops are helping!"

"Excellent!" replied Yakamo, still entranced by the flames. "What about the Crane?"

Tsuru sat taller in his saddle.

"The Crane have been routed. Most of them were killed defending the castle, but a few have escaped into the surrounding countryside. Shall I organize a detail to hunt them down and kill them like the cowardly dogs they are?"

Yakamo shook his head absently. Small droplets of water shook free from the trim of his helmet.

"No," he finally said. "Let them live with their dishonor. We have what we came for."

"And none too soon," said Hida Amoro who walked up the hillock. He was covered in blood and mud. He wore as peaceful an expression on his face as Yakamo had ever seen. "My men report that a large force of Unicorn cavalry is approaching from the northwest. They seem to be intent on coming to the Crane's aid."

All three samurai laughed.

"Well, let them help the poor Crane," Yakamo chuckled. "Meanwhile, we'll take these provisions back to my brother—assuming that, without my aid, he's been able to hold the single most defensible position in all of Rokugan."

21 THE BATTLE OF BEIDEN PASS

The sun climbed toward the peak of a brilliant blue sky. Not a single wisp of cloud lingered from horizon to horizon. This was a day of purity and focus—distractions had no place on the rocky plain.

Hida Sukune rode his warhorse before the formation of Crab samurai in full battle armor. They stood just outside the north end of Beiden Pass, their weapons at the ready—a sea of katana, no-dachi, tetsubo, yari, and every other kind of blade, hammer, or polearm used by honorable warriors.

"If *this* does not make my father proud, then nothing will!"

Sukune wore his crab-shaped armor. He grunted approvingly as he reviewed his troops. It was another sound he'd learned from his father. Sukune himself was more comfortable complimenting the samurai on their preparedness, but most of them seemed to dislike that. The Crab did not take compliments well.

However, a curt, gruff animalistic sound of respect and acceptance never failed to fill the samurai with pride.

"Since the days of the first Hida, we have defended the Emerald Empire against its enemies. Your fathers and all their fathers as far back as memory stretches have been the instrument of salvation for the clans of Rokugan. They kept the empire's enemies outside our lands."

Sukune had practiced this speech alone in his tent for the past two nights. The men and women under his command would follow his orders, but he knew that precious few of them actually trusted that he knew what he was doing. Defending the pass was one thing—they knew how to do that—but going out to face an enemy on an open battlefield, that was not something most Crab had done in generations. Sukune needed to say something inspirational, something to fill his warriors with confidence in themselves and in him. He knew his plan was sound; he just had to convince them.

"But now a different threat has arisen—a threat that comes from within. The clans are on the verge of tearing the empire apart. We cannot allow that to happen. To save the empire, we must fight our own brothers."

This was not going as well as he'd hoped. Samurai shifted from foot to foot, looking across the plain at the Dragon troops deploying opposite them. Sukune raised just the wrong image when he called them brothers. The Crab had no great respect for Dragon samurai—or for those from any other clan, for that matter—but they were at least samurai, not soulless monsters like the goblins and other creatures that assaulted the Great Wall of Kaiu every day. Those same creatures marched side by side with the Crab all the way to Beiden Pass. Even now, the monsters camped at the southern end of the mountains, safe from battle.

"But these are not our brothers. Look! These troops seem to come from the Dragon Clan, yet they march under the banner of the ronin Toturi. These 'defenders of the empire' take orders from a man whose actions were so honorless that he was stripped of his title—indeed, stripped of his name."

Sukune had their attention again. Despite Sukune's personal belief that Toturi was ill-treated by the emperor, most samurai had grown to hold the "Black Lion," as Toturi was now called, in complete contempt. A murmur rose through the assembled Crab, and many shook fists and weapons in the direction of the Dragon army.

"Clearly no true samurai would ever do such a thing! The army you face is merely using our brothers' colors to shake your belief in the ancient Crab duty—to stop anyone who threatens the empire. They dress in Dragon armor in hopes of scaring you off the battlefield. They want to make you doubt the righteousness of our cause!"

Now Sukune had to shout over the angry voices of his troops. They were incensed, ready to take vengeance on Toturi's army for pretending to be honorable warriors. Their discipline held them in place—but only barely.

"Today we fight for Rokugan! We fight to uphold the duty of our clan! We also fight for the honor of all the clans! Commanders, move your men out! Fight with honor, die with glory, and remember—we cannot fail. If we do the empire falls!"

▲ ▲ ▲ ▲ ▲ ▲ ▲ ▲

"How could I have been so wrong?"

No answer came, but Sukune did not expect one. He was alone in his tent, kneeling before a small altar. Incense burned in a tiny brazier and wafted across a carving representing Lord Moon, Lady Sun, and their son Hida—the father of the Crab Clan. Sukune did not often seek answers at the altar. His father taught him too well to rely on the deeds of his own hand rather than the unseen movements of the kami, but tonight the youngest Hida had nowhere else to turn.

The Dragon troops were indeed under the control of Toturi— a boon from the mysterious Togashi Yokuni, champion of the Dragon Clan. Toturi had a different notion for how to keep peace in Rokugan, one that did not include the Crab shutting down travel through Beiden Pass.

The Crab army fought well. Their ferocity was a terrible thing to behold, but they were completely out of their element. They did not have the experience or instincts for offensive battle. They wanted to center themselves on a particular patch of battlefield and defend it, the way they defended the Wall.

The army needed a real leader today, someone who could order troop movements that would confound the Dragon forces and allow the two sides to fight to a standstill. They needed someone who could thwart the strategies of the great Toturi, for the Black Lion was a brilliant tactician.

Sadly, Sukune was none of these things. He had a strong mind for strategy, but he lacked Toturi's years of experience. He knew that his samurai were the toughest and most brutal fighters in Rokugan, but the enemy had used quick troop movements and deadly magic to keep the Crab off balance and on the move.

When the battle was done, fewer than half the samurai Sukune had spoken to that morning returned to Beiden Pass. In one day, he had crippled the Crab army's ability to hold off an enemy charge into the pass—something that should have been simplicity itself.

"What shall I do?" Sukune asked in a desperate voice.

"What you should have done all along, Sukune-san—use the Shadowlands troops."

Kuni Yori stood just inside the tent flap; the young Hida had no idea how long he'd been there.

"Never!"

"Your father did not strike a bargain with his most hated enemy out of the goodness of his heart. Nor did he send these troops with you on a whim. They are here for you to use and, I must agree with your brother, you are using them extremely foolishly."

Sukune rose from the altar and walked past Yori into the cold night. Fog rose all through the pass, covering what was left of the Crab forces in a blanket of clouds no less chilling than their own thoughts. In the morning, the Dragon forces would surely attack Beiden Pass. The decimated force would have to hold them off, probably for days, until Yakamo's troops returned from Kyuden Kakita. It was not an impossible task, but certainly a difficult one following today's debacle. Sukune had led them to the brink of disaster.

"I believe in my father's vision," the young man said through chattering teeth. "If he believes the only way to prevent civil war is to force peace upon the land, I will support him at every turn. But I cannot believe he dealt with the oni for any reason other than to keep the Wall safe in our absence."

"Even more reason why you should use the monstrosities to your best advantage," answered Yori. He seemed to be directly behind Sukune, breath hot on the back of his ear. When Sukune turned, he saw Kuni was a respectful distance away. "Every goblin that dies in defense of this pass is one that will never assault our great Wall. Every zombie dismembered by the Dragon warriors is a fiend that will never threaten Rokugan. They are remarkably useful tools for your use, especially now that your forces are weakened. You said it yourself this morning: We cannot fail, for if we do, the empire falls."

Sukune shook his head.

"Words," he muttered. "And my father's words at that. I've never believed in them as strongly as he does. There is a line over which we should not cross."

"You sound like a posturing Crane diplomat," Yori said without hiding his disgust. "Perhaps you are as soft as Kisada and Yakamo fear!"

Sukune shot Yori a patronizing look.

"You have a great many talents, Yori-san, but inflaming my familial rivalries is *not* one of them. You and I both know that honor is more than a political concept. There are right and wrong things to do. No matter how right an end may be, some means are never justified—they are too dishonorable. Using another warrior as a shield or allowing someone else to die in your stead is not only honorless—it smacks of cowardice. I would rather die the most painful death imaginable than take on the karma of an unprincipled, frightened failure."

Yori bowed and withdrew. As he went, he muttered to himself, "That can quite easily be arranged, young Hida."

▲▲▲▲▲▲▲▲

"Here they come again!" Hida O-Ushi raised her dai-tsuchi and squared her feet. The warhammer was cumbersome in hand-to-hand combat, but it served her well when she found herself fighting larger opponents or those on horseback.

The samurai-ko was quite upset when Sukune told her she would not be leading her troops into battle on the floor of Beiden Pass. That was where the heaviest fighting was taking place, and O-Ushi wanted her chance to earn glory in the battle for the fate of the empire. She grew even angrier when he ordered her company to climb up to the ridge overlooking the main battle and protect the archers perched there.

"You want us to miss out on the most important battle in history so that we can nursemaid a unit that will never fall under direct attack?" she had yelled so vehemently that she inadvertently spit in his face.

O-Ushi had no interest in Sukune's explanation that the position the archers held would be the key to whether the Crab held the pass or were pushed back out in less than a day. But she did follow orders. For all her headstrong ways, she was still a samurai, and her brother—her younger brother—was her commander.

At first the assignment was as dull as she'd feared. She and eleven other warriors stood on a narrow path looking down on the developing battle as the archers launched volley after volley of arrows over their heads and into the chests of advancing Dragon samurai. Not long into the battle, though, O-Ushi recognized that there was another faction among the attacking troops. The Dragon forces were bolstered by samurai wearing the mon of the Unicorn Clan. Though Unicorn foot soldiers were highly skilled, the clan's true genius lay in their cavalry units, particularly the—

"Battle Maidens!" came a cry from below.

Sukune had placed several pockets of warriors along the path up the ridge—originally another source of frustration to O-Ushi. It now seemed one of the wisest moves her brother had made since the start of the campaign.

The Battle Maidens were an elite unit of the Unicorn cavalry made up entirely of samurai-ko. They had a reputation for being twice as skilled as their male counterparts and three times as vicious. From the sounds of the battle below, O-Ushi suspected that the stories did not do them justice.

The Crab lines held most of the day. As afternoon wore on, O-Ushi occasionally heard the sound of a war-horse whinnying. Finally, with less than an hour before the sun would sink below the peaks, a single samurai-ko riding a pure white steed rounded a bend in the path and urged her horse up the ridge.

Her armor was purple streaked with yellow, and her helmet had a flowing golden mane. She guided her steed using only her feet and rode holding her katana in a classic dueling position. She seemed more graceful and ready for action than many samurai standing on their own two feet.

One of O-Ushi's men charged the Battle Maiden. He brandished a no-dachi and howled like a demon. In spite of his weapon's long reach, the Unicorn easily avoided the Crab's blow. She neatly dispatched him with one slice of her katana. Then she turned her eyes on O-Ushi.

A simple nudge from the rider urged the horse to resume its charge.

O-Ushi waited, her shoulders turned and her hammer resting near her left ear—as patient as a cat by a rabbit hole.

The Battle Maiden locked eyes with O-Ushi. Just before her steed came within striking range, she used her knees to command the beast to stop its charge and withdraw. The Crab unit was too much to handle without the aid of her sisters.

The Battle Maiden rode back around the bend to rejoin the fighting below.

The sun was now less than a quarter hour from setting.

Just when O-Ushi thought they would see no more of the Unicorn cavalry today, the same rider rounded the bend in the path. This time, she was followed by two more mounted samurai-ko.

"Here they come again!" she shouted.

Her fellows aligned themselves in a staggered pattern. O-Ushi had ordered this tactic so that any rider would have to pass through a gauntlet of attackers on both sides to get up to the archers. She might strike down one Crab, and her war-horse might take down another, but a third and fourth would always be close enough to strike back.

However, with three riders, the odds shifted in the Unicorn's favor. They were skilled enough riders to send two horses up the path nearly side by side and still be able to use their swords in combat. O-Ushi did not have enough samurai to counter.

With an earsplitting, "Kiiiiya!" the lead Battle Maiden led the others in a charge. All three were attacking at once.

"Stand back," O-Ushi ordered her men. "If I fall, give the signal for the archers to open fire into our midst!"

"Hai!" said her second in command bravely.

O-Ushi resumed her earlier stance—feet squared, chest facing the oncoming Battle Maiden, dai-tsuchi cocked by her ear, ready to try to unseat the lead rider.

The horses climbed the hill at a lightning pace.

O-Ushi nodded her head in time with their hoofbeats. She breathed slowly and deeply, calmly awaiting the right moment to strike.

She seemed a bit too calm. The Battle Maiden was nearly upon her, and O-Ushi hadn't even tensed her arms. The Unicorn rider lashed out with her blade, striking right for the seam between O-Ushi's shoulder and neck.

But the samurai-ko was not there anymore.

She dropped to her knees. Instead of attacking the rider, she swung her hammer with all her considerable might into the horse's chest. It crusted its sternum.

The beast reared in pain and threw its rider. The Battle Maiden twisted in midair, trying to angle her body toward the narrow path. It was no use. Instead she bounced off the rocks just below the path and tumbled end over end to the canyon floor below. To her credit she did not scream once.

The other riders reined in their steeds and retreated down the path. Crab arrows peppered the path behind their mounts' hooves. As they rounded the bend and withdrew, the sun dropped below the mountains. Dusk settled over Beiden Pass.

▲▲▲▲▲▲▲▲

"It cannot go on. I have no choice." Sukune hung his head in abject defeat.

Kuni Yori's voice dripped with mock compassion. "You are merely following the path your father laid before you."

The young samurai glared at the shugenja. The Hida temper flared so bright in his eyes that Yori took a step backward. If this were not his father's most trusted adviser Sukune would surely kill the man on the spot. Sukune knew when to accept defeat, but he never accepted gloating. Not from his brother, not even from his father, and certainly not from this snake.

"My honor, indeed my soul may be forfeit for a decision I must make," Sukune growled, "but I will not delude myself that this is a good choice."

Yori lowered his shoulders and approached again.

"You must make your own peace with this," Yori said in a more neutral tone. "I am certain you will see the wisdom of your actions tomorrow evening when the number of Crab samurai in the pass still outnumbers the Shadowlands troops in our midst."

At the end of the second day of fighting, Sukune's army was only slightly larger than half its original size. They still held Beiden Pass, but they were now evenly matched with the Dragon and Unicorn forces opposing them—and the enemy had reinforcements on the way.

Of course, with any luck he did as well. Would enough troops remain in Yakamo's army to let the Crab secure the pass once and for all? In truth, they had to hold it only another three or four weeks. By that time, snow would cover the countryside and make further battles nearly impossible. Before spring, the Crab would be able to fortify their position and bring more troops from the Wall. By that time his father would arrive; that would certainly raise the samurai's spirits.

Sukune still had to hold the pass until Yakamo's troops arrived, but he wasn't sure he could, given the losses of the first two days. He had no choice. He had to move at least *some* of the

Shadowlands troops into the contested territory. They were fresh warriors, unscathed by the recent skirmishes. What's more, they were creatures of evil. Their mere presence would unnerve even the most disciplined veteran.

Placing goblins and zombies at important junctions would surely save Crab lives and shift the tide of the battle for at least a day. None of that made the action any more palatable.

"We cannot lose this battle, Yori," Sukune said wearily. "But in order to win, *I* must lose my last shreds of honor."

▲ ▲ ▲ ▲ ▲ ▲ ▲ ▲

On the third straight day of battle, Hida O-Ushi got her wish. She and her troops were relocated to the floor of Beiden Pass. The Crane and Unicorn troops had not yet renewed their assault on the pass, but already on the ridge she defended the day before, Battle Maidens urged their steeds up the narrow mountain trail. The sounds of shouting, neighing, and steel against steel told O-Ushi they had already met the company of Crab warriors positioned at the first bend in the path.

These samurai were not meant to stop the Unicorn cavalry, but merely to slow them. O-Ushi had worked with those troops to prepare them for a cavalry assault. By now, they'd dug plenty of small but deep divots into the ground, deadly for riders. They'd also rolled small boulders into the path to keep the Battle Maidens from having an easy ascent. The Crab would strike hard at the horses and try to keep the Unicorn off balance, and then retreat to the next switchback on the ridge. If all went well, it would take the Battle Maidens most of the day to reach the archers' stations.

"I wonder if they'll like what they find at the top?" She chuckled.

The sound of archers above, shouting and loosing their first volley toward the pass' mouth, told O-Ushi her own battle would begin soon. The Crane and Unicorn troops were inside the pass. It wouldn't take long for the first wave to charge through the deadly rain of arrows and reach her.

"To victory—or a glorious death!" she shouted to her troops.

"Hai!" they responded as one and bowed perfunctorily. Weapons drawn, they stared down the canyon for the first sign of the enemy.

A line of Crane samurai charged around a corner and raced headlong at the Crab defenders. Some of the Crane wore bandages over wounds suffered the day before. Others had fresh arrows protruding from their arms or shoulders.

O-Ushi noticed her breath coming in short puffs of steam. It was a cold day for a battle but a fine day to die.

The Crane reached their position, and the battle began. Some of her samurai tried to challenge two enemies at a time. There weren't enough Crab samurai to stop the entire line, so other Crane continued their charge down the pass. Out of the corner of her eye O-Ushi noted that the vaunted Crane chivalry remained intact. None of the attackers stopped to engage the Crab in groups—even in a war, the code of bushido demanded that duels be settled between individuals. The unopposed Crane quickly disappeared around another bend in the pass.

O-Ushi stood nose to nose with a samurai who was a full head shorter than she. His katana pressed hard against the shaft of her dai-tsuchi, forcing the great hammer against the samurai-ko's chest and pinning her arms back where she could get no leverage. However, the Crane needed both hands to keep her off balance and couldn't draw his wakizashi. The two stood locked in a contest of strength and will. O-Ushi's greater size and power countered the Crane's proximity and leverage.

All around, other duels raged. To O-Ushi's right, her second in command slew his opponent with a brutal crushing blow from his tetsubo. To her left a Unicorn samurai evened the score. The young Crab who fell had joined her company only three weeks earlier. She didn't even know his name.

The whole time O-Ushi and her opponent remained practically motionless, each waiting for the other to make an exploitable mistake. A faint but impassioned battle cry reached the two combatants. As it grew louder, the short man smiled. The second wave of Crane samurai was nearly here. His company's mission clearly was to tie up the Crab defenses and allow the following waves to penetrate deeper into the pass—and it seemed to be working perfectly.

The grin disappeared when he realized the shouts came from the south, not the north. A second later, the Crane who had so bravely charged around the bend rounded the corner again, this time in full retreat. When the short samurai saw the reason, his arms went numb and his katana slipped from his hands.

Now it was O-Ushi's turn to smile. The Crane were being chased by a horde of enraged goblins and, if the powerful footfalls were any indication, at least two ogres. The whole lot ran past the ongoing struggles and back around the first bend. The Shadowlands were taking the fight to the Crane.

One well-placed swing of her hammer ended O-Ushi's first encounter of the day.

▲▲▲▲▲▲▲▲

"We lost fewer men today."

Sukune shot another exasperated look at Kuni Yori. "And I suppose if my brother is in a duel and his opponent takes off only three of his fingers, you'd consider *that* an improvement as well?"

The shugenja was right, though. The Crab samurai suffered much lighter losses today, but because the Shadowlands troops would not take orders from Sukune, they were less help than he would have liked. They killed large numbers of the enemy but did nothing to hold key locations like the northern ridge.

After the fighting ended, O-Ushi reported to her brother that the goblins along the mountain path were only moderately successful in protecting the archers above.

"When the Battle Maidens first saw them they reined their horses to a dead stop. But they could see that the goblins did not have the same fighting spirit as my troops. They were easily frightened and run off by the threat of a full cavalry charge. Luckily for us, the only place for them to run was up with the archers, and the combined group was able to hold off the Unicorns until nightfall. I doubt we'll be as lucky tomorrow."

Sukune had to agree.

He needed a better plan, and he needed it *now*. He was one bad decision away from having to pull the Crab army out of Beiden Pass altogether. If that happened, Yakamo's only escape would be through an enemy-controlled pass. Could he maintain his position long enough to protect his brother? Would Yakamo and his army arrive soon enough to turn the tide of battle? Or were both armies hopelessly outmatched?

"Where are you, Brother?" Sukune said to himself.

His only answer was a chill wind sweeping into the tent as Kuni Yori turned his back and left.

22   HOMEWARD BOUND

"We are surrounded." Yakamo paused for effect. "The Unicorn army has cut off our only escape. They have set their battle lines, most of their troops ride trained war-horses, and they are completely rested. Our troops, on the other hand, are almost exclusively foot soldiers. We've been traveling for five days and fighting for three. We outnumber the enemy, but conventional wisdom says the advantage is theirs. As long as we stay here in the woods, we're safe."

Every ear strained to hear his next words. Every eye focused on his slightest movement. Every heart begged him to say three simple words.

"Prepare to charge!"

The generals were as desperately gleeful as children running to the river on the first day of summer. As the word passed from company to company, Yakamo could feel excitement warm the cold autumn morning. The woods hummed with life and energy. Despite the frost on the ground, he could believe the trees themselves were so stimulated by his samurai's passion that they might burst into full bloom.

In fewer than ten minutes, Yakamo received the same signal from every general—we await your command. The entire Crab army stood ready.

"Forward!" Yakamo shouted and began to march.

The order echoed down the line to his left and right. It would take at least a minute for the message to reach the far ends of the army, but Yakamo knew that the wings of his force would not lag. The Crab army would march across the open fields of the Crane lands as a single, straight line of discipline and impending doom. They focused on a clear objective: to break through the Unicorn lines, return to Beiden Pass, and let *nothing* stand in their way.

To his surprise, the Shadowlands forces lined up alongside the Crab and marched to his orders. They were not nearly as organized or disciplined as Yakamo's samurai, but they were willing to take the battle to the Unicorn.

On the horizon the Unicorn army sat astride their horses. Their commander, Shinjo Yokatsu, was wily. He knew that he held the advantage of position—that the Crab needed to get past him. His samurai simply held their ground and made the Crab come to them. Perhaps he hoped the march would further tire his opponents or drive them into a frenzy of anticipation that would make them careless by the time the battle was finally joined.

All good plans, thought Yakamo, but all in vain.

The Unicorn were closer now. They no longer seemed a single swarming mass. Yakamo could clearly make out individual soldiers and even guess which commander they fought under, based on their stylized armor.

The Crab commander raised his claw in the air and snapped it loudly twice.

As one, his samurai drew their weapons and sped from a marching cadence to a slow trot. Occasionally a group of warriors would howl or bark out their enthusiasm. These were not threats to the enemy or even exaltations to their fellow Crab. They were wordless shouts of desire—wild, primal yearnings for the ring of steel against steel. Invariably, these shouts were echoed by the Shadowlands troops with true calls of wild abandon. The goblins and ogres were nearly frothing at the mouth, seemingly ready to fight anyone or anything just for the chance to release their animal passions.

The enemy was close enough that Yakamo could see the white clouds of their breath and feel the padding of the horses' hooves against the nearly frozen ground. He himself let out a ferocious roar and broke into a full headlong run toward the Unicorn line.

The rest of the Crab army exploded into full fury. The air filled with howls, shouts, curses, and growls. Yakamo felt he was surrounded by an army of wild animals—he felt he was an animal.

With a single slice of his katana through the air, the Unicorn commander released his samurai. They kicked their horses and urged them forward. By the time the two armies met, the cavalry was at full gallop.

Chaos reigned.

Horses thundered past the front ranks of Crab samurai and into the heart of the army. Yakamo repeatedly swung a tetsubo with his one good hand, succeeding in unseating three Unicorn riders as they attempted to pass. One snapped her neck in the fall from her steed. Another rolled directly into the midst of a group of Shadowlands zombies. His screams were terrible, but they did not last long. The third Unicorn landed right at Yakamo's feet with a teeth-rattling thud.

The Crab commander raised his weapon and brought it down toward the enemy's head.

The purple-clad samurai rolled to his left and sprang to his feet. He drew his katana and focused for the first time on his opponent. "By the kami, what *are* you?" the frightened Unicorn asked with unabashed horror.

"I am your death!" answered the Crab commander. His tetsubo knocked the sword from the stunned man's hand, and his left hand reached toward the Unicorn's throat. It was only when his black, metal claw closed around the man's entire face that Yakamo truly understood the samurai's terror.

Yakamo laughed as he crushed the life from his screaming foe.

▲▲▲▲▲▲▲▲

The battle was going well. Although the Unicorn cavalry was faster and better armored than the Crab forces, Yakamo's troops were determined. Their number was so large that once an enemy samurai's progress was stopped, she was instantly surrounded and dragged from her mount. Soon the Unicorn only worried the flanks of the Crab army. They were too afraid to penetrate to the heart of the corps.

"Onward!" shouted Yakamo. He waved his great black claw in the air.

As the force crested a small rise, arrows rained from the sky. Wave after wave of the deadly missiles fell, striking down dozens of Crab warriors.

Across the plain stood a cluster of Dragon Clan archers. As one rank unleashed a volley of armor-piercing arrows, another took aim, and a third nocked more projectiles. The barrage was nearly constant.

Yakamo rolled forward, and his army followed. No fewer than twelve more times, Dragon archers unleashed their fury on his troops. Hundreds of Crab warriors would not return to their stations on the Great Wall. Immediately he banished such thoughts. All that mattered was reaching the Dragon position and stopping the slaughter.

As the Crab drew within a hundred yards of the enemy, the archers changed their targets. Instead of firing into the heart of the Crab forces, they lowered their sights and fired directly at the front line samurai. Yakamo felt an arrow bury deep in his right shoulder and heard three more whistle within a few inches of his head.

He kept on charging.

With a mighty yell, the Crab commander swung his tetsubo in a long, flat arc, breaking three Dragon dai-kyu and solidly colliding with one archer's ribcage. Blades clashed and armor rent—the Crab were back where they belonged, in hand-to-hand combat. But the rising wind carried another sound to Yakamo's ears—a droning chant half-sung by a dozen or so voices.

Two of the samurai whose bows Yakamo smashed drew their wakizashi and flanked the Hida. They made menacing motions but never approached close enough to be struck by the Crab's massive club. Yakamo twirled his tetsubo in his casual way, sometimes feinting a lunge at one Dragon or the other. They were patient and observant—this could be trouble.

Cautiously the little circle of samurai stalked through the battle. Around them warriors from both sides fought and died, but these three had eyes only for one another. As they stepped over the bodies of fallen goblins and kicked aside shattered weapons, the wind continued to rise. Soon dust swirled in tiny cyclones at their feet, and dead summer grass blew into their faces. It was becoming increasingly difficult for Yakamo to keep his eyes clear and focused on his opponents.

Then, past one of his attacker's shoulders, Yakamo saw who was chanting. In a hollow just over the next ridge sat a circle of Phoenix Clan shugenja. Some drew arcane symbols in the dirt, others waved their hands about wildly, and others sat as still as stones. They all chanted in unison.

The howl of the wind rose to a heady pitch. Behind Yakamo, troops shouted in chaos. One voice rang clearly through the din, his uncle Tsuru's: "The very ground is alive! Fall back! Move aside! Get out of—"

Yakamo made a quick turn to see what had become of the general, but he could not find him anywhere. The wind battered his men mercilessly, and the ground roiled like a pot of boiling rice. Tsuru's horse dashed madly away from the chaos, but of the man himself there was no sign. Then, with a sound like a ruptured bellows, the missing samurai fell from the sky and landed not twenty yards away. He coughed and gasped for air like a drowning man just pulled from the water.

One Dragon mistook Yakamo's shift of focus for complete distraction. He lunged at the Crab commander and nearly had his nose taken off by a reflexive snap from the Hida's claw.

"Tsuru!" Yakamo shouted to his uncle. "I've two very green dragons here. Would you care to help me make sure they never grow more seasoned?"

The dazed general stood and drew his wakizashi—he'd lost his katana in the fall—and took a few halting steps toward his nephew. He was going to be no help at all, but Yakamo *knew* that. He had no intention of drawing his uncle into the fight. Instead, his plan was to draw his opponents' attention away from him— and that ploy worked perfectly.

Both Dragon samurai shifted their positions to account for another combatant.

Yakamo dropped his head and shoulders and bulled into the nearest one. He collided with the force of an earthquake and knocked the man fifteen feet backward. Yakamo could easily have followed up and slain the Dragon, but his attention was now focused squarely on the Phoenix shugenja. If they weren't stopped, their spells could decimate the entire Crab force.

Thankfully, such spells required complete concentration, which was why the shugenja were hidden in this hollow. Yakamo charged into the middle of their circle without raising a single cry of alarm. He swung his tetsubo in a looping figure eight, striking one spellcaster after another. At the same time, he lashed out with the flat of his claw, bashing it against the skulls of the few shugenja who scrambled for somewhere to hide.

Behind him, the winds dropped off almost immediately. The panicked retreat of his troops halted soon after. The allied forces were in even greater disarray. They'd done quite a bit of damage to the Crab army, but in the end the ferocity of Yakamo's samurai drove the Unicorn, Dragon, and Phoenix from the field.

Hida Tsuru's war-horse came trotting up to its master. Even in the midst of battle, the creature came to his uncle's side.

Yakamo approached the general, who was just beginning to regain his breath.

"Spread the word," he said grimly, "this battle is over. We don't have time to clean up the enemy stragglers. Only one man could get these three clans to put together such an organized defense on such short notice. And since Toturi isn't here, he *must* be leading the assault against my weakling brother at Beiden Pass!"

▲▲▲▲▲▲▲

"Ha! Three quarters of their troops on horseback, and they can still barely keep up with us!" Hida Amoro turned and ran backward for a few steps, admiring the way the Crab army outpaced the Unicorn cavalry that followed them. The grassy plains of the Crane lands grew rockier as they neared the mountains called The Spine of the World.

"We have two advantages," said Yakamo curtly. "We know where we're going, and unlike their horses, we are willing to run for two days and nights without rest if the cause is sufficient. However, we may still fall prey to our own overconfidence."

Amoro stumbled as the ground became more uneven. Embarrassed, he faced forward and returned to his double-time march.

"They may not be able to worry us just now, but our Unicorn shadows will be able to keep us from veering too far off our current path as we approach the pass."

Yakamo drove his army harder than any other commander in the empire would—even his father. But he did so because he *knew* that Toturi waited at the north end of Beiden Pass. At least he *hoped* Toturi waited and hadn't already taken the pass from Sukune.

To the west, the sun dropped closer to the horizon. In less than three hours, the chilly day would turn into a freezing mountain night. Fortunately, they were less than an hour from the pass.

Yakamo thumped Amoro in the chest with the back of his hand.

"Drop back and tell the generals that when we get within sight of the entrance, we break into a full charge. No one is to stop to engage the enemy unless absolutely necessary. I want the entire army in the pass before darkness falls."

"But what if your brother has failed to hold it?" Amoro asked.

"Then we will take it back."

▲▲▲▲▲▲▲▲

"They've surrounded us! We're doomed! We'll never make it out alive!"

The Dragon lieutenant was only one third correct. The Crab and Shadowlands warriors attacking their rear were not from the same force as those in the pass, so they were not technically surrounded. The attackers were more concerned with getting past his men rather than crushing them, so they were not technically doomed. The lieutenant, however, did come face to face with Hida Yakamo, who reached out his claw and crushed the man's skull without breaking stride, so he himself never did make it out alive.

Nearly half the pass was now disputed territory. Sukune's forces, bolstered only slightly by Shadowlands warriors, fought to keep Dragon and Unicorn samurai from solidifying their hold on important junctures.

Yakamo's arrival turned the tide. Terrified by the appearance of the new howling, blood- and sweat-covered troops, the enemy withdrew back to the north end of the pass. But Sukune's samurai were in no shape to hold such gains.

Yakamo turned to Amoro and said, "Take your men and Tsuru's to the final bend in the pass. Do not allow the enemy more than twenty yards into the canyon. Make *certain* they do not take the ridge overlooking the entrance."

"Hai!" said the exhausted samurai. He ran off at full speed to complete his orders.

Sukune's troops gathered around Yakamo and his men, clapping them on the back and saying things such as, "It's about time you got here!" and "Your timing couldn't be better!" and "Now we'll hold the pass for sure!" They did not, however, seem at all glad to see the Shadowlands troops. In fact, they looked at them with deep suspicion.

"What is wrong?" demanded Yakamo "Has one week with my brother made you so finicky that you would pick and choose who saves you from honorless defeat?"

The samurai rubbed the back of their necks and gritted their teeth.

"It's just that the goblins have been of no help to us," said one man.

"Hai!" said another. "They sit at the southern end of the pass and wait for their orders to march home while we die trying to hold the pass."

Now it was Yakamo's turn to grit his teeth.

"Is that so?" he said. "Well, the forces who traveled with us were the first to assault the walls of Kyuden Kakita. Perhaps the fault lies not in our comrades but in your commander."

A low murmur went up among the samurai. None of them were willing to speak out against Sukune—but neither were any of them willing to defend him.

"Where is my brother? Who can tell me where to find him?"

"He is in his tent, son of the Bear. Would you like me to bring him a message?"

Kuni Yori stepped from behind a hulking samurai and walked up to Yakamo. His face was hidden beneath his cloak, but his eyes glowed within the shadows.

Yakamo spat on the ground.

"Tell your new master that as of this moment he is relieved of his command!" he growled. "I will not stand by and watch him throw away our only hope of victory! Tell him I will deal with him properly once we secure the pass!"

Yori's eyes actually sparkled at these words.

"Hai, Tono," he said gleefully. "I will say these words to your brother—and some words from your father as well."

23   THE PRICE

My time is short."

Sukune spoke aloud, though he knew no one was there. Still, he was not talking to himself. To the stars, then? They shone and sparkled above in the kind of crisp night sky that comes only in winter. Rather than go to his tent, Sukune had climbed to one of the perches along Beiden Pass's upper ridge. As he inhaled, the air constricted the insides of his nose and throat, and as he exhaled, it escaped in great billowing plumes. It was cold, colder than it had been so far on this uncomfortable campaign. But there was something more—the wind.

The pass was always windy—such is the way in the mountains—but tonight was different. The wind did not blow particularly hard, yet it howled and moaned like a dog baying at the full moon.

"My father will certainly be here in another day or two," Sukune continued. Perhaps he was speaking to Beiden Pass itself—to the spirit of the place—appealing for support in this vital mission gone terribly awry. "If I can just hold on until then, he will see what desperate shape my forces are in and commend me for achieving so much with so few resources, instead of damning me for failing in my one task. Take and hold the pass—it sounds so simple. And based on every principle of warfare I've ever learned, we should have lost fewer than fifty men in its defense."

He paused and looked at the sky. Lord Moon was nowhere to be seen. Tonight he turned his back on the world completely—a time when anything could happen. The greatest and most terrible of events happened on nights like this, nights with no moon.

"Perhaps my brother is right. Perhaps I am a failure."

Somewhere in the darkness, the frozen gravel of the path crunched as if under an approaching foot.

"Who is there?" he demanded. He had gone to some trouble to get this far away from interruptions and prying ears. "Kuni Yori, is that you?"

"You have failed," Yori said, and took a silent step closer. The faint light from the campfires below flickered across his form. He held both his hands inside the sleeves of his black velvet robe, and his face was entirely swallowed in shadow. For a moment, Sukune thought he was an apparition—a ghost of some Hida ancestor come to punish him for failing to hold the pass.

"One more day, and Toturi will be crushed," Sukune said with a confidence he didn't feel. For most people, a convincingly spoken lie was more powerful than a silent truth.

Yori took another step forward. "I have a message from your father."

"For me?" asked Sukune failing to sound casual. He hoped for orders that would render his current situation less precarious.

"No," said Yori, "for me."

As he spoke, his eyes began to glow. Somewhere in the darkness, another footstep crunched on the rocky path.

Sukune looked over Yori's shoulder but saw no one. "What does the Great Bear have to say?"

Yori now stood directly in front of Sukune. Arcane patterns glinted on the shugenja's robes. His eyes glowed pale yellow in his shadowy face. The long ends of his mustache bobbed and twitched as he spoke. "A great many things," was how Kuni Yori chose to answer the question. Did he smile as he said that? Sukune could not be certain.

The Crab commander's mouth was suddenly dry. He coughed once and licked his lips.

"I would like to see the message my father sent you," he finally said. It was not an order—Sukune did not feel up to ordering anyone to do anything—but he needed to know what was in the missive.

Yori slowly withdrew one hand from his robe. It held a small scroll tied with a red silk ribbon. The shugenja held it gingerly, lovingly, like a prized possession.

Another gust of wind howled, carrying more sounds of footsteps—yes, several sets of slow steady footsteps from down the path.

Sukune snatched the scroll from Yori's hand. He nimbly untied the ribbon and opened the fragile rice paper. Even by the weak firelight, he recognized his father's bold brush strokes. It was a brief message, but one that turned Sukune's blood colder than the mountain night. His eyes stopped focusing on anything— not the scroll or the shugenja or anything on the ridge. Sukune was looking at his future, and he did not see much of it.

The scroll read: Toturi must die. If my son fails, you know what to do.

"What do you read in that paper that turns your skin the color of porcelain?"

The youngest Hida snapped back into focus. Suddenly they were no longer alone on the ridge. Behind Kuni Yori stood four samurai, even more cloaked in shadows than he.

So this was how it would be? A group of turncoat bushi would remove him from authority before he had a chance to prove he could do the job.

"I need more time," Sukune said. He was not begging or even cajoling, merely stating a fact. He *knew* he could succeed.

"There is no more time," Yori said and stepped to one side.

The samurai lurched forward and grabbed Sukune's arms.

"Let go!" he said. "I order you to let me go!"

Yori laughed darkly. "I'm sorry, Tono," the shugenja's words dripped sarcasm, "but these warriors do not take orders from you—they never have."

The young Crab looked closely at his captors. Between the seams of their armor he could see rotting flesh and crawling maggots. Zombies!

"Yori!" Sukune said, panic making his voice high and thin. "I have not yet failed. We still hold the pass. I might yet prevail tomorrow."

The shugenja's eyes sparkled like the stars above.

"Yes, that is exactly what has kept you safe these past few nights. Despite your inept opening foray, you had it within you to upset my carefully laid plans. But no longer. You see, your brother has returned and, seeing the army in such a shambles, has assumed leadership over all the Crab forces." Yori giggled absently. "You have been relieved of your command. There are no more chances. You have failed."

The zombies' hands tightened around Sukune's arms. Another undead warrior moved behind the young Hida and slipped a putrid arm around his neck, holding his head forward so that he would see what came next.

"This is a plan that took years to execute," Yori gloated, "and for the past month only *you* held the power to stop me. Do you know when you failed, when you guaranteed my victory?"

Despite the zombie holding him still, Sukune shook his head.

"The minute you lost your resolve."

It was clear Sukune did not know what Yori meant.

"Of all the headstrong members of your family, *you* were the only one who recognized my counsel for the subtle moral erosion that it was. You refused to apply the Crab motto to every situation in life—for you the ends did not always justify the means. You were the only one willing to take a stand and say that some tactics were simply without honor, and you were willing to die for that principle."

Sukune stood proudly. "I still *do* believe that."

Yori laughed. "If you truly believed that then you would have died in defense of the pass and taken all your samurai with you.

Instead, your resolve shattered, and you brought the Shadowlands army into the battle. If you had died in the pass, your sacrifice would have shown Kisada the truth of your words. Instead you gave up your honor just as he surrendered his—quietly and in a moment of weakness. To protect your own life, you compromised the only principle that could have saved your soul—and those of your father and brother."

Yori leaned in so close that the steam from his breath dampened Sukune's face.

"And now, you will obstruct me no longer."

As the shugenja turned away he made a sharp stabbing motion with his hand.

The remaining zombie drew a rusted and chipped wakizashi from a rotting scabbard and advanced on Sukune. The young Crab struggled to get free, but the undead strength of the zombies was too much for his frail muscles.

Even as the sword stood poised over him, Sukune made no sound. Blow after jagged, painful blow ripped through his flesh, but still he held his tongue. If he was to die tonight, he would die like a samurai—like a Crab. After a while, he no longer felt the blows, or the life and heat of his body seeping out into the cold night.

"Stop!" commanded Kuni Yori. "That is enough. We don't want him dead—yet! Lift him and follow me."

As the cold, decayed hands lifted Sukune into the air, his eye caught the shugenja's.

Yori smiled evilly. "You see, you still have a part to play in my plan. You will be the instrument of your father's downfall."

Sukune let out one tortured scream, but it was carried away by the mischievous mountain wind.

24 THE FINAL WATCH

Atop the Great Kaiu Wall, a dozen Crab samurai stood with legs tensed and arms loose. Moonless nights were the worst. They made it impossible to see Shadowlands troop movements. But the samurai could hear their enemies approaching, scrambling over ancient stone.

The Crab were tired. They would never admit it, and they certainly would never allow weariness to keep them from battle, but they were tired to their bones. The assault had continued for nearly a week, and this was the third attack they had to repel today. The enemy forces were relentless.

Only a few weeks ago, Kuni Higeki was just another veteran in a company brimming with experienced samurai. The section of the Wall to which he was assigned must have been near a goblin village, because it was frequently and heavily attacked. Higeki fought well and was liked by his comrades, but he never showed any inclination toward command. He was simply a good samurai.

Then the daimyo announced the Crab were going to take and hold Beiden Pass. Higeki's commander read off names, indicating who would serve under Hida Sukune and who under Hida Yakamo. When the commander was done, one name had not been read—Kuni Higeki.

"Your assignment," the commander said, "is to remain here and lead a troop of samurai from other companies in defense of our position. The fighting will be lighter all along the Wall, but it will not cease. You must make sure we have a Wall to come back to!"

Higeki couldn't tell whether this was an honor or a punishment.

As the days passed, he realized it was a nearly impossible task. At Higeki's post, the goblins came in the same furious numbers as always, but now the turret was manned by novice samurai under an inexperienced commander.

Higeki was proud of his warriors and, by extension, of himself. At first there was no way goblins, ogres, and other creatures scrambling up the Wall could tell that the post was manned any differently than usual. After a week of nearly constant assault, though, the greener samurai showed fatigue.

Their eyes were wrung with dark circles. Their weapons hung loose at their sides. Their blows became less powerful, their movements less crisp, and their tactics more predictable. Sooner or later they would begin to drop where they stood, leaving the tower undefended and the gateway to the Crab lands open for all of Fu Leng's creatures.

"We cannot fail!" Higeki shouted to rally his troops.

"For if we do the empire falls," answered a dozen lackluster voices.

This could well be it, Higeki thought. These men have given all they have. They simply are not up to the task.

A huge, pale yellow forearm crashed over the top of the Wall. A raging ogre pulled itself onto the parapet. Seven goblins clung to the creature's shoulders and matted hair. The goblins had tanto clenched between their teeth. Feral glints shone in their eyes.

"Charge!" shouted Higeki as he led his warriors forward. He and four others moved to attack the ogre. The remaining seven each took on one goblin.

The ogre leapt directly into their midst, landing squarely on top of one samurai and crushing him beneath tremendous feet. The other samurai stood frozen. They'd never seen an ogre move so quickly, and this was the first casualty they'd had in days.

Higeki kept his wits. He spun on his heel and slashed over the top of his head with his yari. The polearm whistled. Its blade slashed down and through the jaundiced skin of the ogre's back.

Now the creature's full attention turned to the unfortunate commander.

It backhanded the yari from Higeki's grip, nearly tearing his arm from its socket. Opening its hand, it reversed the blow, scooped Higeki up, and pulled him tight against its chest. Before the startled Crab could do anything, the ogre wrapped its other arm around him in a painful bear hug.

Higeki's arms were pinned at his sides—there was nothing he could do. Try as he might, he could get no leverage, and his wakizashi scabbard was pinned against the ogre's midsection. Pain shot through his lower back where the creature squeezed, and flashes of bright white light clouded his eyes.

The white explosions became a wave of red clouds across Higeki's vision. Thunder rolled in his ears.

So this was how it ended?

Abruptly, the ogre loosened its grip. It gently put Higeki down on the ground, loped back to the parapet's edge, and climbed down the Wall. The surviving goblins followed as quickly as they could disengage from their melee combat. All of them looked at the sky, wonder and awe in their eyes, and broad smiles on their lips.

It took Higeki a few moments to realize he had indeed escaped death. Instead of being overjoyed, he too stared skyward.

The red clouds and thunder had not been part of his near-death throes. A blanket of crimson flowed from the north to the south. Heat lightning danced, lighting the sky in brilliant red flashes. A low, resonant thunder rolled relentlessly through the air, shaking the Great Wall.

The display lasted for more than ten minutes before the clouds broke up. Thunder slowly faded into the southern distance.

The clear, moonless sky returned, seeming even more ominous than before.

Sunrise brought no answers. The Shadowlands troops were gone. There was no sight of them anywhere across the landscape. In fact, there was no sign of any living or unliving thing for as far as the eye could see.

As the day wore on, no further attacks assailed the Wall. The siege was over, but why?

Eventually, runners came from other sections of the Wall. All of them carried similar stories. The red clouds and thunder apparently filled the skies from one end of the Great Wall to the other and caused all Shadowlands creatures to halt their assaults and return to the depths of Fu Leng's realm. It meant *something*, the clouds were some sort of signal. But a signal of what? And what did it mean for the Crab Clan?

25 THE TEN-THOUSANDTH STEP

Hida Kisada spurred his horse to a gallop. After nearly two weeks of travel, planning, and more travel, he hoped there would still be some action when he arrived at Beiden Pass.

He was not at all prepared for the sight that greeted him as he approached the southern entrance.

In the failing daylight, wounded and dying Crab samurai lay everywhere. Healers tended to those who had strong spirits, and priests tended to those who did not. What kind of army did Toturi have? Even if he matched the Crab man for man, Beiden Pass offered sufficient protection that Sukune's losses should have been less than a quarter of the enemy's. If the south end of the canyon was this crowded with casualties, at the north, they would be stacked like firewood. How had Toturi managed to raise such a massive army so quickly?

The Great Bear heard the sound of ringing steel. Beiden Pass was miles long, yet the battle was close enough to hear. His thinking changed entirely. No force was large enough to displace a Crab army the size Sukune commanded, not in two weeks. Something had gone terribly wrong.

To the west of the pass entrance stood the command tent. Sukune had better have a lot of damned good answers, thought the Great Bear as he rode to it and dismounted.

"Explain yourself!" Kisada demanded, stepping through the flap and into the small room, but Sukune was not there. His go set was, stopped in the middle of a particularly intriguing game. So was the tiny altar he insisted on carrying with him. The smell of incense still hung faintly in the air. It had not been very long since Sukune was here.

Perhaps he was at the front, leading his samurai. So many things could have gone wrong, and Sukune was a brilliant tactician. The answers to Kisada's questions lay with his youngest son.

The daimyo emerged from the tent. He was about to remount his horse and urge it toward the canyon, but the sounds of battle had ceased. A shiver shot up Kisada's spine, and the world grew dark around him. The last sliver of the sun sank below the mountainous horizon.

The fighting was done for the day. Kisada would wait here for Sukune to return.

But it was the Great Bear's eldest son who led the troops out of the canyon mouth. Though most of the samurai seemed weighed down by fatigue, Yakamo walked tall, strong, and proud.

"Oy! Yakamo!" Kisada called out.

The younger Hida raised his left hand—or what now took its place—and waved enthusiastically.

"Father!" Yakamo answered. "You have arrived! Tomorrow we will drive the hated Toturi from the pass for certain!"

He turned to his samurai.

"Let us raise the call—the Great Bear has returned!"

The other Crab, though, were too weary from the day's battle to raise more than a mild cheer. They appeared gladdened, even relieved, by Kisada's presence. But all they really seemed interested in was hot food and a warm bedroll.

"How fares the army, my son?" the daimyo asked, ignoring the lukewarm reception. Kisada did not blame the samurai for their lack of enthusiasm. War was a terrible business. And though these men and women had been practicing their craft for years, it was tougher on one's spirit to kill fellow samurai than it was to strike down inhuman monsters.

Yakamo shook his head despondently. "We've lost about a third of our troops, Father," he finally admitted. "Shadowlands casualties have run closer to one half."

"How?" Kisada demanded. "How did this happen? What trick did Toturi use?"

"He needed no trick," answered Yakamo, his voice as sharp as a katana. "My brother practically gave him the pass. He refused to use the Shadowlands warriors and—"

His father held up a hand.

"Let us see what Sukune has to say for himself. Where is he?"

Yakamo made a dismissive gesture. "I do not know," he said. "Last night I assumed command of our combined forces, and Sukune has not shown his face since. For all I know he is sitting in his tent crying over his lost command."

Kisada shook his head. "He is not in his tent. And despite your brother's physical weakness, he recognizes that *you* make the better commander and would not stand in your way."

"Yes," Yakamo agreed, "but now that you are here, we can really make some headway! Let me clean off this Dragon filth and then we can . . ."

The young man's voice trailed off. Behind his mask his eyes widened visibly. Throughout the camp, samurai had grown disturbingly still. All eyes stared at something beyond the Great Bear's shoulder.

Kisada turned and followed his son's gaze. Coming over the rise was a retinue of Shadowlands creatures. Ogres, ghouls, ghosts, and other monstrosities marched proudly before a single towering figure—Yakamo no Oni!

"Ah, my old friend," the oni said. "Here we are at last. What a glorious future awaits us!" Its voice was less grating than before. It still echoed faintly with pops and crackles as its ropy throat flexed and stretched, but the overall effect was smoother—more natural. Its expressions and mannerisms seemed even more familiar than before.

"What is the meaning of this?" demanded the Great Bear. "What are you doing here? And what gives you the right to call me 'friend'? I've killed honorable men for such familiarity—don't think that our agreement will prevent me from doing the same to you."

Yakamo no Oni raised its hands innocently—an unnatural expression for this monstrosity. It seemed truly shocked by Kisada's outburst.

"I don't understand," it said. "Aren't you preparing for an assault on the capital? Aren't you bound to spend this winter seated on the Emerald Throne?"

Yakamo stepped between his father and the towering Shadowlands general.

"The daimyo made it clear when last we met," the young Hida barked. "He has no intention of taking the throne. Your offer, and now your presence, is wholly unwelcome!"

The oni looked confusedly back and forth between father and son. Its bewilderment changed quickly to annoyance. "Surely you knew that when you accepted my offer—"

"We accepted *nothing!*" Yakamo shouted with such fury that spittle sprayed across the oni.

Kisada gazed back and forth between the oni and Yakamo. He realized why the creature's mannerisms seemed so familiar—it was slowly transforming into a tremendous, hideously perverted version of his son. Yakamo had not just given this creature his name. He'd also given it his personality, his visage—everything that gave him identity.

"Oh, but we did." The voice of Kuni Yori came from beyond the ridge that the oni straddled. "And we did so at the daimyo's order." His velvet clothing was brittle and soiled. Under the shadow of the hood, the shugenja's eyes were bloodshot and wild.

"Shugenja!" bellowed the Great Bear. "What is going on here? And *none* of your riddles! I want a straight answer. And I want to know where Sukune is!"

"All your questions," Yori said as he crested the rise and stood next to Yakamo no Oni, "will be resolved with one answer." He extended his tiny, fragile looking hand from the depths of his robe and motioned someone—or something—forward.

A handful of goblins responded to Yori's summons. They held ropes tied to a great standard that another group of goblins struggled to carry to the top of the hillock.

"What in the name of all that is holy—?" Kisada said.

Yakamo just stood there mute.

The standard, painted on tattered yellow scraps of cloth, was stained with dark splotches of blood. It was covered with strange symbols and glyphs—black magic. One word was legible, and it chilled the samurai to his very soul. The word was "Fu Leng."

An evil wind whipped the cloth to and fro, causing it at first to obscure something else strapped to the standard's wooden frame. It was something soft and white—no, pink and splashed crimson in places, like a body covered with wounds and dried blood.

Kisada's tremendous frame shrank as he let out a long, mournful breath.

It *was* a body strapped to the standard. No, not just strapped—crucified. And it wasn't just any body, not a Shadowlands zombie or even a Crab bushi who fell during the fighting. The body splayed across the terrible standard of Fu Leng was none other than Hida Sukune.

The Great Bear fell to his knees and stared helplessly at the lifeless body of his son.

"What have I done?" Kisada whispered.

Yakamo continued to say nothing. He simply stared at his brother's tortured body with a hateful sneer curling his lips.

"Done?" asked Kuni Yori with glee in his voice. "You've done everything you ever wanted."

"No!" Hida moaned. "I never wanted this. I never told you to do this. I never meant . . . I never knew. . . ."

"Liar!" the shugenja challenged. "You knew exactly what would happen the minute you gave me my orders. 'Toturi must be killed,' you said. 'If my son fails, you know what you must do.' Well, your son failed. And the only way to kill Toturi was to get reinforcements. I did exactly as you ordered. You simply assumed that your weakling son would not let things come to this point. You *chose* not to think of the real consequences of your orders, but you certainly did know what would happen when it came down to a choice between victory and defeat."

"No!" Kisada yelled. "No! I was wrong! I was so terribly wrong! Sukune! My son! I have killed you!"

"All you have done, Tono, is follow your passions. You let your pride lead you to the brink of greatness and did not allow the mewling of weaklings to distract you from your goal. Now instead of striding boldly to your just rewards," the shugenja said derisively, "you kneel in the dusty remains of those who opposed you and failed."

Kisada knelt completely motionless, completely still.

Yakamo no Oni extended a tremendous, blood-red hand to the Great Bear.

"Get up, Kisada-sama," it said with unexpected compassion. "Your future awaits!"

The daimyo stared uncomprehending at the hand. He was insensate.

Yakamo knelt down and placed a hand his father's shoulder.

"I killed your brother," the poor man finally whispered. "I gave the order. I am to blame. Can you forgive me?"

"No!" growled Yakamo. "You do not need forgiveness! Sukune did not want you to succeed. He never supported this action. By placing him in charge you nearly cost the clan everything. For that I might never forgive you. But you had enough insight to give an order that turned defeat into victory. For that, I offer you my hand."

The son reached his great black claw down to his father. Still half-blind, Kisada accepted the gesture and pulled himself to his feet.

"You have winnowed out the last weakness from our cause," Yakamo continued. "You've focused the Crab Clan on a single vision, the single destiny for which we've fought for countless generations. When you sit on the Emerald Throne, then and only then will the empire truly be safe. You are the only man who can do this. Right now is your moment of temptation, Father. This is your moment of weakness. Step beyond it."

Letting go of Kisada's hand, Yakamo moved to stand next to the Shadowlands creature with which he shared a name and a purpose. "Many good and noble samurai gave their lives in Beiden Pass. None of them thought it an empty gesture. They shared your vision. They believed in your goals. Do not let them die in vain."

"Nothing has yet changed within your empire," Yakamo no Oni said. "So far, all you have managed to do is get the other clans focused on a single problem."

"They do not understand the greater purpose you serve," added Yori. "They believe you are a renegade—a usurper like the honorless Scorpion, Bayushi Shoju. In their ignorance they will seek to destroy you."

"The threat of civil war has not gone away," Yakamo concluded. "In fact, it has moved beyond mere threat—civil war is here."

Kisada blinked. It was as though he were awakening from a deep sleep.

"The empire," mumbled the daimyo. "We must protect the empire."

"If we fail," the younger man began holding out his claw toward his father.

"The empire falls," finished the Great Bear, taking the claw and stepping toward his future.

"With you here, Father," Yakamo said, "and our forces bolstered by our new allies, we will retake the pass and crush Toturi and his traitorous army."

The Great Bear looked around at the fallen Crab—all these lives lost defending the best-fortified position in all of Rokugan. If Kisada did not rally the troops and retake Beiden Pass, did they die in vain? If he did, was it a hollow, meaningless victory? The point of this maneuver had been to shut down the other armies, to prevent bloodshed on a massive scale.

Measured by that standard, it had already failed.

The Great Bear wanted to look up at his youngest son's body, but his neck would not bend.

"No," Kisada finally said grabbing his remaining son by the right arm. "Every general must know when to abandon his battle plan. Forget Beiden Pass. Our karma lies elsewhere."

26   WORDS OF POWER

I have faced death in a thousand forms, but this is the most frightening scene I have *ever* witnessed." Speaking out loud was the only way Isawa Toki knew to keep himself from sliding into madness.

The Phoenix shugenja stood atop one of the towers of the Great Kaiu Wall. The bitterly cold wind whipped his long, graying ponytail behind him like a child's kite. Climbing up to the walkway had been treacherous—winter still held the land in its frigid grip, and the ladder was slick with ice—but Toki braved it because this would be his first chance actually to *see* the Shadowlands after studying them for so many years.

The Wall itself was impressive enough.

Snow covered not only the Wall but also all the scenery beyond. Draped in white, with the wind blowing light curtains of snow across the plains, it looked beautiful—almost inviting. Then the shugenja remembered what was missing from both the landscape and the Wall—people.

The Kaiu Wall and the Shadowlands for as far as the eye could see were completely deserted. It chilled Toki to his heart. The fight along the southern Crab border had been going on for over a thousand years. No one liked the clan much, but nearly everyone pitied them—they never got a moment's respite from the brutality of war. Yet, here the Phoenix samurai stood surrounded by complete silence. No birds flew in the sky. No foxes or rabbits left tracks in the snowdrifts. It was as though Toki visited a poisoned land.

None of the other clans had seen either the Crab or Shadowlands armies since the battle of Beiden Pass months earlier. They withdrew back into the heart of the Crab lands, just as winter settled on Rokugan. Gossip around the snowbound courts of the empire guessed that the two ancient enemies had turned on one another and resumed their centuries-old battle.

Now, standing on the Crab wall, surrounded by complete silence and solitude, it was clear neither army had returned home. The winter had been far too harsh for them to have traveled anywhere since the snows fell. So where had they gone?

Toki pondered the question but couldn't come up with even the beginning of an answer.

In the winter courts all the great generals and philosophers of Rokugan tried to answer the question: what caused the Great Bear to abandon his duty? They wanted an answer by spring—when the clans would march on Crab lands to kill the Great Bear and crush his army.

Once Toki returned with word of the Crab's disappearance, they would have to begin with a new question: Where did Kisada go?

The air was split by a horrendous scream that lasted longer than any man could hold his breath. Toki covered his ears, but the sound seemed to cut through the flesh of his hands and strike directly at his brain. As suddenly as it began, the ear-piercing racket ended with a faint gurgle.

Cautiously lowering his arms, the Phoenix looked toward a strange tower set slightly back from the Wall. It was of the same design but slightly smaller than the rest of the towers. The piteous wail had come from it. Toki's martial training told him the tower held no strategic significance, but clearly it was the one place in all the southern Crab lands that was still inhabited. Inhabited by what?

There was only one way to find out.

After carefully descending the icy stairs and trudging through thick snow, Toki reached the tower. Standing in front of its entrance, he found his legs did not want to carry him inside.

"I've spent my entire life preparing to face any abomination the Shadowlands could throw at me," the shugenja said, trying to talk his limbs into cooperating. "No matter what is in that tower, if anyone in Rokugan is ready to face it, I am!"

The brave talk must have had some effect, because Toki's legs relaxed enough for him to press on through the doorway.

The place was steeped in magic. Toki could feel it. Certainly this tower was home to a powerful Crab shugenja. He thought it odd that he could not make the same determination from outside the tower. Usually sources of such powerful mystical energy were impossible to conceal. If this spellcaster could so effectively mask his presence, he was definitely a force to be reckoned with.

Though from the outside the building seemed dark and deserted, inside it was lit with torches. The tower was one tremendous room, and Toki could see all the way to the ceiling fifty feet above. The upper reaches were masked with flickering shadows. The walls were lined with iron cages, some of which held skeletal remains of creatures that the shugenja could tell were once goblins. Nothing moved.

The source of the scream, Toki reckoned, must be the odd house built in the center of the tower's floor. It was an unassuming cottage. In fact, the Phoenix might even call it charming if it weren't in the middle of such a frighteningly magical building. He took a few steps closer, then thought better of it.

"Are you going to stand outside all day?" asked a voice from within the house. It seemed filled with mirth, as though the speaker was enjoying the Phoenix's caution. "Come inside, please."

The shoji were open, but Toki could see only darkness within.

Toki realized he had two options: Do as the voice said or turn and run. Considering the power of the magic surrounding the house, he didn't think he would get very far.

He stepped up to the wooden deck and into the house, not bothering to remove his sandals as he would at any other structure. He wanted to be ready to leave without delay.

As he passed over the threshold there was no change in the lighting. The building really *was* dark. Away in the depths of the house, he saw a single, faint, flicker—certainly a candle. It showed the pale outline of the head and shoulders of a lone figure hunched over a table. The figure wore a black cloak with the hood pulled up and motioned with one hand for Toki to approach.

"Come in, my friend, or shall I say 'my brother'?" The voice still seemed to chuckle mockingly beneath every word.

"Brother?" As he approached the figure, Toki felt as though he were wading upstream. His breath came in even larger plumes than it did atop the Wall.

"We share so many interests, you and I," the figure said. "Our devotion to the mystical arts being but one."

"You are a shugenja then?" the Phoenix felt the need to say something. His limbs felt numb, and he wasn't sure he wanted to keep approaching the mysterious figure, but he could not stop himself.

"I am Kuni Yori, chief advisor to Hida Kisada and daimyo of the Kuni family."

This was Kuni Yori? Toki had heard many tales of the man. He was responsible for much of the knowledge the Phoenix possessed regarding Shadowlands magic. Toki had hoped one day to meet Yori and discuss his theories, but in his deepest nightmares he'd never imagined the meeting would be like this.

"I am Isawa Toki," he said trying to sound casual. "Yori-san, what has happened here?"

"Happened?" Yori seemed not to understand, so involved was he in his work.

"The Great Wall of the Kaiu stands empty. The largest army in all of Rokugan has completely disappeared. Not a creature moves in the entirety of the Shadowlands for as far as the eye can see!"

Yori lifted his head. For the first time, Toki could see what Yori worked on so diligently. He seemed to be reading or translating a scroll that had been rescued from a fire of some sort. It was blackened and gave off a lingering scent of burnt flesh. Kanji and odd glyphs glowed pale yellow on the blackened parchment.

"Oh, that!" his voice seemed very faraway. "It is nothing you need concern yourself with. Go home. There is nothing for you to learn in the Shadowlands. Not anymore."

"But the Element Masters have agreed, the Shadowlands are growing in strength," insisted Toki. "I am but one of many emissaries sent to these cursed lands to search for clues. It is my duty to do all I can to discover the source of this new power."

Kuni Yori chuckled darkly. "I now know all there is to know about the Shadowlands."

Looking closer, Toki became convinced that the letters on the scroll were not revealed through alchemical or sorcerous means. They were burned into the scroll and still glowed with their own flame. He even fancied he could feel heat coming from the scroll.

"Share that knowledge then, Yori-san," he urged. "The empire stands on the brink of ruin. Our greatest enemy is now beyond our sight, as is the only defense Rokugan has ever known. Revealing the Shadowlands' plans could save your clan from the same dishonor the emperor visited upon the Scorpions. Why would you hold back such information?"

"You Phoenix like to say knowledge has a price," Yori began. The Crab shugenja turned to face Toki for the first time. Although his features were hidden beneath the shadow of his cloak, it was clear that something was wrong with Kuni Yori's face. His voice took on a quality that chilled Toki's blood—it sounded like ice cracking on a not-quite-frozen lake.

With slow, deliberate hands Yori removed his hood. He had been injured somehow. There was blood on his face, and his skin had an unnatural sheen. It almost looked as though he had been badly burned.

Despite the frigid air, Toki broke out in a sweat.

Yori's lower jawbone lay in plain sight, and no lip framed the skin above his teeth. Only one side of his famously long mustache remained—and it was matted with gore. His eyes were so red, no white remained. His skin glistened and pulsed and oozed blood. His mantle of hair was replaced with wide strips of gory flesh that ran from his forehead back over his scalp. Kuni Yori's face had been turned inside out!

"If you would know the ways of Fu Leng, you must be willing to pay," the monstrosity that once was Kuni Yori said. It held aloft the scroll, which Toki now recognized as one of the Black Scrolls that were the original doom of Fu Leng. "It is all in here. The cost is not so dear, really."

Kuni Yori began laughing long, low, and maniacally. The sound built and built until it filled the tower more completely than the winter chill.

Isawa Toki turned and ran. He did not think about trying to grab the scroll. He did not consider attacking Yori, who still seemed to be woozy from his transformation.

No, Toki simply ran. He ran past his horse and north into the heart of the Crab lands. He kept on running until he collapsed in a snow bank. And when he awoke, he immediately began running again.

All the while, Yori's laughter rang in his ears.

27 THE LAST PEACEFUL SEASON

You may not be a warrior, but you are *truly* a Crab!"

Yasuki Taka bowed deeply, his cheeks flushed with pride. Such a compliment from the daimyo was a rare honor for a member of the Yasuki family—even its leader. Merchants were not highly prized, though necessary to keep a clan successful. Like lowly heimin, most samurai considered merchants below their notice. Under Taka's astute guidance, the Yasukis had begun to trade in a most precious commodity—prestige. By gaining Kisada's trust and ear, Taka secured for his family a place of honor in the history of the Crab Clan and, if all went as the Great Bear planned, the annals of imperial recognition.

"I live to serve, Tono," Taka said as he rose. "My apologies that we have not completed our work ahead of schedule, but all the ships will be ready by week's end."

Kisada looked over the cliff edge, down to the sea. A beach of white sand arced from one horizon to the other. Azure water lapped gently at the shore. About a quarter mile down the beach, several Crab samurai played in the surf, splashing and dunking one another.

The Great Bear smiled. It was best to allow his troops some time to romp and release pent-up energy. It had been a long winter, and war was coming soon enough.

Away from the water's edge, as far Kisada could see in both directions, merchant ships covered the beach. Large ships, small ships, ships that could be crewed by one, some that needed a full company of trained sailors to navigate, all built to move cargo from one port to another. And all of them in the process of being refitted to carry people instead of goods.

Certainly the journey would not be a comfortable one. There were no cabins added to the boats, just windows to allow air in and gangplanks to let passengers out. This entire merchant fleet had been transformed into a flotilla of transport ships capable of carrying the combined Crab and Shadowlands army away from their winter camp on Shima Chuto De.

The northernmost of the Mantis Clan islands had been the perfect spot for Kisada and his troops to spend the long winter. It was forbidding, forested heavily enough to supply the shipbuilders with adequate supplies, and nearly uninhabited. The only permanent structure on the island was an abandoned lighthouse. The few hermits and woodsmen who haunted the woods wanted nothing to do with the large camp of samurai on the southern shore. They probably assumed the force belonged to the Mantis Clan anyway. After all, who would *want* to come to such an out-of-the-way place?

An army that wants to remain invisible, Kisada thought.

"You have done a remarkable job, Taka-san," the Great Bear said. "The ice in the bay will still be impassable for another fortnight. Simply be sure that all modifications are completed by that time."

Mainland roads would be nearly open by the time the floes surrounding Shima Chuto De were thin enough for the Crab to put to sea. The other daimyo would come looking for him as soon as weather allowed. The debacle at Beiden Pass made the Crab the clear first target for all the clans. What better way to show worth to the emperor than by destroying the "renegade" who sacrificed his own son to the Dark God and allied his clan with the empire's most ancient enemies?

Looking down at the beach again, Kisada saw his proud, tall samurai working side by side with misshapen green goblins, and giving orders to shuffling undead zombies—some of whom wore Crab armor. It turned his stomach.

"Use every tool available," the daimyo mumbled disgustedly to himself. "All that matters is our success."

"Indeed!" agreed Taka making Kisada jump—he'd forgotten the merchant was still there. "Your navy will be ready to sail on the first safe outgoing tide! And it will sail on to victory!"

"To victory," Kisada replied. But at what cost?

▲▲▲▲▲▲▲▲

Kisada knelt before the tiny altar that used to belong to his youngest son—it was the one remembrance the Great Bear had saved from Sukune's tent when they retreated from Beiden Pass last fall. He would have liked to have taken the young man's go set or some of his favorite essays on the art of warfare, but there was neither time nor space to spare in the rush to evacuate before Toturi's forces descended on the beaten Crab army.

"I did nothing wrong!" he said. "I thought of the clan and the empire. I gave you the chance you always wanted. I made the decisions that had to be made."

He stared at the altar as though he expected it to answer. Although Kisada had faith in his ancestors, he rarely bothered to pray. He believed the kami helped those who helped themselves, so the most sincere form of devotion was action. But it was not a divine voice he hoped to hear this morning. It was the voice of his lost son.

"You were a good son—a good samurai. You were always prepared, and proud, to give your life in the service of the clan. This act may have been against everything you believed, but it will help lead the Crab to glory. Surely you can see that this is a good thing.

Certainly your spirit is proud to have played such an integral part in this victory."

The altar offered no comfort. It simply sat there as it always had.

"Please," Kisada begged. "Please, give me a sign. I have done nothing wrong. I just need to know that you recognize this!"

The Great Bear leaped back as a purple cloud erupted in the center of the altar. Smoke quickly covered the tiny wooden structure and spread throughout the tent. It smelled foul and stagnant, like a swamp in the heat of summer.

When the smoke cleared, Kisada saw a white rice paper scroll case. It bore a round wax seal depicting a pair of crossed crab claws—the mon of the Kuni family. He opened the scroll and read it aloud.

> "Master Hida Kisada—
>
> "The Crane and the Unicorn are on the march, but heavy snows in the mountain passes will delay the Dragon for at least another week.
>
> "The clans bicker heatedly about what to do about the Crab assault on Beiden Pass. The Lion want to absolve the clan but hunt you down as a criminal, Kisada-sama, and bring your head back on the point of a yari. The Crane wish the emperor to assess some penalty for your actions—preferably a transfer of Crab lands to Crane control. The Unicorn and Dragon seem simply to want to crush our army on the field of battle. The Phoenix, typically, want only to better understand the nature of our alliance with the Shadowlands and do not endorse one course of action over another."

Kisada laughed. Of all the major Rokugani clans, he had the least respect for the Phoenix. How like them to wallow in indecision while the other clans got things done.

> "So far, none of the clans seem to be aware that you have left our ancestral home, let alone where it is

you have gone. All eyes turn to the Carpenter's Wall, and all feet march that way. It should be nearly a month until the emperor hears that the Crab are not where we ought to be. I presume that before this time your plans will near fruition.

"May the kami of the sea speed you to our rendezvous, and the swift attainment of your karmic reward.

"Your faithful servant, Kuni Yori."

Kisada did not like that final turn of phrase—"karmic reward." It might have been a blessing for a job well done or a curse saying that transgressions would be punished. Kisada would have been happier if he could have at least looked into Yori's eyes as he spoke those words.

Kuni Yori had spent the winter at his lonely tower in the shadow of the Great Wall, continuing his research and experiments. His ability to spy magically on the other clans' winter courts was a great advantage, and other shugenja's abilities to do the same to the court at Kyuden Hida was what made the army's winter in the field absolutely necessary. As long as no one knew where Kisada was, he could not be spied upon.

Kisada rose and opened the tent flap to let in fresh air. The purple smoke lingered unpleasantly.

After a while it became clear that though the smoke's scent was gone from most of the tent, it clung stubbornly to the wood of the altar. Kisada ordered his page to bring him warm water, and he washed the tiny dais, to no effect. Even the scent of the prayer incense did nothing to cut the gagging odor. Finally, he realized that he had no choice but to remove from his tent this last physical reminder of Sukune.

▲▲▲▲▲▲▲▲

"Faster! Faster! Our destiny awaits!" Yakamo beat on the ship's rail as though he could urge the boat on as he would a horse. His right hand only made painful slapping noises. His claw landed with metallic clangs that sent shudders through the hull and splinters flying through the air.

Kisada placed a hand on his son's shoulder.

Yakamo whirled with fire in his eyes. For a second he seemed not to recognize the Great Bear and reached for the tetsubo that was slung across his shoulder. As quickly as it came, though, the madness passed. Yakamo's face flushed with embarrassment, and he bowed to his father.

"My apologies, Tono," he said quietly. "I am merely anxious to see you receive your karmic reward."

Kisada snapped his head to look directly at Yakamo.

"Why did you say that?"

"What?"

"Those words—karmic reward. Why did you use them?"

Yakamo shrugged. "Because I believe it is your karma to be emperor. It is reward for your selfless devotion to the Clan and to the empire."

Kisada nodded, but in his heart he was not convinced.

Yakamo was acting more and more brashly recently. He had always been an aggressive samurai—he came by that trait honestly, from Kisada—but since the beginning of this campaign he seemed to become increasingly restless. The winter layover had been difficult. At first Yakamo fought occasional practice duels with one of the generals or some other skilled warrior. Soon this became a daily ritual. Eventually the young Hida was not content with a single duel. He spent the last month of the winter stalking from campsite to campsite, challenging anyone he met to a duel. He seemed to live for battle.

At first, the Great Bear thought that his son was practicing the way of the berserker, like his cousin Amoro. Kisada soon saw that Yakamo's madness was different than his cousin's.

Amoro loved the thrill of battle, of being surrounded by enemies as far as the eye could see. Yakamo, on the other hand, just wanted to hurt someone. He derived no pleasure from his actions, as if he were merely answering a primal call.

Yakamo was quickly ceasing to be a worthy heir to Kisada's power.

The Great Bear stopped his reverie. His head grew heavy with guilt. He peered over the railing into the sea below.

He is acting just the way I have for the past year, Kisada thought. I have been chasing my own dreams of power, using the clan to get what I selfishly wanted. The Crab will do anything for me. They will lay down their lives because they believe in my vision. My own son died for no reason other than that I asked him to.

"There it is!" Yakamo's voice rousted Kisada from his melancholy reverie.

Looking up, the Great Bear saw the shoreline and a flat stretch of beach. In the distance, the lights of Otosan Uchi twinkled like stars in the early evening sky.

28 ASSAULT ON OTOSAN UCHI

"**B**y nightfall I will no longer be your daimyo!" Wild cheers erupted from the gathered samurai. "Tomorrow and every sunrise after this one I will be Hida the First, Emperor of Rokugan!"

Sound washed over the Great Bear with a physical force he'd never felt before. For a moment, Kisada imagined himself an ascetic standing naked underneath a mountain waterfall. The cheers from his people—*his* people—were like that cold, pounding water, sharpening his senses and bringing him in tune with the world around him. He could feel every pebble beneath his feet, taste the sweat of brave warriors in the air, and see victory lingering just beyond the horizon. His radiant future lit the predawn sky.

"Resistance at the capital should be minimal, but make no mistake: They *will* resist. The people of Otosan Uchi have been lied to for so many years, they will not know the truth when they hear it. They will not recognize that we are doing what is best not only for them, but for all of Rokugan!"

Another cheer went up.

Kisada hated to think of his honorable warriors cutting down a makeshift militia of merchants and stable boys. The city would, of course, muster whatever defenses it could, but Kisada could not let anything or anyone stand in his way. He thought again about Sukune, but without guilt.

"This is my karma! This is our destiny!"

Destiny would not be denied.

The Great Bear had always trusted his instincts before. Why should he doubt them now? Everything was going according to plan. Using the merchant shallows up the coast, the army landed within a day's march of the capital, and no one was the wiser. Toturi's army was busy on the other side of the empire, scouring the Wall in search of the Crab. Otosan Uchi stood ripe for the plucking.

Still the Great Bear hesitated. His son was dead, but his death brought about the union of powers that would make Kisada's ultimate triumph possible. In giving the order that took his son's life, Kisada put in place all the pieces necessary to achieve his karma. And when he sat on the throne and peace reigned over the empire, he would be proven right.

But if he was wrong, the price of his arrogance and greed would be failure, death, and dishonor—not just for himself but for all who followed him.

▲ ▲ ▲ ▲ ▲ ▲ ▲ ▲

Kisada stood atop a hillock overlooking the plains of Otosan Uchi. Rather than being unguarded, the capital city stood defiantly behind an army in tan and brown armor. The Lion Clan stood watch over the city, not in a protective ring, but in a single formation facing directly toward the hill on which the Great Bear stood.

They *knew* the Crab were coming. Somehow they knew—and they were ready.

"How did they know?"

"It does not matter," croaked Yakamo no Oni. The creature had traveled with the army since they left Beiden Pass, but Kisada could never find it when he wanted to. He had no idea how a creature that large could hide so well. Still, it had the singularly annoying habit of showing up whenever it had something *it* wanted to say. "They will not stop you, Father."

"I am *not* your father!" snapped the Great Bear.

The monstrous creature looked more and more like Yakamo every day. The ropy sinews of its body formed an exact replica of his son's posture, musculature, and even his armor. Sometimes Kisada half expected the creature to lift off the skin that formed its "helmet" and reveal a hideous version of Yakamo's face.

"We all are your sons, Tono," said Kuni Yori. "As daimyo of our clan, you are father to us all—at least figuratively." The shugenja was still Kisada's closest adviser though his experimentation had mutilated him terribly and left him with an oozing bloody wreck for a face. The Great Bear was not squeamish, but the fact that Yori continued to spew his overly polite nonsense through that ruined mouth was almost more than he could stand.

"And didn't you teach me that every Crab is my brother?" asked Yakamo. "We live and die as one family. My namesake has joined us in every way he can—I am proud to call him brother."

"It is not a member of our clan. It is *not* a Crab! *None* of those creatures are Crab!"

Yakamo and Yori exchanged worried looks.

"Would you like us to go, Kisada-sama?" Yakamo no Oni asked with painful politeness. "If we are not welcome in your family, we will leave. There is nothing more important than family, Kisada. The more I learn from my connection with your son, the more I understand that truth."

Hai! The word was on Kisada's lips. One simple word, and every last goblin, skeleton, ogre, and zombie would leave with their unholy master. More than anything, Kisada wanted to be rid of the oni—the creature who took the name of one of his sons and the life of the other. Worse, the creature had not taken anything it was not freely offered by Kisada himself.

Hai! One word and all the nagging doubts would go away—the constant reminder of Sukune's death and display on that foul standard.

Hai! The word that would heal the Crab Clan of all the perversions heaped on it in the past three years.

Then the Great Bear looked behind him. His army stretched away as far as the eye could see. Fully half of that army owed their allegiance to Fu Leng. Kisada knew that with only half an army, he might be able to take Otosan Uchi, but he would never hold it.

"Iie," Kisada said quietly. "No, I do not wish you to leave." The Great Bear's shoulders slumped as he spoke.

"You wish us to join your family, then?" Yakamo no Oni asked.

"Hai," said Kisada even more quietly.

The oni smiled. "Good. You have made the right decision, Kisada-sama. Kicking and screaming in protest, yes, but you *have* made the right decision. And I think you will see that before too very long."

▲▲▲▲▲▲▲▲

"Now *this* feels right!" The Great Bear was so eager for battle he could scarcely stand still while his attendants double-checked the straps on his armor. After months of leading his army like a "proper general" (or, as Kisada liked to call such samurai, a "frightened old man"), he was returning to the only place in the world he felt truly at home—in battle. He had been on the road and in the command tent for so long that he had ceased to keep his armor in combat-ready condition. Now, the leather straps biting into the muscled flesh of his arms and legs made his heart beat faster.

"Tono!" Kuni Yori entered the tent without being invited. The man grew bolder every day. Perhaps the fact that no one wanted to look at the shugenja long enough to question him made Yori think he could come and go as he pleased.

Once Kisada sat on the Emerald Throne, he would disabuse his adviser of that notion. "What is it?"

"The Lion forces stand ready to meet ours on the field of battle."

"Idiot!" spat the Great Bear. It was never too early to begin putting Yori back in his place. "I know that."

"Hai, Tono!" Yori said, though it seemed he wanted to say something more acerbic. "But a rider bearing the imperial mon just came out of Otosan Uchi and is even now visiting the Lion command tent."

"What?" thundered the Great Bear, shoving past to stride from the tent flap. "Let me see!"

Kisada's eyes were still as sharp as ever, and they immediately picked out the opposing command tent. Just to the right of it, a page tended a steed bearing a standard with the emblem of the Hantei. It was true.

"What does the emperor have to say at a time like this?" wondered Yakamo, who stood on the ridge nearby.

"More likely the empress," mumbled Kisada. Hantei the 39th did not have enough experience to offer any advice before a battle, let alone *good* advice. His wife, however, was one of the craftiest tacticians in the empire. Anyone who believed otherwise was doomed to be her pawn.

"But what message is she sending?"

"Wait! The messenger is leaving!" shouted Yori pointing excitedly. "And someone is leaving with him."

A stunned silence swept across the group. None of them knew what to make of the scene they witnessed.

"It is Matsu Tsuko," said Yakamo no Oni, who had not been there a moment earlier. "The emperor has ordered the Lion Champion to withdraw from the battle."

The others turned to the creature as one, but only Kisada responded. "What? Why would he do such a thing?"

"Who can say with you humans?" the oni said gazing down at the Lion army. The posture and attitude of all the troops sagged visibly as the news spread through the ranks. "You always seem to do the worst possible things and somehow convince yourself that it will all work out for the best."

Kisada stepped closer to Yakamo no Oni and, though the creature towered over him, looked him square in the eye. "How did you know what went on in that tent?"

The oni shrugged, an all-too-human gesture. "Though I have made a pact with you, I am not without my resources. You would be surprised what the forces of Fu Leng know about the inner workings of your clans. Yet you still manage to hold onto your precious little empire. Isn't that amazing?"

The creature was taunting him. Kisada stood on the verge of launching himself at the beast's head and throat.

"The time to attack is *now*—before the emperor can change his mind!" Yakamo was already swinging his tetsubo in a threatening manner and noisily clicking his claw.

The Great Bear snarled at Yakamo no Oni one last time and then whirled on his heel. "Give the word—the attack begins *now*!"

▲▲▲▲▲▲▲▲

"Such a slaughter. It is not even right to call it a battle—this is a massacre." Kuni Yori stood alone atop the ridge overlooking Otosan Uchi. The fields ran red, and the city itself seemed to quake. The Crab had not yet breached her walls, but that was only because they weren't quite through routing the opposing forces.

Matsu Tsuko's battle plans had been sound enough. At her order, the Lion forces met the Crab head-on, and then split to flank and surround them. Unfortunately for the Lion, Kisada recognized the tactic and ordered his samurai to breach the ring of soldiers and circle toward the point of the Crab attack, thereby making the Lion troops fight a two-front battle.

It was a fairly standard opening gambit. If Tsuko had been there, she would have recovered. But the Lion Champion was forced to watch from a ridge directly across from Yori as her second in command incorrectly guessed Kisada's response and led the Lion troops into the least advantageous position imaginable.

From that point forward the outcome of the battle was never in doubt. Even Kuni Yori could see that.

The shugenja gazed across the field. His eyes stopped on a familiar figure. Hida Yakamo fought in the unusual, brash style he'd adopted since he first donned his claw—whipping his tetsubo about one-handed, throwing his opponents off balance, then reaching in and crushing them with his powerful pincer. He seemed to be having some difficulty finding opponents to face. Many of them took one look at his size and the claw on his left arm and immediately backed away. Yakamo attacked anyway, so cowards died just as quickly as brave warriors—they just didn't see the deathblow coming.

A bit farther to his right, Yori saw Yakamo no Oni. The shugenja had trouble telling the two apart, despite the fact that one was nearly twenty feet tall and had no skin. For that matter, Yori had trouble telling living samurai from undead zombies. He no longer saw with his eyes. Ever since reading the Black Scroll, he saw people not as creatures of flesh and blood but as patterns of energy, glowing balls of spirit in weak fleshy containers. At one point the spirits of Yakamo and Yakamo no Oni were as different as their physical shells. Now they were nearly identical. Yori would have been hard pressed to say which one had changed the most.

Yakamo no Oni terrorized its opponents the way its human counterpart did. It was literally surrounded by Lion samurai hacking at its ropy flanks. Stroke after stroke from enemy katanas, nodachi, and yari bit into the oni's flesh. Most of the blades left no mark whatever—they simply passed though the oni's hide. The few samurai wielding blades that actually hurt the creature died first, but none of the others escaped the oni's monstrous rage either.

Yori scanned the crowd, looking for Hida Kisada. The Great Bear fought in the most crowded, hotly contested, murderous part of the battle. No doubt, Kisada had purposely made his way there. His soul was at peace only when he faced down death. The Great Bear was not suicidal, but he needed to prove his right to live by overcoming bigger and bigger threats to life and limb. This time, he might have stepped too far.

Kisada was surrounded by four reasonably healthy Lion samurai who cared more about bringing down the enemy commander than about their own lives—or honor. In a very unLionlike display, the four attacked Kisada simultaneously.

It might have been fatigue, it might have been mental anguish, or it might simply have been age finally catching up with the Great Bear. Whatever the cause, Kisada was in trouble.

▲▲▲▲▲▲▲▲

Realizing his predicament, Kisada switched tactics. Rather than trying to kill one opponent at a time, he would simply keep them all at bay and maneuver the fight across the terrain. He hoped to run into reinforcements before his attackers broke through his defenses.

The Great Bear swung his tetsubo in a wide circle above his head, feinted at one samurai, then lunged toward another. The whole group moved another fifteen paces toward the city but no closer to Crab troops. The other two Lion samurai lashed out at Kisada. One bounced his katana off the Great Bear's heavy helmet. The other narrowly missed spearing him through the ribcage with a bladed polearm.

Kisada knew he had only one or two passes left before his opponents actually did him serious harm. Desperate times, and the Great Bear responded with a desperate measure. Completely ignoring the other three, he lifted his tetsubo high over his head and charged headlong at the shortest of his opponents. As he had hoped, the man froze in a defensive posture, waiting for a massive swing of the spiked club. Instead, Kisada lowered his shoulder and ran straight into and over the surprised Lion.

The other samurai sprinted after the Great Bear, but he had enough of a head start to reach the top of a ridge. Kisada ran straight into another Lion samurai, this one in a desperate fight for his own life. A trio of Shadowlands zombies shuffled after him, brandishing rusted and chipped katanas.

Kisada struck the man down with a single blow. He turned just in time to block a thrust from the yari-wielding Lion while the other three finished scaling the ridge.

The Crab daimyo was out of options and out of luck. There were no other Crab warriors around, and the zombies would not respond to his orders. He drew his shoulders up to face what would be his final battle.

The Great Bear blocked one katana blow with his tetsubo, neatly sidestepped a second, but was completely immobile when the yari blade stabbed at his throat. With a meaty sound the blade struck home, but Kisada felt no pain.

A zombie had thrown itself before the blade, which even now jutted from its neck.

Not wasting time wondering how or why this had happened, the Great Bear clubbed one Lion so hard his head bent all the way back to touch the middle of his spine. Another Lion stepped under the yari pole—the zombie had tightened its rotting neck muscles to trap the blade—only to be struck down by the zombie's no-dachi.

Kisada leapt at the immobilized owner of the yari. The Lion tried to draw his wakizashi, but the sight of Hida Kisada flying through the air, tetsubo raised for the kill, unnerved the man. The last thing he ever did in this life was fling the short sword away.

The final Lion attacked the zombie. He swung his dai-tsuchi into the undead thing's chest. The warhammer landed with a dry, hollow thud that sent the zombie flying.

Kisada watched uncaring as the Lion chased after his monstrous opponent. He was glad for the rest. Then the Great Bear looked to the ground where the zombie had dropped its no-dachi. The weapon, though badly corroded, seemed familiar. It had once belonged to a friend.

"Waka?" Kisada said aloud. Could that shambling mass of skin and bones be the remains of his old friend?

Another loud thump came as the Lion landed another solid blow on the zombie.

Kisada picked up the fallen yari and flung it, spearing the Lion through the head. The man stood there twitching through his death throes. The Great Bear climbed the hill once again and stood over the fallen zombie.

Reaching down and removing the creature's masked helmet, Kisada gasped as he saw the badly decayed but still recognizable features of his old friend, Hiruma Waka.

"You are a better samurai than I," Kisada said solemnly. "You do not let anything prevent you from your duties. Even in death you protect my life."

The undead Waka had suffered wounds grievous enough to kill any living man, but it was already trying to scramble back to its feet. Kisada handed it the rusted no-dachi.

"Thank you, my friend," Kisada said as the zombie shuffled off to find more Lion warriors to attack.

"Father!"

Kisada turned to see Yakamo.

"The Lion are routed. Nothing stands between us and the city!"

The Great Bear smiled and looked up to the ridge where Matsu Tsuko sat astride her horse. With a brief gesture, he sent the Lion Champion a salute—she would likely interpret it differently—and turned toward Otosan Uchi.

29 FORBIDDEN CITY

I have seen this before." Kisada stood at the Fudotaki Gate at the threshold of the Forbidden City. Over his shoulder he could hear the roar and feel the heat of Otosan Uchi in flames. The fires were not nearly as bad as during the Scorpion Coup, and the Crab and Lion forces ceased their hostilities to put them out before they could get any worse. At least that much was an improvement over the Bayushi debacle. This was a battle for the soul of the empire, not a petty feud over geography.

There were other differences. The gate was barred, but no imperial troops manned the Wall. Kaiu Utsu's troops set up their battering rams without a single arrow fired at them, never having to worry about boiling oil raining down from above. The walls were still sturdy, but the gates fell quickly to the efficient work of the Crab siege master.

"The last time I came here we failed to secure the empire's future," the Great Bear grumbled to himself as he watched the gate fall. "Removing Bayushi was the easy part. We failed to place a strong emperor on the throne. We let the weak son of a feeble dead man take the reins of power, and every Rokugani has suffered for that mistake. Today, I will make things right."

He stepped through the gaping hole Utsu provided and once again trod the hallowed soil of the Forbidden City. The grounds were like a garden, with strategically placed buildings here and there. The Forbidden City was home to the extended imperial family and hundreds of servants and guards. People came and went at all hours of the day.

Now, though, the grounds were eerily silent. Birds chirped in the elms and sandalwood trees, but the only other sound was the crackle and pop of buildings burning outside the walls. The Forbidden City seemed completely abandoned.

"Where is everyone?" Yakamo asked, more disappointed than intimidated by the incredible silence.

"They're here," Kisada said, "but they know they can't beat us."

"Cowards!" shouted Yakamo shaking his claw toward the Imperial Palace. It stood towering over the gardens, indeed over all of Otosan Uchi. From this perspective, trees blocked out all other structures. The palace appeared to be the only building for miles.

"Oh, they will fight," Kisada chuckled. "These Seppun are not like the other clan samurai. They are more like us. They have only one job—to protect the emperor. They will do *whatever* it takes to stop us. Gather all the men under your command, my son. This is where we test our karma!"

Yakamo grunted.

"And what of my troops?" asked Utsu, a twinge of insult showing on his face. Were his troops not good enough to walk inside the Imperial Palace?

Kisada smiled. "A task for which they are well suited—climb the walls and keep the enemy out!"

Utsu barked a laugh that spread among his troops.

▲ ▲ ▲ ▲ ▲ ▲ ▲ ▲

"Father! Behind you!" shouted Yakamo.

The Great Bear raised his tetsubo and whirled.

A samurai dressed all in white stepped into plain sight, katana in hand. The Seppun knew the palace better than anyone. This one had hidden herself in the shadows behind an ancient folding screen and waited patiently for Kisada to pass. She had allowed several other Crab samurai to go by without making a move, but the second she recognized the Crab daimyo, the Seppun stepped free and launched herself at his throat.

Her katana clanged off the Great Bear's club, but the odd angle of the blow knocked him off balance. The Seppun pressed the attack.

Only then did Kisada realize she was not alone. Other Seppun appeared from hiding places all around. The entire length of this hallway was one tremendous ambush, and his troops had walked right into it.

Fighting inside a building, even one as large as the Imperial Palace, was much different than fighting on a battlefield. It called for different formations, strikes, and focus.

The samurai-ko harried the Great Bear with a flurry of quick strikes. None got through his defenses, but the combination kept the Crab on his heels, unable to counterattack. One tetsubo blow would take the Seppun out of the fight, but the great club was not made for fighting in such close quarters. The walls were too close for wide patterns that kept opponents at arm's length, and the ceiling was too low for an overhead strike to smash through a foe's defenses.

Behind him Yakamo had the same trouble. His extraordinarily tall, powerful body made it nearly impossible to fight effectively in the halls of the Imperial Palace. Yakamo at least had his claw, though. The unholy relic proved quite useful in close quarters.

A male Seppun appeared behind Yakamo and nearly split his spine with a quick strike. The young Hida narrowly avoided the blow by throwing himself against a door frame, rattling the hall with his impact. Wielding his huge weapon one-handed, Yakamo could not get the heavy club head around fast enough to counter the katana. He had to resort to using his claw as a parrying weapon.

Kisada stepped closer to his opponent, close enough that it became difficult to swing even a katana. His left hand grabbed the top end of his tetsubo. Several of the iron spikes bit into his palm. The Great Bear thrust the club forward and pressed the Seppun's blade back toward her chest. With a quick twist of his wrists, he locked the katana between three of the tetsubo's spikes. The two opponents stood face to face. Neither could move without giving the other a fateful opening. It now became a contest of brute strength, and Kisada far outclassed his opponent.

Bending his knees, the Great Bear moved in even closer. Now he looked *up* into the samurai-ko's eyes. He could see fear there. She knew what he was about to do. The Seppun tried to lean backward while still keeping the tetsubo immobilized, but she only succeeded in throwing herself off balance.

Kisada tensed his biceps and extended his arms in a powerful push. He had hoped to knock the samurai-ko onto her back, but his thrust actually sent her flying through the air.

Her arms pinwheeled. She dropped her katana and tumbled away from her opponent. With a raucous sound of snapping wood and shredding paper, the Seppun smashed through a fusuma and landed hard in a tatami room. She rose quickly, but her posture showed that her shoulder was useless.

Stepping out of the hallway, he swung at her head. Even injured as she was, the samurai-ko ducked the blow. She did not, however, avoid the kick the Great Bear launched at her midsection. A rush of air fled her lungs, and she landed on her wounded shoulder. The pain was incredible, but it didn't last long.

Kisada brought the head of his tetsubo down in an overhead strike that released the Seppun from all worldly pain.

The battle continued in the hallway, and the Great Bear was about to step back into the fray when he noticed that the room in which he stood was enclosed on two other sides by fusuma. This was part of a long series of tatami rooms that served as meeting, dining, or sleeping quarters as needed. They could also have their fusuma removed to turn them into a single great hall for banquets and other celebrations.

He looked to Yakamo, who still pitted his claw against the Seppun's katana.

"Come here, boy!" Kisada shouted. "I've found our path to the throne room!"

Yakamo smiled as though he'd been playing with his opponent all along. He snapped his wrist and flicked his tetsubo up to block the katana blade. The blow knocked the Seppun's blade aside while Yakamo reached out with his open claw and crushed the samurai's throat and jaw.

"Come, Father, there are more imperial bugs to crush!" Yakamo said urging the Great Bear to return to the battle.

"No," Kisada said. "The hallways are guarded. We can bypass their defenses the way we Crab know best—by taking the path no one else will walk!"

Tatami rooms were considered islands of refinement and propriety. One did not wear shoes on the straw mats, and one certainly did not run through them brandishing weapons. Simply having someone tread a sandaled foot on one mat meant the entire room's tatami needed to be replaced. So strong was the taboo that it was generally observed even in the heat of battle.

"Will we run from battle?" Yakamo asked.

"No," his father answered. "We will run *to* battle!"

With one firm swing he knocked down the fusuma at one end of the room and stepped into the next. Yakamo followed.

Kisada shouldered through the next set of fusuma, building up speed as he went. Trotting, then running full out and barreling through rice paper screens. In one room he came across handmaidens who scattered to the far wall as he charged through. Another room contained old men, servants or perhaps gardeners, who threw themselves at the invader's feet to slow them down. All they got for their efforts were Hida sandalprints on their skulls and a sharp rap in the ribs from the blunt end of a tetsubo.

When Kisada finally burst through into a wooden hallway again, he stood facing the stairs to the throne room.

"Ai! Invaders!" shouted an imperial guard stationed at the base of the stairs.

Two more guards came from the next floor up. They stood and pointed yari toward the Hidas.

The first guard pulled out his katana and was about to charge Kisada when a soft, melodious voice called out from behind him.

"Stand aside," the voice was at once dainty and as sharp as honed steel.

"My lady—" one yari-wielding samurai began, but he was immediately cut off.

"Your orders are to guard me." The voice moved closer. "And I do not think the Great Bear came all this way to threaten a poor, neglected woman."

Another form stepped into view at the top of the stairs—a distinctly feminine form clothed in a scarlet kimono. "Did you, Kisada-sama?" Stepping into the light, Lady Kachiko smiled demurely at the Great Bear as though they were at an imperial feast, not in the midst of a bloody revolution. Her eyes were covered in a mask of gauze and paint, yet she seemed to be baring her soul to the Crab daimyo.

"My goal today is the Emerald Throne," he growled. "*You* are a matter to be dealt with later."

Kachiko laughed lightly. "My husband, it seems, shares your opinion. He has locked himself in his audience chamber these past five days and ordered that no one disturb him."

"Not even the empress!" said one guard, but he sank back into silence when Kachiko shot him a withering glare.

"I am surprised, given his fragile health, that he could stand such rigorous isolation."

"Not as surprised as I am," Kachiko said mysteriously. "But we know he is alive and robust, for every time we send a servant in to check on the emperor's health he sends the poor man out with a string of curses I daresay would embarrass even *you*, Kisada-sama."

"I think you will find me less easily shocked than you believe, Kachiko-san," Kisada said. "Not to mention more ambitious."

The Great Bear motioned to Yakamo, and the two moved toward the stairs. The three guards stood their ground.

"Do not make me kill you, too," he said.

"Stand aside," Kachiko ordered them again. "You have heard the emperor just as clearly as I—he awaits Kisada-sama's arrival."

"He expects us?" Yakamo asked.

"Hai," Kachiko replied. "That is why he locked himself in the audience chamber."

"He knew five days ago that we were coming?" Five days earlier they had not yet left the Mantis Isles.

"Hai."

Kisada grunted.

"You will not stand in our way?" Yakamo asked, seeming somewhat disappointed. He twirled his tetsubo and clicked his claw absently.

"Iie!" Kachiko said, giving special attention to her guards. "The emperor awaits you—who are we to oppose his wishes?"

Kisada grunted again and motioned to the audience chamber.

"And when will you decide my fate, oh soon-to-be emperor?" Kachiko asked, taking the Great Bear's massive arm in her delicate fingers.

He shrugged her off.

"This will not take long."

30 THE EMPEROR'S NEW SKIN

The emperor's audience chamber was perhaps the single most ostentatious room in all of Rokugan. The walls were covered in murals depicting the history of the empire from the day the children of Lord Moon and Lady Sun fell to earth, through to the assassination of the Hantei the 38th and the ascension of the current emperor. The braziers, created by the greatest metallurgists and sculptors who ever drew breath, stood unlit in a long row down the center of the chamber.

The focus of the entire space was a raised square dais about seven feet on a side. The dais had rice paper walls erected around it and a single set of shoji allowing entrance. The ostentatious audience room was for the emperor's guests, but the pure and austere room upon the dais was for the emperor himself. Only the most honored and respected guests were ever invited onto the tatami where thirty-nine generations of Hantei had sat upon the Emerald Throne— the very symbol of the empire.

The audience chamber was dark as Kisada and Yakamo entered. Flickering light filtered through the slanted wooden window screens. It danced on the solid gold braziers, glinted off the gold foil and precious stones set into the murals, and caressed the audience chamber like a lover returned from war. It did not, however, touch the central dais at all.

"That is the most beautiful sight I have ever seen."

As artful as the room was, Yakamo referred to the view from the window on the west wall.

Kisada looked to his left, to the very window where nearly three years ago the Lady Scorpion urged him toward this day. The fires of battle lit the skyline of Otosan Uchi. Several buildings in the poorer districts still burned, though none of the blazes seemed out of control. The firelight showed that the Lion army and imperial guard still fought their losing battle against the Crab and Shadowlands forces. In the flickering light, even Kisada's own samurai seemed monstrous and deformed. They looked more like a force of invaders than an army of liberators.

"It is nothing compared to the beauty you will see when our enemy's head adorns the gate of the Forbidden City," the Great Bear growled. Then he shouted, "This is the end, Hantei! I will spill your thin, weak blood across the throne your family has held for too long. Rokugan will have the strong leader it has desperately needed for so long."

The Crab daimyo stomped loudly as he approached the dais. He swung his tetsubo in lazy circles, not for any military purpose but just to fill the otherwise silent room with quiet swooshes that would unnerve anyone trying desperately *not* to become the weapon's target. Kisada wanted the cowardly emperor to *know* the Great Bear was coming for him.

Yakamo followed his father and matched him move for move. His left hand itched, a sensation he hadn't felt since his battle with Mirumoto Hitomi. There was an energy in the air—something raw that made the hair on his arms stand up.

This must be what it feels like to reach your karma.

"Come out, little emperor, and I will make your death painless, which is more than you deserve." The Great Bear stalked behind the dais and thrust his tetsubo through one of the shoji. It struck nothing.

Sounds filtered through the window—the clash of steel on steel, the howl of dying men, and the rumble of beasts feasting on human flesh.

"Do you hear that, little emperor?" Kisada teased. "That is the sound of the death of your family. That is the dirge for the Hantei. Isn't it beautiful?"

Yakamo seemed on the verge of adding his own taunts, but something prevented his lips from moving.

The Great Bear prowled back to the center of the audience chamber. The wretched Hantei still remained silent. Was it possible that hunger had gotten to the emperor before Kisada did? Was Hantei the 39th simply lying on the floor of his tatami dais waiting for death to come?

No. The throne—the malnourished whelp must quite literally be slumped in his seat of power, too weak even to whimper in his own defense.

The Great Bear stepped up to the emperor's dais, pulled the doors wide, and gazed into the darkness.

Two glowing red eyes looked back.

The flickering light barely penetrated the dais. It glinted weakly off the Emerald Throne where Kisada could barely make out the Hantei's fragile body sitting calmly. The emperor's eyes, though, glowed like hot coals.

"Things are not always what they seem, Kisada-san, but you should be used to that by now." The voice belonged to the young emperor, but it was rougher than Kisada had ever heard before, as though he had been praying over heavy incense all day. The words reverberated in the audience chamber, a rumbling echo that lasted too long.

"What do you mean?" asked Kisada. Then with a confidence he no longer felt he added, "Tell me quickly. My urge to kill you is far stronger than my curiosity."

"The Shadowlands are your most hated enemy, and yet they are your most faithful allies," whispered the emperor. The sound filled the room. What's more, he seemed to be laughing at the same time. "Your most sacred duty is to guard the borders of the empire, yet you've spent the last year fighting battle after battle against Rokugani citizens. Your sons are the most important part of your life, yet you killed one and allowed the other to be turned into a monstrous freak. Your most trusted adviser uses magic so black that his own body rejects him, yet you keep him close to your bosom."

Hantei stood and stepped into the light cast by the burning capital. He was still a slight, sickly bodied young man, but his entire frame brimmed with power. In his hands, he held a sheathed sword—the Ancestral Sword of the Hantei—and Kisada could tell he knew how to use it.

The emperor continued in a hypnotic voice, "Things are not what they seem—*you* are not what you seem."

The Great Bear laughed. "I am exactly what I seem. I am the man who is about to kill the last Hantei!"

Yakamo stood rooted to the ground, immobile and turnedand then completely silent. The itching in his arm turned to a dull ache.

"The last Hantei is already dead," said the emperor. "*I* killed him!"

The boy was mad. Kisada considered whether this made him more or less of a threat. "And who are you?" he asked, stretching his arm and tetsubo back behind his left ear.

The emperor's eyes flashed fire.

"I am Fu Leng!"

A thunderous retort filled the air and flames shot high into the night sky as one of the burning buildings collapsed under its own weight. The fire was spreading.

"The Dark God seated on the Emerald Throne?"

"Who better? You?" Fu Leng laughed. "Little Crab, you cannot even remain true to your little clan. How could you possibly rule an empire? You built your life, your world around one duty, one precept—and a simple one at that—to protect the borders of Rokugan from evil. What did you do? For the sake of your own personal power you turned your back on everything that gave your life meaning."

The Great Bear fell as silent as his son.

"At least I am true to myself—I *am* evil! You threw away your duty, honor, and family for the sake of avarice. Very soon your greed will cost you your life as well."

Kisada raised his hand to object, but his conscience would not let him. He thought back to every compromise he had made: his decision not to kill the oni; his permission for Yakamo to give his name to that same creature; his abandonment of the Great Kaiu Wall—his Wall; his march arm-in-arm with his most hated enemy to overthrow the ruler of the Emerald Empire. He listened to Kuni Yori, he listened to the Lady Scorpion, he even listened to a demon, but never once did he listen to his youngest son—to his own heart.

Now this truly was his karma—he would reap what he sowed. But all of Rokugan need not pay the price for his folly. At the very least he could prevent that.

Throwing aside his tetsubo, Kisada reached to his hip and drew the katana his father handed to him on the day he took the reins of the Crab Clan—the very same sword that the first Hida used against the minions of Fu Leng—the Ancestral Sword of the Crab.

"I may have lost my way," Kisada roared, "but with my remaining son at my side I will send you back to the darkness from which you crawled, Dark One!"

Had he looked to his son, Kisada would have seen a man a motionless as a statue. Even so, he could not have heard what the Dark God whispered in Yakamo's mind.

Be still, Little Crab. You do not think I would allow you to use my own gift against me, did you?

The claw on his left arm slowly clicked open and closed. Each snap sent fire up Yakamo's arm, but he could say nothing. He pleaded with his eyes for his father to notice, but Kisada remained completely unaware.

Kisada stood with his weight centered on his left foot and slid his right toward Fu Leng. He raised his ancestral sword so that it hung parallel to his right ear and pointed at his most hated enemy. A classic dueling stance, and one he had not used since his days as a student.

"It is not too late. We will redeem ourselves!"

He lowered his weight onto his right foot and spun toward his opponent. Another classic maneuver—he now held the katana low and came from a strong left stance. The purpose was to throw his opponent off guard.

Fu Leng only stood there, holding the still-sheathed Sword of the Hantei and wearing the emperor's malicious smile. "It *is* too late, little Crab."

Kisada focused his chi in his stomach and launched himself in an acrobatic series of leaps, striking at the enemy with each one.

Though Fu Leng never moved, his power deflected each blow. "It is far too late for you to do anything—except die."

With one fluid motion, the Dark God drew the sword that symbolized the honor of all of Rokugan and thrust it through Hida Kisada.

▲▲▲▲▲▲▲▲

"Look at them run!" Kaiu Utsu rarely got to see the tail end of a battle. Being the clan siege master meant being on the front lines, finding a way to punch through the enemy's defenses, and stepping out of the way once a breach was established. Other samurai specialized in exploiting the hard-earned weakness. Utsu and his men were far too valuable to risk in the unpredictable ebb and flow of melee. Their specialties would be needed again the next day.

Today, though, every Crab's duty was to crush the Lion and imperial forces. Today, as night fell, Utsu finally knew what it felt like to *be* the victor!

"It is a curiously appealing sight," said Yakamo no Oni.

"I don't suppose it's one either of us is likely to forget," added Utsu. "This may well be the most important day in the history of the empire!"

"Of that I am certain," replied the oni as it looked toward the heart of Otosan Uchi.

With a sound like thunder in the mountains, a building not two blocks from where they stood exploded. Gouts of flame shot into the air, and the roar of the collapsing structure echoed for miles.

"I wonder what caused that," said Utsu. "The building didn't look *that* unstable."

"Many things are less stable than they seem," said the oni. Utsu's attention was too focused on the ruined structure to see that the creature's grin had turned menacing.

▲▲▲▲▲▲▲▲

"Noooooooo!"

Fire flowed through Hida Yakamo's veins as he willed his magically petrified limbs out of their frozen positions. He heard tendons stretch and muscles pop—sounds that reminded him too keenly of the Shadowlands creature to whom he'd given his name. Only in the past few minutes did the young samurai realize how much power he'd given the oni and how deeply he'd steeped his own soul in the power of Fu Leng.

The Ancestral Sword of the Crab clattered to the floor, released from Hida Kisada's hand as he hung helplessly on the hilt of the Dark God's katana.

One step.

"Your days are through, Kisada," Fu Leng said. "You made the same mistake that all humans do—you thought that you could make a difference."

Another step.

"The funny thing is, you can make a difference. And you certainly did, oh Lord of the Crabs." The Dark God laughed.

Another step . . . and another.

"What you didn't know was that the only way to accomplish good is to work with your rivals. If you had put aside your differences and worked together, I could never have achieved what I did."

Two more steps, following closer together.

"Instead you did what the rest did—what humans *always* do—you believed that your vision was somehow superior to that of your fellows. You decided that everything would be all right if only people would listen to you. And you acted on that wholly selfish belief."

Step after step after step.

The creature that once was Hantei the 39th twisted the sword in the Great Bear's belly, but Kisada did not make a sound.

"It is too bad that a lesson like this will do you no good. Not in this life anyway." Despite the frailty of his host body, Fu Leng raised the sword, and the Crab daimyo, high over his head. "However, with the karmic debt you have amassed, Kisada-sama, I'm certain you will be back to fight this fight again. Good-bye."

Yakamo lowered his shoulder, willed his feet to keep moving, and plowed headlong into the Dark God. Taken completely unawares, Fu Leng released Kisada. The force of Yakamo's blow flung the Dark God through the air. He tumbled over the Emerald Throne and crashed violently through the rear wall of the emperor's dais.

The young Hida caught his injured father and laid him gently on the floor.

"I am sorry, Father," Yakamo said. He collapsed in absolute pain. Once again, he was held completely immobile. He could see blood flowing down the length of the blade that protruded from Kisada's gut.

Fu Leng rose to his feet and held a clenched fist in Yakamo's direction. A wrinkle formed between his glowing red eyes, and suddenly Yakamo's claw moved of its own volition. It opened wide and placed itself around the young samurai's throat.

"Shall I have you kill yourself—in a most dishonorable fashion—or shall I just give the rest of your soul to my minion? Perhaps I should let you choose."

Yakamo howled. "Do what you will and be done with it! There is nothing I can do!"

It is that *particular belief,* said a voice as light as silver, *that led both you and our father to this terrible state.*

"Sukune?"

Who else, Brother? answered the silver voice. A spectral image shimmered into existence next to the trapped Yakamo.

"Help me," begged the older sibling. "Save me. Save our father. You are the clan's only hope."

That may have been true while I was alive, corrected the ghostly Sukune, *but no longer. You killed the hope I represented the same day you killed me. Now it is up to you.*

Yakamo fought with all his will against the burning grip that held him in place, but it was no use.

"I cannot move," Yakamo whined.

Perhaps, then, you are doomed, said Sukune. *Will you simply lie there and accept this fate? Is this what karma has brought you?*

The floor shook with the weight of Fu Leng's approach.

"No!" cried Yakamo. "I will not give up! I will not surrender! I will fight to my last breath, and then fight on until my spirit no longer haunts this world."

Yes, answered Sukune. *That is the answer. That is the way of the Crab. Find a way to win, no matter what.*

"If we fail, the empire falls!"

Look at what has happened here, he said somberly. *We succeeded, and the empire is about to fall. It is not required that the Crab win, only that we fight indomitably for the right cause!*

Yakamo could see Fu Leng's foot. The Dark God was nearly on top of him.

"The empire," said the older brother. "The empire is the unity of the clans. We can overcome anything as long as we face it together."

Correct.

Fu Leng stopped directly above Yakamo. He picked up Kisada's fallen tetsubo and raised it high over his head.

"Hopefully, I will remember this lesson in my next life," said Yakamo.

The light from burning Otosan Uchi shone on the spikes of the Dark God's weapon. It descended.

With a brilliant flash of the purest white light, Sukune materialized kneeling above his brother. He had no weapon, but he reached up and grabbed Fu Leng's wrists and wrestled him to the far side of the room. Flames shot out wherever the two beings touched.

Consider this my final act of obedience to the clan, Brother. After this, I have other battles to fight.

Yakamo's limbs came free.

Nothing has changed yet, said Sukune as he struggled with the Dark God. *It is up to you to act. Do not shame the clan!*

A tremendous burst of flame leaped from the pair onto the wooden floor of the audience chamber. The Imperial Palace was burning.

"I won't," Yakamo began to say, but both his brother and Fu Leng had disappeared.

31 ONE WRONG STEP

I t's not over. It's not over."

With his right arm wrapped around Kisada's chest, Yakamo dragged his unconscious father through a gauntlet of corpses. As near as he could tell, every Crab and every Seppun involved in their earlier battle had died in this hallway.

Flames licked the walls, and smoke crawled along the ceiling. All sound from the outside world was drowned out by the conflagration in the audience chamber. Whatever the outcome of Sukune's battle with the Dark God, the Imperial Palace would not survive the conflict.

Did they fight still?

Can a ghost be killed? Yakamo wondered. What would happen to his brother? And what were these "other battles" he mentioned?

Like so much about his younger sibling, these questions would remain mysteries. Yakamo had to concentrate on getting himself and his father out of the burning castle.

Dragging Kisada was tougher work than Yakamo had expected—particularly because he refused to allow his defiled left arm to touch his injured father. Fu Leng had used the claw to control Yakamo, to wrack his body with pain and hold him immobile and practically insensate. There was no telling *what* the Dark God might be able to do if that same appendage even brushed the injured Kisada.

Yakamo looked back down the hallway. They left a wide, wet trail of blood as they went. His father's injuries were grave. Yakamo had left the sword of the Hantei impaled in Kisada's gut, afraid that removing it would simply make his father bleed to death. If he were not tended to soon, the Great Bear would surely die.

"I am not ready to lead the clan, Tono," Yakamo whispered to his unconscious father's ear. "I cannot do what you did—I am too weak."

Kisada stirred, his eyes clouded by pain.

"No one is every ready . . . my son," he croaked. "Look at me. I led the Crab for twenty years . . . and still I was not prepared. All you can do is follow your heart. . . . That was my biggest mistake, doing what seemed right instead of what felt right. . . ."

Yakamo's head drooped.

"Do not give up, Yakamo. It is never too late. You can undo the wrongs I have done . . . if you root out the evil and remove it completely. . . ."

Yakamo looked at his left arm and the abomination strapped there.

"There is nothing you cannot live without . . ." whispered Kisada, "as long as you have your honor. . . ."

The Great Bear's eyes rolled back, and he collapsed again.

The ceiling beams groaned loudly. They popped and shifted, showering father and son in embers and ash. It would not be long before the entire roof collapsed.

Yakamo tightened his grip around Kisada's chest and pulled harder. They were almost to the stairs that would take them down three more floors. At least then, the young Hida could catch his breath without fear of the ceiling falling on his head. The Dark God's influence had not only taken his will but also sapped his strength. In the back of his mind, the claw cried out to be used.

I can lift your poor dead father, it seemed to say.

"He's not dead!" Yakamo cried out and leaned his weight toward the stairs.

Not yet, the claw seemed to answer. *But you both will be soon unless you get out. I can get you out. I can help. Let me help you.*

The call of the claw was alluring, too alluring. Yakamo had become the living embodiment of all that was wrong with the clan.

"No!" the young Crab growled. "We will make it, and we will do it without your help!"

So it would be. He would get himself and his father safely out. He would purge the clan of the evil that infected it and *make* things right.

Yakamo's foot caught on the outstretched arm of a fallen Seppun—or had Fu Leng ordered the guard to grab his ankle in the first throes of her new unlife? The young Hida held tightly to his father as he fell toward the floor. Rather than sprawling across the bodies, he found himself tumbling end over end down the stairs, dragging his wounded father behind him.

They bounced off several stairs, smacked into the wall, and finally fell off the unguarded side of the staircase. Father and son landed in a twisted heap on the hardwood floor ten feet below. Though he fell on his right side, Yakamo felt stabbing pain run up and down his left arm.

"You seem to need some help."

"No!" Yakamo barked. The voice had changed—become softer, more seductive.

"You are in no shape to refuse. Besides, I am indebted to your father for not killing me when he had the chance—and I detest being obliged to anyone."

It was Bayushi Kachiko, the Lady Scorpion. Without saying another word, she wrapped her lithe arms around Kisada's massive legs and lifted with a strength Yakamo would not have thought she had.

"Neither of us can do this alone, Yakamo," she said sternly. "And at this point I don't think either of us will leave your father here to die. So I suggest you pick up your end and we begin working *together*."

The young Hida considered whether this was another test of his character, but decided that such questions were best examined after they were safely out of the fire's reach.

▲▲▲▲▲▲▲▲

"The emperor is dead." Kachiko smiled as she said the words. "Kisada killed him, and now all of Rokugan will pay the price!"

"No!" cried Yakamo. "Kisada did *not* kill the emperor."

"Are you saying that my husband is alive?" She dropped the Great Bear's feet and crouched. She seemed to be contemplating running back up into the burning building.

"No longer, not in any real sense," he answered, as he gathered Kisada in his arms. "The emperor is dead, but his body is not. Fu Leng has taken control of it, like some disgusting puppet."

"Replaced by the Dark God?" the Lady Scorpion said. "When did this happen? How long ago?"

"Who can say," Yakamo answered, clearly unimpressed with Kachiko. After all he'd heard about this woman, he'd have expected her not to fall apart at such a crucial moment.

"This explains so much," she whispered. Losing all interest in Kisada, she rose and gazed up to the castle's peak, which was now completely engulfed in roaring flames. "Is he still up there?"

Yakamo grunted.

"Yes. May he burn here before he burns in Jigoku."

The Lady Scorpion was mesmerized.

"The empire is dead," she whispered.

"The imperial residence is aflame and beyond all hope of recovery," Yakamo said. "The capital itself is ruined, through actions I am shamed to have led. But the empire lives on. Rokugan will survive."

The sounds of battle no longer rang in the streets surrounding the Forbidden City. Peace reigned within the capital.

"Yakamo-sama! Yakamo-sama!" A Crab samurai came running through the smashed Fudotaki Gate.

"Call the healers. Our daimyo has been hurt—he requires immediate attention!"

"No one is left in the city. They have all fallen back to the Otosan Uchi plain," puffed the man, trying to catch his breath. "You had better come there, Yakamo-sama—there is something you must see."

"Bring the Bayushi bitch with us," Yakamo muttered. "She has much to answer for."

"There is no one here, Tono."

"Do not call me that!" snapped the young Hida. "My father is still the daimyo!"

"Hai!" the man said bowing deeply. He shook his head ruefully as he assessed Kisada's wounds.

The man's other words finally sank in. Yakamo looked around—Kachiko was nowhere to be seen. The Lady Scorpion had escaped again. The only place for her to go was back into the burning Imperial Palace. The young Crab turned his back on her.

"She will bother us no more," he said.

32 THE PATH OF HONOR

hank the kami my father cannot see this. If Fu Leng did not kill him, this sight surely would."

Yakamo stood on the ramparts of Otosan Uchi's main wall. He looked out on the plain where earlier that very day the Crab army had routed their Lion opponents. The plain was a mass of chaos. Minor skirmishes flared here and there, and two conflicts nearly worthy of being called battles raged at the very edges of the field.

Had the Lion army received reinforcements? No. While a few Lion warriors remained in the turmoil, most of the combatants were Crab samurai or Shadowlands monsters.

Then it dawned on Yakamo. "A-are our samurai fighting other Crab samurai?"

"Hai!" said the young man who had led him to the wall.

"How?" demanded the enraged Hida. "How did this happen?"

The soldier was too shaken to say anything. He simply pointed toward the plain, toward a tremendous figure that looked exactly like Yakamo himself, only larger and even more powerful.

"Oni!" Yakamo shouted. His voice took on an unnatural quality—more resonant and powerful than it had ever been before. It echoed across the field, rolling over the noises of battle and leaving an unexpected hush in its wake.

All the fighting stopped. All movement stopped. There was nothing—nothing but the two Yakamos staring at one another across a blood-soaked field.

"What is the meaning of this?" Kisada's son demanded.

With great, loping strides the oni approached the wall. It clambered up the berm and rose to its full height. The two Yakamos were nearly eye-to-eye. It smiled and cocked its head.

"Word has spread that the last Hantei is dead," it said with no trace of remorse. "They say that Fu Leng inhabits his body and sits on the throne—a powerful man who will rule the empire with strength and dignity for a thousand years."

"Who says these things?"

The oni smiled again.

"I do!" answered Kuni Yori, who had appeared on the rampart next to Yakamo. His voice also echoed across the field for all to hear. Clearly the shugenja had cast a spell so that the assembled armies could hear this conversation. "The weakling Hantei is dead, replaced by a strong presence—a presence with which we are already allied."

The words hit the young Hida like a tetsubo. He took a step backward, nearly tumbling off the Wall.

"What's more, the Great Bear is dead—or as good as dead," the shugenja looked to the street below, where healers tended Kisada. The old man was alarmingly pale. From this height it was difficult to tell if he were still breathing. "The Crab Clan requires guidance. The soldiers are uncertain what to do."

"We must rally our forces," Yakamo said, keenly aware that every samurai in his army could hear his words. He was not ready to lead—not in his heart—but he had no choice. "The Dark God

Fu Leng sits on the Emerald Throne. We must gather our strength to drive him out!"

"And replace him with whom?" asked Yori. "Kisada is dead."

"Stop saying that!"

"We must face facts," the shugenja said not unkindly. To the others he must seem to be consoling Yakamo, but the young Hida saw the mocking twinkle in Yori's eye. "The Great Bear was a man the other clans could accept on the throne. You, though every inch his son, do not yet have Kisada's presence and authority. You would be just another usurper—and one they would overthrow. If your father's death, indeed his entire life, is not to have been in vain, we must continue down the path he chose."

Yakamo growled at Yori. The shugenja's eyes widened, and he took a step back. Yakamo turned to face the oni and fixed it with a similar glare—one that vowed defiance no matter what the cost.

Placing both hands on the Wall, he spoke.

"We have gone the wrong way," he said, his voice reaching every ear on the field. "We came to a fork in the road, and we chose the wrong path."

Kuni Yori waved his hands as if casting a spell—or perhaps breaking the one that allowed Yakamo's voice to be heard. The young Hida shot the shugenja another dangerous glare, and Yori ceased.

"No, that's not right," Yakamo continued, his voice still echoing. "*You* did nothing wrong. You followed your daimyo. You remained loyal to your clan. You acted in exactly the way samurai should. After all, my father is a great man—a great daimyo. He saw a chance to change the empire for the better, and he took it. And we took it with him. We used every tool possible to achieve his goal for the sake of the Crab Clan, for all of Rokugan. After all, if we fail, the empire falls."

A murmur of agreement rolled across the field.

"Well we have succeeded—and the empire is about to fall!"

Silence.

"Our daimyo . . ." He paused. "My father stormed the Imperial Palace and discovered the last Hantei completely in the thrall of Fu Leng. He uncovered a plot that threatens the future of Rokugan. But he was wrong to do so!"

The crowd grumbled in confusion.

"How can that be?" called out a samurai at the bottom of the Wall.

"Because he should never have been in Otosan Uchi to begin with," answered Yakamo. "The Dark God needed our help to shatter the empire. Fu Leng is not strong enough to break the bonds between the clans. Only our own greedy souls could do that.

"The Crab have *one* duty—we have always had just one duty—to stand on a wall and protect the empire from the evil of Fu Leng. It is not our job to right the injustices or inequities within the empire itself. No, our job is to protect the land, the people, and the spirit that is Rokugan so that we all can find our way without being crushed by the evil outside.

"My father failed to remember that duty, and so we have failed to carry it out."

A faint, mournful wind blew across the plain.

"Some say that the hardest part about living an honorable life is never giving in to temptation. They are wrong. The hardest part is picking yourself up after you've failed, standing up, and resuming your place on the Wall."

The crowd murmured, but whether in agreement or dissent remained unclear.

"I fell off the Wall just like the rest of the clan, but the proof of my fall is much more evident!" Yakamo raised his left arm in the air, showing the vile claw to the crowd. "I lost my hand in a fair duel. Instead of bearing my wound with pride and honor, I invited evil and dishonor into my very body."

Some of the samurai raised their katanas and other weapons above their heads and shouted encouragement. Others scuffed their feet and spat on the ground. Yakamo could get no sense which group was in the majority.

"My father's adviser," he said glaring menacingly at Yori, "would have you believe that we have no choice other than to continue down the path we're on, despite how wrong that path is.

But we do have a choice. We can choose to do what is right and honorable, no matter how difficult it might be—no matter how far we've wandered, and no matter what the other clans think of us. There are many other choices we can make, but there is only one right choice."

Yakamo now raised his right hand. In it he held the Ancestral Sword of the Crab Clan. With a mighty swing, he struck the bindings that held the claw to his left arm. Pain wracked his body, and the leather straps bled a thick, black ooze where the sword had struck. Still the claw remained attached.

"Hida Kisada made a wrong choice—one single wrong choice—a small step off the path of honor. It led to other choices and on to others, each but a small step away, but it was that one first wrong step that led us to this day—led me to this state."

Again Yakamo raised the blade, this time striking the straps where they connected to the claw. Sparks flew as he struck again and again until at last the straps fell from his arm to the ground below.

Cheers rose from at least half of the assembled Crab, but they quickly transformed into gasps of horror. The Shadowlands forces, on the other hand, winced in pain as Yakamo struck the claw but cried in glee when they saw what had silenced the samurai.

Though the straps were gone, the claw itself clung tenaciously to Yakamo's arm. The metal dug into the flesh where his wrist used to be and held tight, like a drowning man clinging to a log. And where it touched him, Yakamo's skin had turned black and putrid.

"But it is not too late. We cannot undo all the harm done to the empire and to our own spirits in the past two years, but we can return to that right path. We can do what must be done."

The Shadowlands creatures nervously huddled together. Trying not to attract attention, they shifted toward samurai who seemed unhappy with Yakamo's speech.

"My father's mistake was in not listening to the opinion of his adviser, nor accepting this *creature's* aid." He pointed his weapon toward the oni. "No, the mistake he made was sitting eye to eye with this monster—to whom I later gave my name—and not immediately splitting its skull!"

Yakamo no Oni seethed with fury. It reached up toward its namesake, tendrils writhing, transforming its hands into claws.

With a smile, Hida Yakamo raised the Ancestral Sword of the Crab Clan over his head. He held it there as if frozen in time, then brought it crashing down on his own arm with all the strength he could muster.

Yakamo no Oni flinched and clutched its chest.

Kuni Yori disappeared from the Wall as quickly and mysteriously as he'd arrived.

Hida Yakamo howled in triumph.

The claw fell to the battlement, dripping the last of its black life out onto the cold Rokugani stone.

Yakamo's arm bled again, his wound reopened by the katana, but it was a good, rich blood—red like the coming dawn.

"There is no mistake that cannot be redressed. Our karma is what we have made it—it is not beyond correction. I don't know about the rest of you," Yakamo said through clenched teeth, "but I intend to do what's *right*!"

Thousands of voices, loyal Crab voices, raised a mighty "Banzai!"

Yakamo clutched his father's sword in his one good hand and threw himself off the battlement toward the startled oni.

33 LEAP OF FAITH

"**B**ack! Back to the unholy pit that spawned you!"

Yakamo landed on the oni and swung his ancestor's sword with reckless abandon. Though he had only one arm and fought with a weapon he hadn't wielded in years, the ferocity of his blows forced his foe to the defensive.

The katana was the traditional sword of the samurai—indeed, it represented his very soul. The young Hida considered the fact that he had kept his katana in its sheath for so many years, occasionally taking it out and polishing it but never actually putting it to use. It was a decoration to him, another piece of ceremonial gear to be strapped onto his armor each day.

But in this darkest hour, when the fate of the entire clan hung on his action, the Ancestral Sword of the Crab Clan felt like an extension of his arm. Unlike the thrice-damned claw, the katana did not come with any pain or imbalance.

It simply filled his heart with light and gave him the will to fight on.

Yakamo no Oni waved its arms wildly. The sword cut them. Finally its fist connected with the human and sent Yakamo tumbling to the ground.

All around him, other battles raged. Very few soldiers came to the aid of their fellows—it was too difficult to tell who was friend and who was foe. Was your lifelong compatriot supporting Yakamo's cause? Indeed, which Yakamo's cause?

Yakamo no Oni growled something unintelligible and struck out with its giant fists.

Hida Yakamo leapt out of the way. He stared at the Shadowlands leader with unmasked horror. He was looking at himself, looking at exactly what he had become over the past few years. This creature, with its crimson sinews and glowing eyes, was a direct reflection of Yakamo's soul.

The thought filled the Crab with rage.

"I take back my name!" he cried. "I take back everything! I deny you, oni! You are *not* a Hida! You are not a member of this clan! I will drive you and your misbegotten army off the blessed soil of Rokugan, back to the fetid Shadowlands!"

The oni laughed. "Little Crab," it chuckled, its voice regaining much of the scratchy, strained quality it had when they'd first met. "Was it only this morning that you called me 'Brother'? You do not know your own mind, let alone your heart. Your grief for your father has blinded you to the truth you know deep in your soul—the cause for which we've fought all these months."

Yakamo launched another round of attacks. The Sword of the Crab bit shallowly into the ropy tendrils of the oni's left hand. A sizzling sound filled the air, along with the smell of burning flesh. Steam escaped the open wound.

The creature pulled its hand away but did not resume its assault. It seemed reluctant to hurt Yakamo.

"Stop this senseless battle before I have no choice but to kill you," it implored. "We are family, we are the same. Join me, and I will put you on the throne. Fu Leng has no need for such petty things. You can accomplish everything your father set out to do—you can rule the Emerald Empire!"

Did the creature really think Yakamo could be tempted?

The sound of clanking armor made him turn. A dozen zombies converged behind him as quietly as their undead shuffling allowed. He was surrounded.

"Never!" he yelled. "I do not want to rule! I am a Crab! I want only to fulfill my ancestral promise to keep the empire safe from you—or die trying."

Yakamo launched himself at the oni, hoping his quickness and ferocity would take the creature by surprise. All he got for his troubles was a mighty backhanded blow from the oni's ropy fist. It rattled his jaw and sent him flying back into the bloody muck. Tumbling head over heals, Yakamo could not hold on to his sword. Skidding face first through the mud, he came to rest at the feet of the first zombie.

"That, I cannot allow," said the oni with a malicious grin. "My samurai will make sure that your life is safe, but they have no compunction about making it unpleasant—painfully unpleasant."

The young Hida clawed his way to his hands and knees. Of course the oni wanted him alive. The creature drew power from its connection to him. A name did the oni no good if it belonged to a dead man.

Several pairs of zombie feet, all clad in Crab armor, surrounded him. Undead hands grabbed Yakamo's arms and pinned them back. Helpless, he looked up into familiar, if lifeless, eyes.

"Hiruma Waka!" Yakamo gasped.

It was indeed his father's old friend, his own former mentor. In its hands, the Waka zombie held the Ancestral Sword of the Crab. It seemed somehow fitting that the forces of darkness would use that against him. The zombie raised the sacred sword over its head.

Yakamo did not avert his gaze. He looked Waka right in his unseeing eyes and shed a single, bitter tear of pride.

The creature that used to be Yakamo's teacher paused. Beneath putrid flesh, decaying muscles twitched, but the sword did not fly.

Suddenly, the creature that once was Hiruma Waka let loose a sound like all the demons in creation baying at once and launched itself at Yakamo no Oni.

Taken completely by surprise, the creature raised its hands defensively and took a step back. The Waka zombie landed on its chest anyway. With one swift motion—swifter than any of the zombies had moved before—it slashed the oni's shoulder and breast with the Ancestral Sword of the Crab.

The oni howled in pain.

Waka motioned to his fellow undead warriors. Come, fight for honor! he seemed to say. Your lives may be lost, but your souls may yet be redeemed!

One by one the other zombies heeded the cry—and not just the dozen or so standing by Yakamo. All across the field, zombies who had once been Crab samurai (some dead for hundreds of years) ceased their fight with the living and shambled, ran, leaped, and crawled toward Yakamo no Oni. Soon they covered it entirely, the red tendrils of its body completely obscured by a writhing mass of gray, undead flesh.

Yakamo watched, dumbfounded by this supernatural display of passion and will. Though the zombies outnumbered the oni hundreds to one, they had no hope of real victory. They owed their reanimation to the creature—and it could remove the spark of unlife just as easily as it had granted it.

With a deafening roar and one shrug of its mighty shoulders, Yakamo no Oni sent the bodies of the Crab zombies flying. In the same motion it sent all their souls to eternal rest.

Once-again-lifeless bodies rained all around Yakamo. He smiled proudly as he recognized the one closest to his feet— Hiruma Waka, still gripping the Ancestral Sword of the Crab. The young daimyo bowed deeply to his fallen mentor.

"Arigato, Waka-san," he said quietly as he retrieved his family's katana.

Shaking its head dizzily, Yakamo no Oni looked around for its namesake.

They locked eyes.

The next pass they made would be the last—both Yakamos

knew it. One would die, and the other would hold the fate of Rokugan in his hands.

They tensed their legs and struck identical dueling poses.

Sound seemed to cease. Neither could hear the ring of steel from any other battle. No shuffling, no scuffling, no cries of triumph or defeat reached their ears. The wind became eerily cool and blew noiselessly by their ears.

Then the air was split by three long blasts on a war horn.

Gazing up, both Yakamos saw an army poised atop the ridge from which they themselves had charged earlier that day. Not just one army—three armies. The Unicorn mon flew above the troops to the east, the Crane mon above those to the west, and the troops in the center stood proudly below the mon of the ronin Toturi.

The allied forces had returned to defend the capital.

Hida Yakamo nodded to the samurai. They would be sure to restore order to the capital should he himself fail in this last battle.

He turned to his opponent, ready to let the cataclysmic duel begin.

But Yakamo no Oni was no longer there.

Looking around, Yakamo spied the creature atop the ridge directly opposite the one the allied forces now controlled.

"Another time, my brother," Yakamo no Oni shouted with a grin. "Only a fool fights in a burning house!"

Before Hida Yakamo could even think of a reply, it was too late. His opponent had already taken four gigantic steps and disappeared beyond the ridge. Goblins, zombies, and other horribly mutated creatures followed in its wake.

The Shadowlands army was in full retreat.

Much to Yakamo's dismay, a large number of still-living samurai also followed the creatures of darkness. His clan was sundered.

Briefly Hida Yakamo considered standing his ground and forcing Toturi to take the plain. But in he knew that the best thing for his soldiers—for his family—was to fall back. If they retreated in a different direction than the fleeing Shadowlands troops, it would make it nearly impossible for the newly arrived forces to chase them all down and make sure Otosan Uchi was safe. The capital was more important to Toturi than routing fleeing troops.

He was about to yell "retreat" to his forces but thought better of it.

"We are through for the day!" Yakamo finally shouted. "We have undone all the evil we can for now! Gather up the wounded and move out!"

"But where are we going?" asked a foot soldier wearing the Hida family mon—some distant cousin.

"Back to the Wall! Back to our home! We must protect the empire! That is what the Crab do!"

34 KNOWLEDGE AND KARMA

It is a good day to die." Hida Yakamo smiled as his tetsubo messily tore a goblin's head from its shoulders.

He felt alive—more alive than he had in months. Here atop the Wall, *his* Wall, he truly was master of all he surveyed. He was now daimyo of the Crab Clan. The responsibility for protecting the Emerald Empire from the Shadowlands fell directly on his shoulders. And he would have it no other way.

"But it is a better day to crush our enemies!" Hida O-Ushi replied. Yakamo's sister held two goblins under a single arm in a vicelike head-lock while she used her dai-tsuchi to parry the attack of a zombie wielding an ono—a great two-headed axe.

The parapet was awash in combat and blood. In the gray twilight, it was hard to see that the blood was mostly green, but Yakamo could smell the Shadowlands taint in it. He *knew* his samurai were winning the day.

Yakamo stepped forward, and his tetsubo crushed the skull the zombie menacing his sister. In the first days after his return to the Wall, Yakamo carried the Ancestral Sword of the Crab Clan with him into battle every day. It was his way of reminding himself that *he* carried the clan's honor with him always. But remembering the day his father lost his weapon, he soon began to leave the blade in a place of honor in his father's command tent. Though Yakamo was now daimyo, he could not think of that tent as truly belonging to anyone other than Hida Kisada.

O-Ushi tightened her grip and twisted her hip suddenly. The satisfying sound of goblin necks snapping was her reward.

"Oy!" yelled a samurai from the other side of the tower. "They're sending up an ogre! Reinforcements! Reinforcements!"

Yakamo turned without a word and sprinted to the far end of the parapet, with O-Ushi hot on his heels.

This was *his* fight.

▲ ▲ ▲ ▲ ▲ ▲ ▲ ▲

"Ai! For a minute I thought you were the Great Bear himself! You look just like your father!"

The generals and servants around the command tent always made inane statements like that when Yakamo returned from a day on the Wall. The daimyo always waved off the comments. Why this resemblance should be any revelation was beyond him—from the time he was ten years old, people told Yakamo how much he looked like Kisada. Still, deep down, he considered such remarks the highest of compliments.

He dismounted and strode into his father's command tent.

"Make sure I am not disturbed," he instructed Hida Tsuru.

"Hai, Tono!" his uncle responded.

Inside, the tent remained exactly the way it had been when Kisada was daimyo. The center of the space was still occupied with a tremendous map of the Crab lands, with pins stuck in it to denote troop locations.

"You did well today. I can smell it on you," said a gravelly voice from the corner.

"Hai!" Yakamo said, bowing deeply. Then he walked over to the chair in which his father sat. "It was a fine battle. We lost only one to their thirty-five."

Kisada grunted. "You lost one, you say?" the elder Hida teased. "In *my* prime not one samurai fell until fifty of the enemy lay cold!"

"Then I still have room to improve," answered Yakamo, hanging his head in mock shame.

"The runners arrived an hour ago," Kisada told his son. "The news is good from all stations along the Wall."

Yakamo grunted. "The Clan is recovering, as are you."

Kisada's wounds were healing well. After only a few months he was able to walk unaided. His appetite and his dark sense of humor were returning rapidly. But he clearly was not the same man who strode defiantly into the imperial throne room. His once-robust face was now sallow and pale, and he kept his head shaved like a monk's. His shoulders did not seem as broad as they once had been, mainly because he spent so much time sitting. And while his temper was as great as ever, he could not raise his voice for very long without becoming fatigued. The Great Bear seemed to have shrunk to about two-thirds his previous size.

"Bah!" Kisada spat. "We are stronger than ever before!"

Yakamo knew his father believed that, and eventually it would be true. But at the moment, the Crab army—much like Kisada himself—was significantly reduced. So many samurai had decided to follow the oni. . . .

Some had believed in Kisada so fervently that it bordered on religion. They did not question the Great Bear's choices, but only obeyed. When he fell, they followed the path he'd led. The key to saving the empire had to be taking the throne—and if Yakamo was not wise enough to see that, they would follow someone who was. They might have been wooed back by the announcement that the Great Bear yet lived, but Kisada insisted that the empire continue to believe he was dead. Yakamo, like any good son, acquiesced to his father's wishes.

A few of the samurai had been tainted by their contact with the Shadowlands, as Yakamo so nearly had. Despite their mortal forms, they were now creatures of darkness. Their souls were dedicated to the cause of Fu Leng, and they would fight all who opposed their dark master.

Still others left after the Clan returned to the Wall. They believed Kisada had been insane with power and that Yakamo was even madder. They believed he had not lost his hand in a duel but had cut it off himself in order to wear the claw. Following Yakamo, they believed, would lead only to more dishonor and failure. Most of these samurai had joined Toturi's army.

"We may be powerful, but so is Yaka— . . . the oni," said Yakamo. "He has more troops than ever before."

Kisada grimaced at the near mention of the creature's proper name. He had given one son's name to the beast, and the other son's life. The Great Bear took full responsibility for both sacrifices. Those burdens weighed down the old man's shoulders.

"You must always keep yourself better prepared than that creature. Its fate and yours are still inextricably bound. You will meet it again, and you must be ready!"

"The beast will not come back here anytime soon," Yakamo responded. "It finally has an army and access to the heart of the empire. It is having too much fun fanning the fires of war. I heard that the Lion and Crane forces are at one another's throats."

"Do not believe idle gossip," Kisada said. "That could be a rumor spread by the Shadowlands."

"Hai!"

"We make the mistake of thinking we understand too much," Kisada mused. "If we cannot even know the truth of what is happening today, how can we possibly know what karma we have earned?"

Yakamo moved behind his father and placed a strong hand on the old man's slumped shoulders. "No man knows his own destiny. Anyone who claims otherwise is a dangerous fool."

"Eh?"

"Something Sukune told me."

"Your brother was wiser than either of us knew."

"And stronger."

Kisada sighed. "Hai. And stronger, too."

Yakamo straightened his shoulders and looked at something that wasn't there. "I will carry his strength with me all my days."

"You will need it," said Kisada. "Fu Leng still sits on the Emerald Throne, and the clans can barely stand to be in the same room with one another. This war will get worse before it gets better."

The daimyo looked to the small wooden shrine that sat in the corner. His brother's katana lay upon it.

"The empire will not fall," he said, low and strong. "*I* will not let it fall. The Crab stand on the Wall as we must, as we always have!"

Yakamo picked up his tetsubo and walked briskly toward the tent flap.

"Where are you going?" asked Kisada.

"To make sure no evil comes over the Wall tonight!"

GLOSSARY

Amaterasu—the Sun Goddess

ashigaru—foot soldier

bokken—wooden practice sword

bu—a coin, money

bushi—warrior

bushido—the code of a warrior

-chan—suffix, young master—an endearing term for a child or lover

chi—the seat of the soul, the power of a samurai

daisho—the katana and wakizashi sword combination worn by samurai

dai-kyu—long bow

dai-tsuchi—warhammer

doji—castle

domo arigato—thank you very much

domo arigato gozaimasu—thank you very, very much

engawa—roofed veranda

eta—the unclean, the lowest caste who do the dirtiest jobs, such as burying the dead

fundoshi—loincloth

fusuma—an interior paper wall (see *shoji*)
gambatte—fight on
ganbari masu—don't give up
gempuku—coming of age ceremony
hai—yes
hakima—wide trousers
hanko—"chop mark," signature
haramaki-do—heavy lacquered armor
heimin—the peasant caste
iaijutsu—fast-draw sword technique
iie—no
ishii—a game played with stones on a board
Jigoku—the underworld, the afterlife, or hell
jigokuni ochimuratachi—"the lost," warriors fallen into hell
Kabuki—melodramatic theater
kami—the ancient children of Lady Sun and Lord Moon; also, a nature spirit or a god
kanji—characters, letters, runes
katana—the samurai long sword, part of the daisho
kata—a series of exercise or martial arts forms
konbanwa—good evening
kosode—narrow-sleeved kimono (undergarment)
-kun—suffix: old friend
kyuden—palace
matte—halt
maho—dark, blood magic
nage-yari—short javelin
naginata—polearm topped by a sword blade
natto—sweet bean paste
nezumi—ratlings, a race of human-sized rats
ninjato—ninja short sword
ninjitsu—the art of ninja
no-dachi—two-handed sword, taller than a samurai
Noh—minimalist theater
obi—a belt of folded silk
on—emblem or symbol
oni—demon

onikage—demon steed

Onnotangu—the moon god, husband of Amaterasu

ono—battle-axe

otennoo-sama—great lord, highness, exalted one

ratling—nezumi, a human-sized rat creature indigenous to the Shadowlands

ronin—samurai without a master

sake—rice wine

-sama—suffix: most esteemed, lord, master, highness

-san—suffix: honored, sir

seppuku—ritual suicide

shamisen—guitar played with pick

shiburi—flicking technique used to clean blood from a sword

shiro—castle

shiruken—throwing star

shoji—paper walls, exterior (see *fusuma*)

shugenja—a wielder of magic

shuriken—throwing stars or darts

soba shop—a shop offering food and drink

sochu—strong sake

sumimasen—sorry for causing you trouble

sutra—a meditation or precept

taiko—large drum

tanto—dagger or knife

tatami—mat for sitting upon the floor

torii—wooden archway with two pillars and a crosspiece

tetsubo—wooden clublike staff with iron studs

tono—lord

tsuba—hand guard on a sword

udon—soup with flour noodles

wakizashi—samurai short sword, part of the daisho; the "soul" of the samurai, used in seppuku

yari—a 6-foot-long spear with a straight blade

yojimbo—bodyguard

yosh—"good" an assenting grunt

yumi—a type of bow, fairly short, can be fired by a standing man

zori—straw sandals

Counselors and Kings

ELAINE CUNNINGHAM

Under the blazing sun of Halruaa, intrigue stalks the land.
Skilled wizards compete for power and wealth, threatening to
destroy any who interfere. Only the society of Counselors,
impervious to the effects of magic, can maintain balance and order.

Book I: THE MAGEHOUND

Matteo is a rising counselor, intent on
serving his wizardly masters well. Yet when
a spark of magic is discovered within him,
he must flee the wrath of one sworn to root
out such talents: the magehound.

Book II: THE FLOODGATE

As Matteo and his companion Tzigone
search for clues to their mysterious pasts,
Kiva the magehound, now fallen into
disgrace, plots in secrecy to destroy those
who opposed her. To accomplish her ends,
she plans to unleash a power that could
sweep away all Halruaa.

April 2001